Praise for

Nocturne

"An enchanting and lyrical fever dream bursting with dazzling prose and dark romance, *Nocturne* enthralled me."
—Erin A. Craig, *New York Times* bestselling author of
House of Salt and Sorrows

"Richly imagined and heartbreakingly told, *Nocturne* is a lush gothic romance that will dance you dizzy."
—Hannah Whitten, *New York Times* bestselling author of *For the Wolf*

"No one writes the way Alyssa Wees does, and *Nocturne* is her latest masterpiece. Like the ballet pulsing at its core, the story is both sinuous and quick on its feet, leading the reader through a labyrinth of emotions that range from the brightest passion to the darkest grief. . . . A powerful, haunting read."
—Joan He, *New York Times* bestselling author of *Strike the Zither*

"A beautiful nightmare and a fairy tale all at once . . . Wees's lyrical prose swept me away in this unique story about the battle between love and despair. *Nocturne* is not to be missed."
—Evelyn Skye, *New York Times* bestselling author of *The Crown's Game*

"In *Nocturne*, Wees robes the classic story of Beauty and the Beast in lush prose and infinite splendor. It's a fever dream of a novel, surreal and intricate, and enchanting in every way."
—Ava Reid, author of *The Wolf and the Woodsman*

"Haunting and immersive—like a dream poured onto a page . . . Alyssa Wees has deftly spun a dark tale of romance, betrayal, and destiny. *Nocturne* kept me in its sinister grip from the first page to the last."
—Heather Walter, author of *Malice*

"Darkly beautiful and threaded through with an undercurrent of magic and madness, *Nocturne* is a captivating tale replete with layers of illusion, where true enchantment lies hiding beneath the manufactured witchery and gossamer splendor of the ballet."
—Leife Shallcross, author of *The Beast's Heart*

"*Nocturne* reads like a fable, a mythical tale full of magical power, but imbued with the very real and wonderfully graceful power of ballet. Its heroine is a prima ballerina for whom nothing—life, death, love—is as important as the dance. You will be enchanted!"
—Louisa Morgan, author of *A Secret History of Witches*

"Absolutely captivating, *Nocturne* is a delicious and radiant treat of a novel. Prepare to be spellbound!"
—Sarah Beth Durst, award-winning author of
the Queens of Renthia series

"*Nocturne* is an utterly unique, lyrical play on the Persephone and Hades myth for fans of Neil Gaiman or Madeline Miller. The beautiful language creates an atmosphere of darkness, grace, and foreboding that sets up a haunted and mythical story."
—*Booklist* (starred review)

"Enthralling . . . a lush, impressive fantasy from a promising new voice."
—*Publishers Weekly*

"Set in 1930s Chicago, Wees's lyrical fantasy has hints of *Beauty and the Beast*, *Phantom of the Opera*, and Greek mythology. . . . Perfect for fans of Erin Morgenstern and fairy tale retellings, with great character development and a mystery that will keep readers on the edge of their seats."
—*Library Journal*

Nocturne

Nocturne

A Novel

ALYSSA WEES

DEL
REY

New York

2024 Del Rey Trade Paperback Edition

Published in the United States by Del Rey, an imprint of Random House, a division of Penguin Random House LLC, New York.

DEL REY and the CIRCLE colophon are registered trademarks of Penguin Random House LLC.

Originally published in hardcover in the United States by Del Rey, an imprint of Random House, a division of Penguin Random House LLC, in 2023.

This book contains an excerpt from the forthcoming book *We Shall Be Monsters* by Alyssa Wees. This excerpt has been set for this edition only and may not reflect the final content of the forthcoming edition.

LIBRARY OF CONGRESS CATALOGING-IN-PUBLICATION DATA
Names: Wees, Alyssa, author.
Title: Nocturne / Alyssa Wees.
Description: New York: Del Rey, [2023]
Identifiers: LCCN 2022017366 (print) | LCCN 2022017367 (ebook) |
ISBN 9780593357491 (paperback) | ISBN 9780593357484 (ebook) |
ISBN 9780593722664 (international edition)
Subjects: LCGFT: Fantasy fiction. | Novels.
Classification: LCC PS3623.E4226 N63 2023 (print) | LCC PS3623.E4226 (ebook) |
DDC 813/.6—dc23/eng/20220521
LC record available at https://lccn.loc.gov/2022017366
LC ebook record available at https://lccn.loc.gov/2022017367

Printed in the United States of America on acid-free paper

randomhousebooks.com

246897531

Book design by Virginia Norey
Art used throughout has been adapted from Anna Ismagilova/stock.adobe.com,
Dušan Zidar/stock.adobe.com, Olga/stock.adobe.com, vat2522/stock.adobe.com,
and jenteva/stock.adobe.com.

For Frank,
My sun and stars. Ti amo.

Part One

One

THE MASTER CAME INTO MY LIFE LIKE THE DUSK. SLOWLY, until all the city was covered in night. And I, a star waiting to burn.

It was winter, or nearly so, the cold before the snow when the air goes still around you and inside of you. The radiator in my little room in the boardinghouse was shaky at best and I shivered getting dressed, frost in the corners of the window. With the heel of my hand I wiped away the condensation, an unchanging view of the brick alley beyond. Though it was early I had eaten already—eggs and toast with margarine—but still my belly rumbled because it was not enough and never would be.

My breath quickly misted the glass again; I stepped away. Nine years into the economic depression and my basic needs were met, even if this was the coldest of rooms in the creakiest boardinghouse on the North Side of Chicago. Granted, the matron, Mrs. O'Donnell, served us more for dinner than most: baked beans with cornbread and Hoover stew. Dandelion salad, and potato pancakes, and potato soup. Boiled carrots and spaghetti, cabbage and dumplings—all of it fine, though none of it appealing. I knew I was fortunate, I did; and yet, even the guilt of ingratitude was not enough to banish my growing discontent.

This can't be all there is.

I was thinking of running away forever when there was a knock on my bedroom door.

I had made it part of my routine every morning, imagining how I would manage it: out the window, down the alley, through the park.

Hurrying, but not so fast as to appear suspicious, or as if I were going anywhere in particular. Hair up, no wind, a half-melted moon in the dim afternoon guiding me toward the open water, the lake like one long shadow. There I would wade into the water and the waves would carry me to another world entirely—to a place I had never been, and from which I would not be able to find my way back again. Or, at the very least, to a crack in *this* world, a place where magic coats everything like a layer of dust, where the wind smells sweet and night never comes. A place that has no edges and no end, where there is always *more*. More life, more light, more to see, and more to explore.

It was the fantasy of a little girl. A girl I had not been for some time and of course never would be again. One that still had a mother who would stop her if she tried to leave; one that still had the whole world open to her, and dwelled in that sacred place before a perfect, cherished dream became a less than satisfying reality. For years in the company of Near North Ballet, I'd been another girl in a row of perfect girls, another face, another body in a line of similar faces and bodies. Symmetry and seamlessness, every step and angle of the chin; every curve of the arm and lift of the leg, precisely the same as the girls in front and behind. After a while I'd begun to feel as if I'd run eagerly, wildly into a labyrinth of possibility only to find that it was instead a straight aisle, pressed among a crowd of equally eager girls all trying to unlock the same door at the end of this infinite corridor.

And so, stuck in one place, growing stagnant and unsure, a new dream had been born: If I couldn't dance the way I wanted to—ecstatically, with all eyes on me—I would run. As long as I was still in motion, my heart would keep beating, and nothing, not even death, could touch me.

More. There has to be more.

"Coming!" I called, as another knock came at the door, louder and more insistent. I turned from the window and hurried to pull on my favorite pale pink dress for church: the last dress my mother had ever made for me, a gift on the day I turned thirteen. A little worn around the seams, and tight across the chest, but seven years later it still fit, and I would wear it for seven years more as long as it didn't fall apart. I tugged on my stockings, hoping the tiny rip near the hip wouldn't reach my knees and become visible to judging eyes. Sunday was the only day of the week I wore my hair down, shadow-black and falling in bouncy spirals well past my shoulders, much longer than Mamma ever used to let me keep it. Finally I slipped on my brown penny loafers and went to the door.

"Mistress is here." It was Emilia, slightly breathless even though she stood absolutely still, her dark hair set in pins to curl. It was still half an hour before we would leave for church and she was never early for anything without a pressing reason. "She asked to see you right away. She's waiting in the parlor."

My heart gave a vicious kick.

"What do you think she wants?" It was barely a whisper. We looked at each other, and both of us knew, but neither wanted to say it in case it didn't come true. The prima position—*Emilia's* position—would be open soon, and though it was all anyone in the corps could talk about, I had refused even to think of it, as if my own hope was a monster that would turn me to stone if I slipped and looked it directly in the eye. I wanted the position; I burned with the wanting, the sun in my throat, and maybe that was the true reason I had not run away yet: There was still something to wish for. *Prima ballerina of Near North Ballet.* It was utterly impossible—and right within reach.

"To demand that you dance for her morning, noon, and night," Emilia said in that way she had of teasing while also being perfectly serious. "So that she'll never have to live for even one second without gazing upon your unparalleled grace and beauty."

I smiled, but it was more for her sake than for mine. Was it the touch of destiny I felt then, or was it simply nerves pinching in? Of late Mistress reprimanded me more than anyone else in the corps, barking my name as she clapped her hands once, sharply, so that we stopped in a flurry, the music cutting out. She ordered us back to the beginning of the phrase each time I strayed even slightly out of formation, each time I smiled a little more widely than the others, or spun just a smidgen too quickly. It was a failure, she'd admonished, to stand out from the corps. Weakness, not strength, to draw the eye to only one part of the whole.

But, if I were a soloist, I would be a whole unto myself. Never again would I need to blend in.

And so I could think of no other reason for her visit but that she was about to promote me—or to fire me for my mistakes. There was, after all, another, perhaps more obvious choice, than me: Beatrice Lang, whose upper middle class family had enrolled her in ballet lessons practically the moment she'd learned to walk. Despite the war and the depression, she'd never known a day of wanting or weeping, of hunting for dandelion greens in the park to cook into a sauce, or watching her veteran father gamble away his meager savings. Sometimes I wondered if we lived in the same city at the same time at all, or if she had crossed from some other reality into our own, so far removed was she from the life I had known. Tall, and with hair so fair it shone almost white in the stage light, she was delicate in demeanor but powerful in execution, possessed of that elusive gravity we called *presence*. An ability that had never come easily to me, the radiation of an undeniable energy that turned eyes toward her as soon as she entered a room. She was very much like Emilia in that way, and so seemed Emilia's natural successor. As I thought of this my smile slipped, a short-lived thing, and Emilia must have seen. She took my hand, as gently as lifting a sculpted angel made of glass, and said, "Come, Grace. I'll walk with you."

The hallway was narrow and there wasn't much light, an electric bulb protruding from the ceiling every few feet. The stairwell was even darker, and though we were forced to descend single file, I never let go of Emilia's hand. Between the thick walls of exposed brick our footsteps echoed like the whispers of a growing crowd around a crime scene. Halfway down, I squeezed her hand and stopped. She stopped too, turning toward me with a question posed on her lips, but before she could ask it I threw my arms around her, hugging her tightly.

"What was that for?" she said, laughing, as I released her. I stood one stair above her, and she seemed so small as I looked down, even though on level ground we were precisely the same height.

"I'm going to miss you," I said. "That's all."

Emilia was leaving in the spring to get married, to make a home and start a family. Though I'd had plenty of time now to get used to the idea, my throat still burned the way it had the day she'd told me, as if I were inhaling shadows instead of air. Emilia was the only family I had now, the only family I'd had for the last seven years. Was there a place for me in her new life, or would I linger like a splinter stuck deep into her palm, and it was only a matter of time before her protective skin pushed me out, the thing that didn't belong? I began to miss her, even while she was still right there in front of me.

"Not so fast," Emilia said as we stood in the stairwell, the ache of her imminent absence even more pronounced. "You're not rid of me yet."

She took my hand firmly and led the way again, our footsteps slightly heavier than they were before. Two floors down and we emerged into a much brighter corridor, the walls here papered in forcefully cheery stripes and the floor carpeted in soft beige that swallowed our footfalls. A smell of burnt coffee, strong enough to choke. At the end of the corridor was a closed door, looming like the entrance to the underworld. My heart seemed separated from my body somehow, its mad, mortal beat in my ears belonging to someone else. A monster, maybe. It was like that when I stepped onstage too. I became the tiniest bit inhuman.

Emilia stopped before the door and turned to me. "All right, let me look at you."

I stood at attention while she fluffed my hair, raking her thin hands through my curls, and then pinched my cheeks to coax a rosy glow to the surface. When Emilia was satisfied she took a step back and nodded.

"I'll wait here," she promised. "Just outside."

The thought of her presence—even on the other side of the door—calmed me. But only slightly.

As if sensing us standing there, a voice came through the door, a voice like a gray cloud holding on to its lightning for just a minute more. "My colombina, is that you? Come in."

"Well," I said, and could think of nothing else to say or do but to face whatever awaited me.

"*Merde,*" Emilia said as I turned away: the wish of good luck that was usually reserved for the stage. I nodded once, then twisted the heavy doorknob and stepped into the parlor.

Though Mrs. O'Donnell was the matron, it was Mistress, in fact, who owned the boardinghouse. It used to be her home, before she'd moved elsewhere—I'm not sure where, as she never invited any of us over—and began renting out the rooms in order to keep her dancers close to the studio. And so, when I entered the musty parlor, I marveled as always at Mistress's taste—or lack thereof—in décor, the room replete with several faded chintz chairs and long gray curtains obscuring the windows, catching and killing the sunlight before it could trespass. It smelled old. It *was* old—the house had been built fifty years ago, in the 1880s. Now, in 1938, it was all rotted wood and mothballs, mildew and dust. Mrs. O'Donnell burned scented candles but it only enhanced the stench, not banished it.

Mistress sat in a chair with her back to the window, dressed in a navy tunic-top dress belted at the waist, a matching tilt hat resting in her lap. As always, her long, graying auburn hair was twisted on top of her head. She was much older than she looked, her back straight and her chin held high. When she danced she moved like moonlight—precise, direct, but still with an air of otherworldliness about her, of night. Not that she danced much anymore; she was at least sixty—though she never did complain of aches and pains—and she had a company to direct—a severely underfunded one. It was rumored she'd had a steady patron twenty or so years ago—back when her daughter, also a dancer, was still with the company—but either he had left to apply his patronage elsewhere, or he'd lost all his money in 1929 when the stock markets first took a severe tumble. Either way, I suspected that now it was only through the sheer force of her will that Near North Ballet still functioned at all—her fists clenched around it, her refusal to let go.

She managed her dancers in much the same manner.

"Close the door behind you," she said to me, and I obeyed. The latch clicked like teeth, a hard bite. "Sit."

I sat across from her, my stomach roiling. Sometimes, after a long day of rehearsals, fresh bloodstains in our shoes, the other girls and I would whisper behind our hands, calling her a harpy, a witch who wanted to bathe in our blood and steal our youth. But all the while I knew she wasn't a witch, not the way we meant it, because heroes and villains did not exist in life as they did in stories.

Here there were only those who smiled when they said something kind, and those who smiled when they said something cruel.

Mistress was both.

"Colombina, how are you sleeping?" she said, and my heart spun in my chest, tripped, and fell flat. *Just tell me why you're here.* "Are you eating well?"

She knew I ate as well or as badly as anyone else in the company—as anyone in Chicago, for that matter—and sleep was parallel to a miracle when it came without a fight.

"Yes, Mistress," I said, staring at the pinched skin of her neck instead of her eyes. I wondered if Mistress's daughter—whose name I didn't know because Mistress rarely spoke of her—had ever felt like this beneath her mother's gaze, pinned like prey. I'd never met the daughter, or seen her, and I didn't know where she was now, if she was dancing for another company—which had possibly caused the rift between her and Mistress—or if, like Emilia, she had retired to start a family. Did Mistress have a nickname for her daughter like she had one for me? No other girl currently in the company could say the same, and I clung to this, that I alone was Mistress's colombina. That though she had been cross with me lately, I was still special, still deserving of my place.

There is always my little window, I thought, reassuring myself in case things were about to go terribly wrong. *Out the window, down the alley, through the park. No matter what happens, this is not the end.*

"Look at me." Mistress leaned toward me, a cup of steaming coffee in her hands.

I raised my gaze, trying to keep my face blank. "It's very important we keep you in perfect condition, now that you're rising from the corps."

I inhaled so sharply that I almost choked. "I'm . . . ?"

"Yes. Can you believe it?" Mistress said, watching me keenly. "Grace Dragotta, prima ballerina assoluta."

Prima ballerina assoluta. It was like she had cast an enchantment, and for a full minute I could say nothing, do nothing, display no reaction at all. I was dizzy, more so even than when I'd stood at the top of the Tribune Tower with my older brother, Lorenzo, beside me—*Come on, gotta surprise for you, bearcat. How'd ya like to touch the sky?*—and gazed down at the city below for the very first time, as high as I had ever been or would be again. I had come so far, I had worked so hard; but still the moment held an air of unreality, a second of lucidity in a dream when you look around and think, *No, none of this is happening.*

"You haven't said a word." Mistress set her coffee on the low table between us. It clinked against the glass. "Your evident surprise at this is almost insulting. Are you not my colombina? My sweet, shy bird? You flew through my window, and I did more than mend your broken wings. I gave you new wings, bigger and better, stronger, so you could soar higher, faster, so you could tear through the night and bring me back stars." She clicked her tongue against the roof of her mouth, startling me with the sudden, staccato sound. "Haven't I molded you into the proud ballerina you are today? Haven't I shaped you into the beautiful young woman I see before me? Why shouldn't the artist responsible for such a transformation be rewarded for her fine work? Answer me."

"I never doubted you, Mistress," I said quickly, and it was true. Only overwhelmed, I didn't know whether to laugh or to cry. In the end I did neither—Mistress loathed strong emotions, claiming they only belonged on the stage. I settled on a smile, not too wide, and I showed no teeth. "I'm honored. Truly."

Mollified, Mistress sat back with a sigh. "There's more, colombina. Would you like to hear it?"

"Yes," I said, and concentrated very hard on not scratching an imaginary itch in the corner of my eye, or picking at the skin around my nails. Mistress didn't take kindly to fidgeting either—one's movements should always be deliberate, she said. "Please, tell me."

"You will be dancing the Golden Firebird this season."

This time I couldn't hide my bewildered delight, and I covered my cheeks with my hands to obscure at least some of it, the flush that had risen to my face. The Golden Firebird was the lead role of *The Firebird*, the Russian composer Igor Stravinsky's breakthrough ballet. As far as I knew, it had not been performed in America yet, but was regarded overseas as a masterpiece. It was the story of a prince named Ivan and the Firebird he finds in the forest that helps him rescue thirteen sleeping princesses from the clutches of the sorcerer Koschei the Deathless and his scheming demons. A pure fairy tale, with good triumphing over evil and true love conquering all.

"But . . . Emilia . . ." I said, still trying to wrap my mind around all of this. It was true that she was leaving, but she had not left yet. "This is her farewell season. Shouldn't she dance the lead one last time?"

"Are you the ballet mistress here, or am I?" Mistress sounded as close to *amused* as I'd ever heard her, exasperated but not angry. "Miss Menendez will serve as your understudy, in case something goes wrong."

A deep coldness swept through me, hardening in the spaces between my bones.

"Goes wrong?" I echoed, my voice as small as a child's.

"Yes, well, you could fall and break your neck on the stairs, or suffer some other hideous disaster." Mistress's gaze drifted toward the window. "If it makes you feel better, your friend will be featured prominently, as always. The role of Princess Ekaterina will suit her just fine."

I nodded, relieved. She did believe in me, but of course, every prima has an understudy. And the princess was the next best role—some would even argue that it was equal to the Firebird. So really, there was no reason to feel guilty about pushing Emilia out early. Her farewell season would still be a great one, perhaps even her best yet.

Mistress took a slow sip of her coffee.

"You look worried," she said, eyeing me over the rim of her cup. "Don't be. I have known that same fear of center stage, even while longing with all my soul for it. Stars burn—and burn out. Sometimes the fire is slow to consume and sometimes it happens quickly—too quickly, and your career is over. The dance is done. It's frightening, but there is no stopping it once it has begun." She leaned across the space between us and put two fingers beneath my chin, a light tap, before letting her hand fall away. "But if you must burn, colombina, why not burn the brightest?"

She had misinterpreted my anxiety over Emilia, and I inhaled a breath to explain, but then decided against it. I simply nodded, smiling a little as if her words had soothed me, when really the opposite of what she thought I was feeling was true: If anything, I feared *not* burning, of staying still with my feet stuck to the ground.

"Thank you, Mistress," I said at last, and though I meant it with all my heart, the words felt insignificant. "Thank you for trusting me with this position, and this role."

"Well deserved, little bird," she said, and with that I was dismissed. I stood and left the room, forcing myself to move at a normal pace. I felt Mistress's eyes on me, and tried very hard not to tremble beneath that dissecting gaze.

The hallway was darker than when I'd been there before, the shadows thinner and longer. Emilia waited right where she said she would be. She took my elbow and guided me back to the stairwell where Mistress would not overhear us, my steps so light it was almost like floating.

"Prima?" she whispered, when we were sure we were alone. Her eyes were bright like a beginning, like once upon a time. "Is it you?"

"It's me," I whispered, and suddenly it was real; it wasn't just a dream. Joy filled me like midday light touching every corner of a room. No longer would I be another faceless girl in the corps; after all, wasn't it my inimitability that had first gotten me noticed? Seven years ago I'd been brave enough to enter Mistress's studio and ask for what I wanted: to learn and to grow under her wing. I would burn, burn the brightest, and in burning become untouchable; no hand of god or man could hope to hold me down.

"Oh, Grace, I'm so happy for you." Emilia embraced me, closing the space between us so suddenly that I was nearly knocked off my feet. A laugh escaped me, a high, girlish sound. "I knew you would get it—I just *knew*."

I smiled, though Emilia couldn't see as she continued to cling tightly to me. Maybe Beatrice had been the conventional choice for Emilia's replacement, but I was special too—and this promotion was the proof. More like the moon than the sun, bright and a little strange, a touch of mystique that made you marvel at it night after night. Beatrice was bold and exciting, but I was ethereal, haunting, and mine was the performance the audience would remember long after it was done, lingering.

"I couldn't have done it without you," I said, thinking of all those long hours we'd spent in the studio after dark, Emilia acting as a second mistress to my instruction. At thirteen years old I'd been sorely behind the other girls in the ballet school, a thin, tired orphan who'd had no formal training in her childhood. Emilia had been a patient teacher, gently if relentlessly adjusting my legs and feet until I'd achieved near perfect turnout, leading me through stretches to expand my extension until I could penché with my leg in a six o'clock arabesque, my toes pointing perfectly to the sky. She watched me execute the same combinations, at the barre and in the center, over and over until I could do a triple pirouette without hopping, land a tour jeté without stumbling, a brisé volé without fumbling. Until Mistress could find little fault with me, and I was ready at last to join the corps.

"Oh, you would've gotten there on your own eventually," Emilia said modestly, and when she pulled away I saw that she was crying, just a little. She wiped her eyes, and as soon as hers were gone I felt the tears start in mine, as if we could only express emotion one at a time, passing it between us like shared food at a table, drinking from the same cup.

"I'm not so sure about that," I said, and sudden footsteps at the top of the stairs made us both jump. A moment later Beatrice and her close friend Anna, who was also in the corps, appeared above us, slowing when they saw us.

"What's all this?" Beatrice said, her voice flat as her eyes darted from Emilia's face to mine. Our drying tears, our tremulous hands, evidence that something had happened—something momentous.

Emilia and I glanced at each other with secretive smiles.

"Perhaps we should leave the breaking of the news to Mistress. I'm sure she'll make an announcement soon." Emilia's hand flew to her head, as if only just remembering that her hair was still in curlers. "Oh! We're going to be late for church if we don't get going. Shall we, Grace?"

"What news?" Anna said plaintively as we inched around them and ascended the stairs, but we pretended not to hear.

"I'm guessing we have a new prima," Beatrice said with a touch of bitterness, and the echo of it—*prima, prima, prima*—followed me all the way back to my room, where I pulled the curtains over my little window, and finished readying for church.

Two

REHEARSALS BEGAN A FEW DAYS LATER, HOURS UPON HOURS spent in the high-ceilinged studio from first light to sunset, learning the choreography and then perfecting it. Every day in the studio brought us closer to the stage; every day I grew stronger. Sinew and symmetry, fire and finesse. Never slouching or slacking for even a moment, striving for perfection from every angle and finding something close. *So close.*

The first week was pure elation, sweat and breath and the beat of my heart—wild, insistent, *I am here, I am here*—and I couldn't take my eyes off myself in the mirror, even after Mistress admonished me. *The mirrors are only a tool, like the barre. They are not for vanity.* But I ignored her, greedily tracking my reflection, relishing the sight as well as the feel of every stretch and every bend, every chassé and fouetté and arabesque, reveling in the way my muscles obeyed my every command. I began to feel that if I couldn't see myself then I wasn't actually real, and that all of this—prima, Emilia, the Golden Firebird—would slip away from me when I wasn't looking. So I looked, and eventually, not even Mistress tried to stop me.

"Let's go out," I said to Emilia as we left the brownstone building two blocks north of the river where the studio was housed and headed back to the boardinghouse on Friday, the end of the first week. We had been rehearsing the scene where Prince Ivan meets the Firebird after he becomes lost in the woods, and so there had only been four of us in the rehearsal: Emilia as my understudy, plus my partner, Will, who played Ivan, and his understudy. And me, of course. I was tired but not sleepy, famished but not empty. "Let's go dancing!"

Emilia laughed, the cold burning two red spots on her cheeks. "*More* dancing? Haven't you had enough?"

"Never," I said, looking up at the buildings rising around us, their windows gleaming like a hundred eyes, glowing yellow against the darkening sky. "If I stop dancing, my heart will stop beating."

"All right, all right," Emilia said, taking my elbow and steering me out of the path of a man walking toward us, briefcase in hand, his trilbyhatted head bowed against the wind. "Let's get cleaned up first."

Club DeLisa was a jazz club with no drink minimum and no cover charge, and though the owners were Italian (which of course made them suspicious, even to me), they weren't gangsters like the ones that ran the Green Mill or Friar's Inn. Located in Washington Park, a predominately black neighborhood, Club DeLisa was the most prestigious integrated club in the city. Emilia's fiancé met us at the boardinghouse, wearing a slightly out of style gray suit and his brown fringe styled like the actor Errol Flynn, wavy and thick. Together, we caught the bus at the stop on the corner; thankfully we didn't have to wait very long. No need to engage in any lengthy conversations while we stood in our evening dress, restless for our glamorous night out to begin. On the bus I sat alone behind Emilia and Adrián, staring alternately out the window and at the back of their heads.

About nine months ago, Adrián Ramos had come into the Mexican panadería that Emilia's parents owned in East Pilsen while she was working behind the counter, filling in for her cousin who had taken ill. He'd seen Emilia in the window while walking by; he said he'd felt as if he'd been asleep all his life and only finally woke up when he saw her for the very first time. He had come into the panadería looking for work, and Emilia's parents had hired him as a baker. In only a few months he'd been promoted to lead pastry chef, and was even expected to take over the business someday with Emilia. He was kind, if quiet, timid with a wide, sweet smile. He was successful and reliable, and he would take good care of Emilia as well as the children they hoped to have, so what was there to find fault with? Nothing, nothing—I knew this. But still, I couldn't help fancying that if Adrián hadn't come along, Emilia would have danced with me forever.

The ride across the city was long.

Half an hour later we arrived, but the tedious trip was worth it. The outside of the nightclub didn't look like much, only a short building with an awning over the door and enormous letters spelling Club DeLisa on its front, but the inside of the main room was inviting if a bit cramped: a square, high-ceilinged room host to a maze of tables and tightly packed chairs, a raised stage at the far end in front of which was an open floor for dancing, the wood shining in the cloudy light of the hanging lamps. Curls of cigar smoke and puffs of floral perfume; murmurs like wind under the door, gusts of laughter and shuffles of feet like a prelude of soft thunder before a storm. It was still early in the evening; most of the tables were unoccupied, so we picked one on the edge of the dance floor, nearest to the stage where a brass band had set up their instruments and began to play. Emilia and I sat together while Adrián went to buy drinks—a beer for himself, and martinis for Emilia and me.

"You were right," she said as we waited for Adrián to return. We'd worn our best dresses, though Emilia's was finer than mine, made of a red, silky fabric that fell all the way to the floor. Mine had been Mamma's, and so was at least ten years out of style, pastel pink with a dropped waist and fluttery sleeves. Normally I didn't like to wear it—sometimes, when I let my guard down, I felt a warm weight on my shoulder, a hand that belonged to someone that, when I turned, wasn't there—but now I wanted her close to me, to share my joy with her in the only small way that I could. "We deserve a night of fun, don't we? To celebrate all that we've achieved?"

"Absolutely," I said, thinking of my reflection in the studio mirrors, the girl I'd seen flying in the glass. "A celebration."

The music was like a rush of blood to the head, smooth and quick. I felt it in my chest like a second heart, a fevered pulse behind my eyes and in my throat. I watched Emilia dance with Adrián while the club filled with bodies—men in suits just a little bit wrinkled, women wearing paste diamonds, sparkling so viciously in the light it was almost easy to believe they were real and not made of lead glass. Then Adrián rested while Emilia and I took a spin together, laughing as we led each other in a lurching foxtrot, the liquor blazing in us like shooting stars. My feet were sore but I didn't mind it, and my curls grew limp and loose from their pins. All three of us were at the table, finishing up our second drinks, when a voice at my shoulder startled me.

"May I have this dance?"

A young man, about my age, held out his hand as he bent near to me, imploring. I stared, seeing not his face, but another's—one that had faded over the years despite my best efforts to remember, to hold him uncorrupted by time in my mind. The man before me had hair that was rich and dark, like mine, and his skin was olive like mine too. Definitely Italian, likely Sicilian, and yet, it was the way he carried himself—tall and loose, thin through the waist but broad through the shoulders, slightly hunched—that reminded me the most of Lorenzo, albeit a slightly older version of him. For a moment, I couldn't move or even speak. A touch on my shoulder, dreaded but familiar, a soft pressure pushing me down and down and down.

"Go on," Emilia prompted, and her voice, though gentle, tugged at me violently, wrenching me from a memory. The weight lifted from my shoulder, as if it had never been. "Grace, don't you want to dance?"

Without a word, I took the man's hand.

"So, where's your family from?" he asked as we swayed, the music having slowed, and I knew he didn't mean Chicago. His hands on my waist were cold—too cold. I could feel the ice of his palms through my clothes.

"Cefalù," I said, trying to focus on his face and not the one in my head. Of course, I had never been to Sicily, but Mamma had told me stories of her small fishing village near Palermo where she'd lived until the age of fifteen. My father's family had emigrated from Corleone, an inland town, but I didn't feel as much of a connection to it. He hadn't been around much to tell stories.

"Ah. I'm from Messina myself," the man said, and I was afraid to ask his name; Lorenzo was a common one. He didn't have an accent, so he must have come here when he was very young. "The shit on the tip of

Italy's boot, my old man always called it. Whole island overrun by the mob." He laughed, or I thought he laughed; it was more like a grunt. "As if Chicago's just chock full a' saints, right?"

I nodded, unsteady. "Right."

I'd grown up in Little Sicily—nicknamed Little Hell for the factory furnaces that turned the sky orange at night—and adjacent to Death Corner: an otherwise unassuming intersection where mobsters had often been murdered or where they simply left their dead. Some of them I had known: Vincenzo LoCascio, a veteran friend of my father's; Don Rizzo, who'd taken to shining shoes outside the El station after he'd lost his job at the Kraft factory; Jimmy Cassata, a boy my brother's age, who'd delivered the daily newspaper to the porch of our two-flat every morning for years. I knew all too well that this city had more sinners than smokestacks, more killers than church bells chiming out the hour. I didn't recognize the man I danced with now, but it was possible he'd grown up there too. Chicago was big, but not *that* big, and the hot breath of grief reached far, blown about on the wind.

The man continued to chat, but I was barely listening. It was Lorenzo who had first taught me to dance—not ballet, naturally, but a wild, spinning waltz, my toes balanced on the tips of his boots as he twirled me around and around the living room of our flat, the windows and the radiator and the porcelain figurines in the china cabinet blurring into a haze, rendering his smile the only thing in focus, the only thing in the world that mattered. Mamma would shake her head in the doorway as we stumbled apart, me landing hard on my rump, dizzy and dazed, while Lorenzo extended a hand to help me to my feet, always right there to set me straight. He'd been six years older than me—born before our father served in the Great War, while I'd come along after Papa was honorably discharged for a wound to the shoulder—so that when I was seven he was thirteen, already tall and lean with the makings of a man, the hint of who he would become in the seriousness that gradually replaced the mirth in his eyes, that ate his ebullience like dusk devouring day from the sky, so that it was almost entirely gone by the time he died.

Mamma didn't like me to dance after his death, because if I was dancing I was not mourning and if I was not mourning, my brother's soul would not find the light of Heaven. I'd tried to explain to her once, twice, a dozen times that dance was the *only* way I could mourn or grieve—a release for restless energy—and if I did not dance then I would lose myself to dark dreams. But she would not have it, so I danced in secret.

In my bedroom in the early morning, in the alleys on my way home from errands, in the kitchen when Mamma took naps, her fingertips poked full of needle holes from her work as a seamstress. I raised my arms and pointed my toes; I twirled and leaped. I danced until I felt my heart beating past perpetual midnight so dawn could rise through my ribs again. I had no formal training—only a clawing desire and stolen minutes spent watching through the wide windows of the Near North Ballet studio, which was not so far from Little Sicily, only a ten-minute ride on the Brown Line. Mamma and I had been on our way to deliver a suit she had tailored to a banker that worked near the river the first time we'd walked by, my little hand held firmly in her soft, warm one. I had tugged her to a stop in front of the window, my four-year-old eyes opening wide, and together we had watched the dancers as they leaped in the air and seemed to hang there a moment, as they spun so fast it should have left them dizzy and stumbling but didn't. A secret glimpse into another world, one of girls untethered to the earth, floating like stars and brightening the dark. It appeared to me a kind of paradise—I couldn't imagine anything bad ever happening in a place so full of light. Eventually Mamma had pulled me away, and I had felt a crack run through me, as if a piece of my heart had broken off from the rest and lodged there in that very spot, waiting for me to come back for it.

Before I was old enough to venture outside of our neighborhood on my own, I accompanied Mamma on her deliveries to River North with great enthusiasm, or begged Lorenzo to take me on a stroll down Grand Ave directly past the studio. In snatches I studied the ballerinas' movements, their poses and postures, the strain and stretch of their muscles, delicate and powerful at once. At home I imitated them as best I could, aided by the square mirror in our bathroom as I twisted myself into the glorious and sometimes confounding shapes I'd seen through the window—the closest I could get to the real thing, the dancers in their tights and tutus and shiny pink pointe shoes. There was an air about them, this untouchable quality, like their bodies were firmly in this world but their hearts and their heads were in another where they could never die. It was a world I wanted to claim as my own.

"Thank you for the dance."

I had not realized the song had ended, that the dance with the man who was not Lorenzo but looked like him was over. He bowed, and kissed the back of my hand, but the gesture barely registered, and when I hurried back to the table, Emilia's bright smile did not make sense either.

"Well? Who was he?" she said, as I stood there wringing my hands, my shadow falling over both of them. I was so tired, tired like I had never been in my life, all those hours in the studio folding in on me at once. My lower back hurt, as did my shoulders, my ankles and knees; a heavy throbbing behind my eyes, a pain like rot, like meat gone rancid. Emilia dimmed when I didn't reply. "Grace, what is it?"

"Another round?" Oblivious, Adrián gathered our empty glasses. His cheeks were flushed, his pupils wide, his tie hanging slack around his neck.

"No." Emilia's eyes never left mine. "Adrián, I think we'd better head home."

Adrián blinked. "Why? What's wrong?"

"Nothing," I said, because it really was nothing, only a moment of tripping over a memory, a flash of sun in my eyes, somehow, at midnight. "I'm fine," I said at Emilia's dubious frown, and I *did* feel fine—the past was only an echo, a shout dying down. "Really, I am."

"Well. Great," Adrián said, and somehow I managed a smile. "Another round, then?"

"*One* more," Emilia acquiesced, and when he was gone she put her arm around my shoulders, pulling me close. I leaned into her and sighed, fading like a star in the dawn.

THE NEXT WEEK of rehearsal was not so smooth as the one before. I was restless; I couldn't sleep. Every time I closed my eyes, I felt a dark presence at the foot of my bed, a phantom leaning over me. A dirty hole in the chest where a heart should have been, bruised, swollen cheekbones, and crust of blood between the teeth. "Mamma? Lorenzo?" I whispered, my pulse as heavy as a stone in my throat, but of course it was nothing, it was no one—a shadow, or the dream of one. For the first time I realized—in a concrete, inescapable way—that no one I loved would come to see me dance as prima, that all eyes on me would be strangers' eyes (with the exception of Emilia's family, of course, but though they had been kind to me they couldn't truly replace my own). Somewhere between midnight and morning, I went to my little window and cleaned the daily grime from the glass with an old scrap of a threadbare pillow, until my breath had steadied once again. Still, I was too tired even to think.

"Mistress begged Emilia to stay, you know." Beatrice cornered me that day in the dressing room during a break, with Anna beside her, as always. I sat on a bench, sipping from a cup of water, my legs stretched straight out in front of me while I rolled my ankles in large, slow circles to keep my muscles warm. The music from the studio was blunted through the walls, but I could hear Mistress's voice rising above the piano as she praised Emilia for her footwork in the scene where the princess and Ivan meet. "I heard there was a new patron ready to hand over all his cash, but he backed out when he discovered that Emilia was leaving."

This was a rumor Emilia had already denied, several times, but gossip was a free currency, and no one really cared if it was counterfeit.

"Oh?" I said, my attention squarely on my feet as I pointed and flexed them, pointed and flexed. My current pair of pointe shoes was almost dead, the shank too malleable, the box too soft, but shoes were expensive and Mistress insisted we wring every last ounce of support out of them before tossing them into the trash.

"If you're not at your absolute best for every performance," Beatrice continued, undeterred, "we'll never get a patron and we'll all lose our jobs."

"The company can't survive much longer," Anna added. "Maybe not even another season."

"Pity you're an orphan," Beatrice said, with no pity at all. "No family, no connections. You'll have to work doubly hard to attract audiences, since you're completely unknown."

The music in the studio trailed off, a pause between sentences, and in the silence Mistress called my name, summoning me back to the scene. I stood, giving Beatrice and Anna a thin, polite grin. "A company is only as strong as its *weakest* dancers," I said, and left the dressing room with the heat of their stares on my back. I tried to forget their words, to push them aside, but they became like ghosts inside me, stubbornly treading the same path through my mind, again and again as they had in life.

If you're not at your best, we'll never get a patron.

We'll all lose our jobs.

The company can't survive.

The shadows in my room, in my heart and in my head, only thickened as the weeks passed, and soon it was nearly time for costuming and lighting and practicing with a full orchestra. A nasty cold ripped through the company at the end of January, two weeks before opening night, and I was one of the last to fall ill with it, just when Emilia had finally recuperated. I spent a full day and night in bed, sleeping but not really resting, tossing and sweating through thick, tangled dreams. I'd been born in October of 1918, in the midst of the carnage wreaked by the Spanish influenza, upward of eight thousand Chicagoans killed in under two months. Growing up, Mamma would startle at every cough, cringe at every sneeze, instantly on alert and convinced that the flu was once again standing on our doorstep like a man from the Black Hand, extorting us for a sum we couldn't afford. Her anxiety had been infectious; even now, nearly twenty years after the pandemic had come and gone, I was convinced that every illness would be the end of me. Alone in my room, with Mrs. O'Donnell occasionally bringing a fresh glass of water or a bowl of watery soup, I pressed my face into my pillow and prayed—*not yet, not yet, please, not yet*—until the very moment I felt my fever break.

Back in the studio, mostly better though not without some lingering congestion, every errant noise and movement distracted me: the dancers of the corps stretching at the barre when they were "offstage"; Elsie the pianist tapping her fingernails lightly against the keys while Mistress directed us between scenes. Whispers, scratching, Mistress's cane as she tapped out the tempo on the floor. And the door, opening and closing every time someone came in or out while fetching a glass of water, or swapping an old pair of pointe shoes for a new one to break in.

"*What* is so very interesting over there, colombina?" Mistress slammed her hand down on the top of the piano, and Elsie cut off abruptly. It was the last rehearsal in the studio, a full run of the scene when Prince Ivan summons the Golden Firebird to the secret lair of Koschei the Deathless to help him wake the sleeping princesses trapped under the evil sorcerer's spell. I was so startled that I stumbled out of a pirouette and would have fallen if my partner, Will, had not caught me around the waist. The other dancers—Koschei's demons—stopped too, and Emilia looked at me from across the room. In the corner by the piano Mistress stood rigid, waiting for an answer.

"I—nothing," I said, and bowed my head like a penitent before a priest. *All those eyes, all those eyes on me.* "It won't happen again."

"Oh?" Her heels clicked on the floor. Mistress came across the room until she was standing right in front of me. "All day you've been looking at the door, almost as if you are desperate for escape. Tell me, are you planning to fly away?"

"No." All I could hear was my heart. My heart, and her voice. "No, of course not."

"This is not a cage." Her hand was cold as she patted my cheek. She lowered her voice, but the room was so quiet that it did nothing to keep her words private. "But where would we be without our little bird to sing for us so sweetly?"

"I'm sorry," I murmured, and she leaned even closer. "I'm tired, that's all."

"Tired? Would you like your understudy to step in for you, since you're so very *tired*, my poor dear?"

Emilia and I locked eyes from across the room. She shook her head, just slightly. Of course she would dance for me, but if I let her, Mistress would see it as weakness. As failure.

"No," I said, raising my voice now for the room to hear. "I'm fine."

Mistress smiled, like a slow cut into an apple, a knife sawing at the surface of something unyielding. After a moment she stepped back, and a sigh shivered through the room.

"All right," she said, and rapped her knuckles on top of the piano. "Let's back up to the beginning of the manèges. *Places.*"

I didn't look at the door again. Occasionally I watched myself in the mirror, but only to make sure that I was still there. Still prima, still the Golden Firebird; still moving even when it felt as if I had come to a standstill again, stuck in one position, one pattern, one place.

IT SNOWED THE night before the first performance, so heavy and thick it was like the stuff of myth, a phenomenon that could only have been prompted by a great god's wrath. Or else by his indifference, coldness, and utter abandonment. I sat on my bed reading a copy of *Vogue* five months out of date when Emilia knocked on the door, holding up two cups of after-dinner coffee brewed—and burned—by Mrs. O'Donnell. I didn't feel I had room for much of anything in my belly besides butterflies, but the warmth of the mug in my hands was soothing. Emilia perched on the bed beside me, my room so narrow, so cramped, that I imagined our breaths filling the space like mist. If not for my little window, this would be less of a room and more like a closet, the place where you tuck away those things that don't require sunlight, like clothing and keepsakes and secrets.

"How are you feeling?" she asked, eyeing me over the rim of her cup. "Your solo debut is here at last."

"Well, I'm still alive," I said with a wry smile. "That must count for something."

She laughed.

"It really is a feat, with how hard Mistress has been pushing you." Her laughter curled away like the steam rising from our cups. "But she's only tough on you because she believes in you. She wouldn't bother otherwise."

"I know." I set my coffee down on the nightstand, an ancient piece of furniture whose top drawer remained forever jammed. I curled my legs to my chest, resting my chin on my knees. "But . . . sometimes I wonder why she picked me."

"You were the only choice." She said this so firmly, so assuredly, that it was easy to believe her. And I wanted to—really, I did. "I know you often still feel like that lost thirteen-year-old girl who didn't know a tendu from a tour jeté, but trust me, Grace. You're going to be marvelous."

I reached across the space between us and hugged her tight, a bit of hot coffee sloshing onto the blanket beneath us, but I didn't care about that. Tears swelled but I closed my eyes against them, closed my eyes tight. How fortunate I was to have a friend who understood me so well.

A few months ago, when Emilia had first told me the news of her engagement and her subsequent retirement, I had not been at all surprised.

"Oh, Grace, are you happy for me?" She had come to my room—hers was one floor below, bigger and warmer than mine—and we had sat on my bed, the light from the window turning the edges of her dark hair red. She had laughed but it wasn't a full sound. More like a breath to blow a candle out. "Please, please say you are. Lie if you have to."

I was, and I'd said so, and it wasn't a lie; I'd only felt a little bit sorry for myself. So many nights we had stayed up late, imagining our futures, and always we talked of mysterious strangers whisking us away to a life of penthouses and parties where we'd wear gowns that went all the way to the floor, where we'd have more to eat in one evening than we'd had in the last year alone. Of course, when it came down to it, all we really wanted was a kind husband to walk us home when we got blisters on our feet from dancing all night, a husband to keep us safe and warm, someone to love and to love us in return. For Emilia, this dream was real and breathing and right within reach and I was glad she'd realized it at last. But for me a life like that had always seemed so very remote—not because I didn't want it, but because I couldn't quite picture him, the kind of man who might become my husband. When I closed my eyes and tried to imagine him, I only saw a shadow. It stretched over me, and covered me completely, and when I looked up his eyes glowed like little stars.

"But why does this mean you have to leave the company?" I asked after the congratulations were through. "Surely you can still dance after you're married? Unless you plan to have children straightaway?"

I had to fight to keep my voice free of disbelief as I posed the last question. It wasn't that I didn't like children—I'd liked *being* one quite a lot until Lorenzo took all the light away with him and the remainder of my childhood went cold and dark—but I couldn't quite fathom the desire for them, especially when the choice was between ballet and giving birth. The havoc it would force on my body, stretched and bloated and gripped with nausea, unable to dance or even to move very far or very fast. At least until the baby came, but even once the pregnancy was over nothing would really be the same as it had been before. Suddenly there would be another mouth to feed, another person to guard and protect, a precious little life whose youth and vitality did not shield them from the frozen touch of death.

"I do want children," Emilia said, with a little smile I didn't quite understand. The thought of a family of her own made her happy—why couldn't I be happy too? "At least three, but I'm open to four."

She laughed, seeing the incredulity on my face. I'd known she wanted to have a big family someday, but when we'd spoken of it in the past, *someday* had always felt so far away. It made me feel strange, detached from myself, to find that someday had arrived already.

"Well, even if children don't come right away, I'll keep working shifts at the panadería, because we do need the money," she said. "But when it comes to the company, I've been prima for four years now, and . . . Oh, Grace, I'm *tired*. You know how hard ballet is on the body, how it will wear us down to nothing eventually. Sometimes I feel a hundred years old."

I nodded, because I did know. But despite the sore spots and the muscle pulls, the aches in my back and the blisters on my feet, when I thought of stopping or even slowing, panic swept through me. I must not stop moving, I must not stand still; dancing or running, it didn't much matter—though dancing was, of course, preferable to running—because the longer I stayed in one place, the heavier the weight on my shoulder became. When I danced, the hand fell away.

"What I really want is to teach and to choreograph. It's not nearly as demanding as dancing, and then I could teach my own children when I inevitably force them into lessons as soon as they're old enough." Emilia laughed again, but her smile faded quickly this time. "I asked Mistress a while ago, but she said she doesn't need an assistant."

Need? No—more likely she couldn't afford one. But either way, a part of me would never forgive Mistress for not moving heaven and earth to keep Emilia by her side. To keep Emilia here, with me.

Now Emilia drained the rest of her coffee, and we sprawled out on my bed, side by side, staring at the ceiling. Tired, but not ready yet to part for the night. She took my hand in hers, and I felt the pulse at her wrist fluttering like a little bird's wing.

"A girl died in my room downstairs, you know," she said, fighting valiantly against a yawn. "Twenty years ago now. I think about her quite a lot, but most especially the night before a performance. I always have."

Beyond the window, the snow fell on a slant. The wind filled in every silence.

"Poor girl, no one knew she was sick; she hid it as long as she could. Tuberculosis, I think. A sickness that steals you slowly. She didn't want anyone to fuss over her, or tell her she could no longer dance. So she wore herself out, dancing until she couldn't anymore, and died in her sleep. At first the other girls thought she'd killed herself but no one could figure out why. She had a family, a place in the company, a fiancé . . . eventually the autopsy revealed her illness, which I imagine was even more confusing for those who loved her but didn't know." Emilia sighed. "How very strange and sad."

I had heard this story several times before, even from Emilia. It was stuck in our collective consciousness, a legend of transcendence.

I think this was because it could have happened to any one of us.

"Do you think it's true?" I asked. I had already claimed Emilia's room after she moved out of the boardinghouse, and of course, I didn't relish the idea of sleeping in a dead girl's room. But what troubled me most about the story was that she died alone.

"Yes," said Emilia at once. "Don't you?"

I thought of my mother, and of all the people I had lost. I believed in ghosts, but not the restless, frightening kind. I wanted my ghosts to watch over me, to look out for me and love me, until the day I would be held by them once again.

"Yes," I said finally, and fell asleep that night dreaming of the dead.

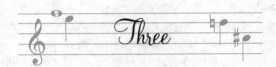

Three

THE FIRST TIME I THOUGHT I HEARD THE VOICE OF GOD IT was really just a gun going off down the street. We ran outside, Mamma and I, my small cold hand in her long warm one. It was counterintuitive, surging toward that sound and the danger it signaled instead of away—instead of *far away*—but death in those days asked for witnesses and we were compelled to oblige. We ran outside with all our neighbors and there it was: my brother's body on the sidewalk. His mouth was open and his chest was ringed by a wet black halo, his dark hair covering his eyes. I froze when I saw him, feeling a warm weight settle on my shoulder, steady and sure, and I thought, *Here is the hand of Death; he has come to take me too.* But I jerked and the weight lifted, a sudden and dizzying release, and when I dropped to my knees it was almost like church, except the bells were my heart and the pulse in my wrist and the pulse in my throat and the pulse in my belly and Mamma's screams.

The second time it was a brown bird flying into the clean glass of my closed bedroom window. I felt the impact as if the bird had slammed into my own body, and an unfamiliar dull heaviness settled deep in my belly. When I stumbled to the bathroom I found a dark red stain between my thighs, sticky and cloying. Mamma and I had just returned from our daily walk to the cemetery, and as I watched the red trickle down my leg I pictured my own grave, the dirt soft and clogged up under my fingernails. There would be no headstone, no name—we couldn't afford it. I bled without pause for the next five days and I was sure if people knew, they would call me a saint. But the red receded eventually and when it returned the next month I knew I was still alive but in a different way.

The third time it was thunder. The sky cracked open like dry lips as I rushed home from the park with the dandelion greens I'd picked all afternoon. With my head down I passed the shops—many of them closed and boarded up—remembering all the things in the windows I used to pine for before the depression hit two and a half years before: a cloche hat with a great big bow on the side, an Iver Johnson bicycle (which I did not know how to ride, but that didn't stop me from wanting it), a pair of lattice pumps with a two-inch heel. I made it home and through the front door just as the rain began. Bringing the greens straight to our cramped kitchen, I started to sauté them in olive oil for dinner, watching their edges curl and brown. When I was done I found Mamma in the living room, hunched over her sewing machine, with a spill of white silk for a wedding dress commissioned by the owner of the local grocery store for his daughter, and it took me a few seconds to realize the machine had gone still, her foot hovering over the pedal.

"Mamma?" I said, taking one step into the dim room. It was cold despite the radiator clanging in the corner, and a dozen candle stumps working as hard as they could on the windowsill. Mamma looked up and there was a line of bright red running from her left nostril to her chin, dribbling over her parted lips. A drop fell on the silk, staining it permanently, but who cared about that now? The room was too hot and I blew out the candles in one trembling breath, as if that would help. In the dark we stared at each other, and Mamma licked her lips, eyelids heavy.

Mamma slipped away in the night. Curled on my side in a nest of blankets on the floor by her bed, I knew it the moment it happened, startled awake by a warm weight at my shoulder, a gentle pressure. I reached up without thinking, and for a second, a split second, I held the hand of Death, large and strong, and my heart was still, quiet, and calm. I let go before comfort curdled into terror, and I wept under the veil of a shadow that wasn't mine.

After that there was silence, and the silence went on, and on.

PERHAPS I COULD have swallowed the silence more easily if it weren't for the music that had come before, the music and the dancing. Before the North Side Gang shot Lorenzo on the sidewalk in retaliation for the murder of one of Bugs Moran's men by the Outfit—the gang that was led by Al Capone at the time Lorenzo belonged to it—Mamma loved to dance. Everywhere, and often. In the evenings, especially in the winter when it was so cold the electricity cut out and the radio wouldn't work, the widower that lived in the flat below ours would visit, bringing his violin. Several years before, Signor Picataggi had retired from a small symphony orchestra, but he missed playing so much that we had the pleasure of enjoying his company and his music. Mamma and I would push all the furniture to the edges of the living room so we could dance while Sig. Picataggi played in the corner, laughing with us as we skipped and stepped, as I raised my arms over my head and twirled like I'd seen the girls do behind the wide windows of the ballet studio in the Near North neighborhood. When Sig. Picataggi finally lowered his violin, always with a heavy, contented sigh, his balding head shiny with sweat, he would clap his hands and say to me, *Brava, Grazia!* and I would curtsy, gracious and deep. Those nights I went to sleep smiling.

On the occasions when Sig. Picataggi was too tired, or too sad, or too sick to come up, Mamma brought out her old wooden tambourine and taught Lorenzo and me the tarantella, a folk dance from southern Italy. There were two types of tarantellas: One was quick and light, a courtship dance, with couples circling around each other. Then there was a darker, frenzied version, ecstatic movement that was thought to cure the lethal bite of a wolf spider. Mamma made sure we knew the steps for both.

Twice a week Sig. Picataggi gave me violin lessons after school in exchange for Mamma mending his socks and his trousers and for running his errands. I was an attentive pupil, eager to learn. He offered to teach Lorenzo too, but my brother said nah, he already knew he wouldn't be any good. I didn't understand how he could know that, though, if he hadn't even tried.

"Then we'd be in competition, see," he said, with a too-rough affectionate tug on the end of my stubby braids. With Mamma we spoke Italian, but with each other we settled into English, the way we were required to do at school. "Only room for one Dragotta in the Chicago Symphony Orchestra, and I'm placing my bets on you, bearcat."

"Well, I do love the violin, but I'd rather be onstage where everybody can see me." I shook my head, yanking my braids out of his grasp. "I want to *dance*."

Lorenzo smiled, his teeth white and crooked. "Whatever ya say, Gracie girl. I'll be front row at your show, either way."

My desire to dance was more than merely wanting to be seen, but I couldn't have explained it then. Playing the violin was like breathing, but dance was the thing that kept my heart beating, wild and free. Breath or blood? Air or ichor? If I had to choose, I chose my heart.

On my tenth birthday in the fall of 1928, when Lorenzo was sixteen—the oldest age he'd ever reach—he bought me my very own violin. Used, not new, but it was made in Germany, and must have cost a fortune, the nicest thing any of us owned, besides Mamma's old wedding ring. Mamma gasped when I lifted it out of the box, the varnish shining icy red in the low lamplight, and asked my brother in a sharp voice where he'd gotten the money for it.

"Tips," he said, innocently enough. "I've been working hard down at the flower shop. Lotta deliveries lately, what with Sweetest Day and all."

Mamma eyed him but I was too distracted—and too young, really—to understand why she was so upset. I ran straight downstairs and pounded on Sig. Picataggi's door to show him Lorenzo's gift, and I watched with pride as the signore marveled over the fine craftwork, the sound body, and the gleaming strings. While I sat with him in his living room, Lorenzo's and Mamma's voices came through the ceiling, a muffled argument, and my heart felt like a ball of string becoming more and more tangled with every quickening beat.

"Why don't we have a lesson right now, hmm?" Sig. Picataggi said, with a grim upward glance, and then went into the bedroom to fetch his own beloved instrument. His violin was made of a very dark wood, nearly black, and he'd carefully carved his late wife's initials into the underside, near the tailpiece: *GP*, for Giovanna Picataggi. "I'll teach you a special song for your birthday, and you can play it for your mother and your brother as a treat. How does that sound?"

I nodded, and we played until there was nothing but music, and the music warmed us, like light.

WHAT I REMEMBER most about my father is his voice—not the sound of it, necessarily, but the cadence. He was always so soft-spoken, murmuring, and every evening before bed he poked his head into my room and said, *Sogni d'oro, cara, cara mia. Dormi bene, buona notte,* like the beginning of a lullaby. *Golden dreams, dear, my dear. Sleep well, good night.* I was four when he left home, forever and for good. Just disappeared one day, maybe to another city or maybe to his grave. A gambler even before he'd served in the army during the Great War, his addiction had worsened after he returned home, and Mamma hadn't known how to help him. He'd gambled away our scant savings, and Mamma kicked him out of the house. I forgave him for never coming back, but not for what he'd left behind. At only ten, almost eleven, years old, Lorenzo felt burdened under a responsibility Mamma never placed on him, this idea that he now had to provide for us, that he was the man of the house. Mamma was a seamstress, working long hours on alterations for the local tailor's shop, and we got by well enough—but Lorenzo wanted more for us.

I only wish he'd wanted more for himself.

He began to leave home for hours at a time, until soon he was gone all night. Often he returned with bleary eyes, his pockets full of cash, and a furtive look about him, becoming defensive when Mamma asked where he'd been and whom he'd been with. It took me a long while to realize what was happening, and not only because I was so young. I simply could not reconcile the idea of Lorenzo—sweet, charming, *mine*—committing crimes, or even associating with men like Al Capone or Lucky Luciano. Mobsters were thieves and murderers, violent and corrupt; Lorenzo was neither, never had been, but desperation scraped away his goodness like paint from a wall, chips and cracks over time until he was nothing but bones and teeth, raw and irascible beneath. He was still kind on the surface—how can someone kill and be kind? I don't know, I don't know—but in the night he was bootlegging, and even if he was not the one physically pulling the trigger on his rivals—the Poles and the Germans, Irishmen, Chicago law enforcement—he was still aiding and abetting the Outfit's extortions, still taking their money and digging himself in deeper and deeper.

"Don't do this," I heard Mamma shouting at him often. Usually after I'd gone to bed; I would creep to my bedroom door, open it a crack. "*Basta*, Lorenzo. *Basta!* These are bad men, and you are not bad, only lost. *Ascoltame, figlio mio. Per favore.*"

But he'd only lean down—he was tall at sixteen, towering over her—and kiss her forehead, an easy smile in place. "Ma, don't worry. I know what I'm doing."

But he didn't and he paid for it, in blood on the sidewalk, in a heart stopped too soon. On the corner where so many others had been murdered, yet another sacrifice to an insatiable god. Death took them all, everyone important to me: First Lorenzo, outside for all to see; then Sig. Picataggi, quietly, in his sleep. And, Mamma, who was sick; Mamma, who starved herself out of grief. Mamma, who caught a cold and couldn't recover, who not only left, but left me alone, and I was still trying, trying to forgive her.

I KEPT THE wedding dress Mamma had been altering; I even tried it on. It hung loose on my shoulders and over my hips, and I couldn't fathom ever being elegant enough, full enough, old enough to wear it. There were still pins in the hem. The blood spot lay right over my heart.

With a small sack filled with all the food we had in the house, plus the dress, folded up, and my violin in its case, I slipped outside to the streets.

Late night tipped toward early morning, black smoke curling from the chimneys like crooked fingers beckoning. The sky had a silver glow like clinging ice. The street was quiet—as quiet as a city block in Little Hell could be, even so early in the morning, the thunderous hiss of the gashouse furnaces reaching me from several blocks away, columns of flame rising up to singe the sky. Somewhere there were skyscrapers, but it was impossible to see their points through the haze of the smokestacks. A rush of warm wind tangled my hair and slipped through the narrow alleys between the nearly identical two-flats huddled shoulder to shoulder like tombstones in the oldest part of the graveyard.

This can't be all there is, I thought, as I left the only home I had ever known. More, more, I wanted *more*—to crawl beneath the skin of the world and touch its bones, to find some kind of magic I could keep as my own. I wanted stars that would burn the death out of me; I wanted skies filled only with light.

My heartbeat as I walked the streets of Chicago was a love letter to the city that I would never send. As I made my way west, I had this feeling like I was already dead but didn't know it yet. Not real. Even the sunlight shone right through me. There was nowhere for me to go, and yet, I knew where I was going. The world had made a ghost of me, and I would do my best to haunt it.

IN A DAMP alley in Little Italy, I raised my violin. Most people who passed me on the street as I played let their eyes slide to their battered shoes, walking quickly, almost tripping, but a fair number stopped to watch for a while, and some of those who stopped tossed me coins or bills. At night I stayed with Zia Vita and my myriad cousins in the flat above the butcher shop that was owned by her son-in-law on Taylor Street. Vita was my father's sister, a widowed, recalcitrant woman who didn't much care where I went or what I did during the day. Every morning I moved to a new location, but there were a few regular visitors who always seemed to find me, no matter if I went north, south, or east toward the lake. Never speaking, only watching, shoulders hunched against the cold, faces wrapped in scarves so only their tired eyes were visible. Perhaps it was the only form of art they'd see or experience all day, all week, throughout their entire lives. Despite the hard times, a young girl alone inspired more charity than I'd hoped. Half the money I earned I spent on food, and the other half I saved, stuffing it in a slim pouch and wedging it in my brassiere, the safest place, nearest my heart. After only five months, I had saved enough.

I bought a pair of ballet slippers. New, pink canvas, the elastic straps forming an X over my arches. I slid them on and pointed my toes, and for the first time since Mamma had gone, I did not feel so alone. So see-through and half-there. The sun shone on me instead of through me, and I was no longer a ghost.

I wore my slippers out of the shop. On the sidewalk I rose on tiptoe and stretched my arms over my head. Now I could finally go to the one place in the world I thought I might be safe—a place of grace and heart-hunger and girls who become gods in chandelier light.

If magic exists anywhere, surely it is wrapped like muscle around the bones of Near North Ballet.

It looked like all the other long, narrow buildings on the long, narrow street, with only a plain sign on the door to distinguish it. I stood on the sidewalk for three minutes, breathing deeply, then I walked up the steps and let myself inside.

A dark hallway, filled with girls and boys my age or a little older, some of them on the floor stretching their legs, and others leaning against the walls and chatting in low voices. A few glanced over their shoulders as I passed by, but most didn't even seem to see me. Or maybe, I thought, they saw my slippers and knew immediately that I belonged there, that I was one of them.

There was music coming from somewhere near the end of the hallway, a piano slightly out of tune, and a voice rising above the notes, spilling like hot tea.

"Wake *up*! Isabelle, extend your leg. Shoulders *down*! William, please, relax your fingers! You're always so *tense*. No one wants to see you straining, for God's sake. *Hide your pain*."

I followed the music and the voice to an open doorway at the end of the corridor, and when I stepped close to peer inside I saw about twenty dancers in a square studio, the girls in pink tights and black leotards, the boys in black tights and white shirts; a tired brown piano in the corner and a wall of mirrors, crystal clean, reflecting the dancers as they pirouetted and then planted their feet in a firm finish, arms flourished over their heads. And there I was too, as I leaned farther over the threshold, my pale thin face reflected back at me. I took a step into the room, and then another, until I could see my whole body in the glass, my slippers pink as kissed lips. I watched myself as I pointed my right foot and my reflection did the same, and I was so entranced that I didn't hear the music stop, or see the woman in the long, loose skirt approaching from the other side of the room.

When the woman was close, she clapped once. I jumped and stumbled back, noticing for the first time that twenty pairs of eyes were on me. The woman before me had her hands on her hips, her red hair in a bun very high atop her head. She smiled at me and I wrapped my arms around my waist, making myself small.

"Who opened the window and let this little bird inside?" she said, her eyes never leaving mine, though it seemed as if she was speaking around me rather than to me. "Hmm? How did this little bird get in?"

I wasn't sure if she expected me to answer; anyway, I couldn't. My voice was gone, snatched by a sorcerer in exchange for a wish that never even came true. What had I been thinking, coming here? That I could walk in and forget my hunger and dance like the girls I'd seen in the window, girls who had been training properly for years and years and nearly killed themselves to reach the top? How could I ever be like them? Me, a skinny girl with a violin, who'd never had a real ballet lesson in all her life, who had no mother and no father and barely enough food to eat? Dreams were liars, and only nightmares told the truth. I didn't belong here—when I chanced a glance to the front of the room, I couldn't see myself in the mirror anymore.

"You," the woman said to me, and I startled again. She hooked her thumbs and made a motion with her hands like wings flapping. "How do you say *little bird*? If you tell me, you can stay."

She thought I didn't speak English. She thought I didn't understand. And if I didn't say something right now, she would toss me back out to the streets. But some of her words were magic words, and I seized on those: *You can stay*. All I had to do was speak.

"*Colombina,*" I said, dropping my arms and straightening my spine. "I am the colombina that came through your window."

For a moment there was silence and stillness and my heart knocking around my ribs, and I thought I had done something wrong. But then the woman's smile turned warm and she reached for my hand.

"Follow me, colombina," she said, and pulled me to the center of the room. "Let's teach you how to fly."

Four

WHEN YOU'RE IN THE THEATER, NOTHING EXISTS OUTSIDE OF it. Not the wind, or the trees, or the stars, or the snow slickening the sidewalks. Not the foxes in hibernation, or the swallows gone south, or the cold cutting through skin and bone like light through glass. The coastline, the skyline, the line that separates sleeping from waking—all of it, gone. There is only this: a wide bright stage in a long dark room, red velvet curtains, and music rising like the moon. Girls dancing like souls come back from the dead, ethereal; pale shoes and tight tutus, crystals and lipstick. Boys in black tights landing lightly as they jump and turn in the air.

It was opening night, the breathless first performance in front of an audience, and the show had just begun.

I watched from the wings as Prince Ivan caroused with his hunting party, his bow and arrows strapped to his back. This was just before he would catch a glimpse through the trees of a bright red bird with feathers of flame. Fixed on his prey, Prince Ivan hardly notices when he crosses through the thin veil between worlds and into the enchanted forest belonging to the sorcerer Koschei the Deathless. The Firebird stops and Ivan does too—and when he pulls back his arrow to shoot his prize, the Firebird sings a song of high sorrow, begging him for her life. The song burns in his heart and he lowers his bow. In gratitude for sparing her life, the Firebird gives him a golden feather from her wing that will summon her should he find himself in dire need of help.

But we were not quite there yet. While Ivan and the men danced,

Emilia stood beside me in a pink Romantic tutu and a silver crown. She squeezed my hand so hard it ached.

"Well," she said quietly, "this is it."

My throat burned, as if from wine, and my hands trembled—not drunk, but *alive*. I looked at the dancers onstage without really seeing them, aware only of the music touching me like wind, the darkness of the wings and Emilia's warmth beside me. I felt, strangely, as if I were about to be born, to leave the world I knew for another, one where magic is real and close and sticks to you like a shadow. And if it was not a *better* world, at least it would have different torments. I was tired of all my old burdens; I was tired of sadness without end.

"I'm ready," I said, and Emilia squeezed my hand again. Ivan was about to stray from his hunting party, which meant that it was nearly my cue.

"*Merde*," she said, and I smiled, because this was my favorite part.

The music went soft and twinkly, somewhere between a bell and a heartbeat. In my bright red tutu with gold accents, and feathers in my hair, dozens of crystals in the bodice meant to catch the light so even those in the back rows and the balcony could see them sparkle, I stepped onstage.

When I am on the stage, nothing exists outside of it. Not the other dancers sliding in and out of the wings to watch or wait their turns, not the brass instruments shining in the orchestra pit, or the conductor's hands graceful like swans skimming a dark lake. Not the lights—no, those are suns, gleaming from every angle—and not even the edge where the stage drops away. The wires, the pulleys, the proscenium arch—all of it, gone. The audience, though—the audience remains.

It was for them that I performed, for the audience that was watching me, hungrily, deciding which parts and pieces of me they'd most like to eat. Which step they liked best, which pose and which leap. Which port de bras, and which pirouette. And I didn't mind it, because I knew they couldn't hurt me, couldn't cross that divide between seats and stage like a child in a bed who is certain that the creature beneath won't seize them as long as they stay tucked up tight under a blanket. Here, I was safe; here, I took my dread and my joy and my fear and my longing and I turned them into energy—into movement and rhythm and story. I danced, and found I was right, after all: Nothing could touch me. Nothing at all.

Mamma was there, and Lorenzo, and Sig. Picataggi, side by side in the very front row. Who was to tell me they weren't, when all the faces out there looked the same in the dark? I danced for them, and felt as though I would never need sleep again. I pirouetted and fouettéd but never grew dizzy; I burned, and the fire was bright. A dream is only a dream until it comes true, and what is it then? Fact? Reality? That doesn't sound quite as lovely, but it is. It was.

Covered in sweat I made my exit, but stayed in the wings to watch Prince Ivan wander deeper into a glade containing thirteen princesses all sleeping in a row. Overcome with exhaustion, Ivan falls asleep and dreams he dances with the princesses, falling quickly in love with the thirteenth among them—Emilia's last, triumphant role upon this stage. I felt tears prickle in my eyes, already mourning her loss. In the dream she tells him how the sorcerer Koschei had put them under a spell, and that the only way to break it is to kill their cruel captor. But Koschei is immortal; he keeps his soul in an egg hidden inside a casket. Prince Ivan vows to destroy the soul and free the princesses from the curse, and declaring this, he awakes.

The curtains closed and intermission began. Those fifteen minutes felt like an eon as I went back to the dressing room to wipe my forehead with a towel and touch up my makeup. The other girls talked and laughed around me, but I felt utterly separate from them. I was the only one wearing feathers, wearing red. Onstage it had made sense, but behind the scenes I felt marked. Like a firebird in truth, an arrow aimed square at my heart.

At last it was time for the second act. Prince Ivan called for me with the feather I had gifted him, and with my song I danced Koschei and his demons to sleep so that Ivan could find Koschei's death unimpeded. When it was done and the princesses were saved, I danced at the wedding of Prince Ivan and Princess Ekaterina, singing a song of joy and victory that would set their hearts ablaze with passion so long as they both shall live.

I took my bow last of all the cast, and the applause swelled and spilled like water, filling my ears and my heart and the entire theater. And after the curtain closed I could hear it still, the cacophony of their adulation, like rain falling wildly all across the city, a long drought ended at last.

As soon as the show was over, I went down to the bathroom beneath the stage and locked myself inside. I wanted to be alone, just for a minute. I leaned against the wall, my beautifully made tutu crushed against my back, the layers bent. When I came out Emilia was there, still in her long pink tutu, so close it was like she'd been pressing her ear to the door.

"Are you all right?" she said quickly, and I realized she *had* been pressing her ear to the door, because she thought I might be crying.

"I'm fine," I said, stepping out of the way so that Beatrice could access the bathroom. She had already changed out of her costume—she was one of the thirteen princesses—and back into a black leotard. "Just nerves."

But it wasn't *just* nerves, I knew it as soon as I said it—it was more like euphoria, quickly cooling. Like gold poured in a metal mold, steaming as it hardens into shape. Now that the performances were beginning, the season would soon be over, and I couldn't help thinking of the end and how empty I would feel then.

"Well, you were stunning," Emilia said, taking my elbow and steering me around a quiet corner where we could have some measure of privacy. "Everybody's talking about it. About *you*."

My feet were swollen in my shoes and I needed to take them off, the ribbons too tight now, an ache like a cloud too full of rain. But I forgot that dull pain as my heart began to dance. I kept my voice low. "What are they saying?"

Emilia smiled and lifted her chin like she had a secret, a good one. "Oh, only that tomorrow night's show is almost *completely* sold out. Your admirers are clamoring to come see you again. Fistfights at the box office, a parade of young men all eager to meet you."

This news stopped my breath, though I didn't entirely believe it could be true. Even with Emilia as the prima, beloved though she was, the company hadn't sold out a show in years. I was about to express my skepticism when Beatrice came out of the bathroom and walked around the corner past us, taking a circuitous route back to the dressing room that was completely unnecessary unless you wanted to eavesdrop. We stayed silent until she was gone, and then Emilia took my hands and leaned so close she was practically breathing in my ear, ensuring only I could hear.

"I heard that there's one man in particular, sitting alone in box number one—you know, the one directly to the left of the stage—who fell in love with you at first sight. And that he's so mad about you he refuses to even *look* at anyone else, the world rendered ugly and unbearable in comparison to your great beauty." She lowered her voice even further, a wisp. "I heard from Anna that he's a *prince*. Very rich and *very* handsome. Beatrice is quite upset."

"And you believed her?" I said, but the words sounded thin and faraway. I clasped my hands together to keep them from trembling. Emilia was still smiling, half-teasing, half-delighted. If it were true—and I was not convinced it was, for how could anyone possibly know of some lovesick suitor (and a *prince*? Certainly not!) when the show had only just ended, when he was sitting alone with no one beside him with whom to express this sentiment? Yet if it were true, could this be a potential patron for the company at last?

Just then Mistress came stamping around the corner, a long strand of pearls looped twice around her neck. Her pale green gown fell all the way to the floor, with a short train trailing behind her. I had seen her wear that dress many times before, and wondered that it still appeared so pristine, seemingly untouched by time.

"There you are!" she snapped, and Emilia and I let go of each other's hands. "Why are you two still in costume? Go change! The public is waiting to meet you."

There was to be a post-performance reception hosted in the lobby of the theater. Mistress had paid to retain a string quartet from the ballet orchestra for the event, and hors d'oeuvres would be served on silver trays, as well as some champagne—one glass per guest. But for me it felt like less of a party and more of a parade—an opportunity for Mistress to put me on display, to entice any of these supposedly enamored young men to donate. In accepting the prima position, I had made a deal not only to dance but to dazzle, to ensnare. And though I'd known that these were the terms of the bargain, the full reality of it clawed at me, a long scratch down my throat and into my chest. The stage acted as a boundary—even if it *was* only imaginary—a shield from the world and everyone in it. But at the party, that protection would be gone.

Mistress led us back to the dressing room, muttering about insolent girls and a decided lack of *time management*, and I was somewhat jarred to find that the room was mostly empty now, only a few girls in their party dresses, fluffing their hair and carefully repainting their lips with less garish hues than the ones we used for the stage so our features could be seen all the way in the back rows.

"You're going to be late, but I suppose that's all right." Mistress hovered as Emilia and I began pulling pins from our tightly coiled buns. "My primas, best for last."

I reached into my bag under the makeup counter for my dress, the same one I'd worn to the Club DeLisa all those weeks ago, but Mistress stopped me with a hand on my shoulder. She held a box I hadn't noticed before and passed it to me with a smile.

"Wear this," she said. "A gift."

I accepted it mutely, and let it sit on my lap while Mistress brushed my hair, smoothing out the crimps with each pass of the bristles scraping along my scalp. I eyed the box as if it held a beating heart, wondering what I would find inside. And how I could possibly get out of wearing it if it proved to be hideous.

"All right," Mistress said, and I started as if I had been caught doing something I shouldn't, even though I'd only been staring at the mysterious gift she'd given me. She nodded toward the bathroom and turned to take the brush to Emilia's hair next. "Go and change."

THE GOWN WAS white. So white it made my teeth hurt. It had long sleeves and a low back, draped with no embellishments, and when I put it on it felt like cooled candle wax against my skin, smooth and clinging but not too tight, absolutely opaque. I felt like I could go to war wearing it and it wouldn't rip; I could sleep and it wouldn't wrinkle. I never knew clothes could be like that, like armor. It was the nicest thing I'd ever worn.

Emilia's dress was red and belled at the hips, not unlike a long tutu. After we'd oohed and aahed and generally swooned over each other's exquisite beauty, we linked arms and followed Mistress as she led us down a long brick corridor to the foyer.

"We've switched places for the night," Emilia said in a trembling hush, and I couldn't help feeling a little giddy, a little moon-mad, like there were bubbles in my blood and my heart was filled with air. I had just danced my first performance as the prima of Near North Ballet, and it wasn't a dream, it was as real as my shadow.

"Tonight I'm the Golden Firebird," she said, "and you're the beloved princess."

The sounds of the party reached us before we saw it, mist-like— footsteps and laughter and the clink of glassware. An adagio playing in the background, soft and sweet. As we crossed through a door at the end of the hallway the party grew louder, closer, though still out of sight. We were on the second floor of the foyer, the party at the bottom of the wide staircase, beneath a grand Tiffany chandelier. I slowed to a stop, and sensing my hesitation, Mistress and Emilia stopped too.

"You go on ahead," I said to Emilia, and she nodded, glancing quickly from me to Mistress. My stomach twisted as I watched her disappear around the corner to the stairs.

Beside me Mistress waited, huffing an impatient breath. It shook me to realize that in my heels I was slightly taller than her, looking down. It had always seemed like she loomed so large over me.

"Mistress, please," I said quietly. "Won't you tell me . . . where you got this dress? It's beautiful." *And expensive*, but I didn't say that.

It was not the question I'd meant to ask. *Was there really a potential patron sitting in box number one?* But it was a safe question, innocent enough. Or so I'd thought.

"Ah, colombina." Mistress surprised me by pressing a wrinkled hand to my cheek, the knotty skin over her knuckles the only part of her re- vealing her true age. I had always appreciated when women looked their age, unashamed—it made me feel less afraid of growing older. Her palm was warm and dry. "That dress you're wearing—it once belonged to someone I loved very much. You reminded me of her tonight."

"Who?" I said quietly, surprised again. My exposed back felt so vulnerable then, all those vital organs unprotected. How had I imagined even for a moment that this dress was a shield? Not even my heart was safe.

"My daughter. She left it behind when she . . . left," Mistress said, and dropped her hand from my cheek. I stared at her hair, hanging in gray-streaked red waves around her face, instead of her eyes. The intensity of her gaze was overwhelming. "You did well, my little bird. I believe you have sealed our fate tonight."

"What do you mean?" I said, suddenly breathless. *Fistfights at the box office, a parade of young men all eager to meet you.* "Do we have a patron?"

"Oh, dear." Mistress took my hand and tucked it beneath her arm. She began walking forward, and I had no choice but to be pulled along. "No fretting, not here and not now. Only joy, and *triumph*."

"I'm not fretting," I lied as we rounded the corner and found ourselves at the top of the stairs, a swirling confection of brightly colored gowns below. The string quartet playing in the corner, a long table with items for auction—including several pairs of pointe shoes I'd used for rehearsals with my signature on the vamp—and tuxedoed waiters serving bruschetta on tiny white doilies. I spotted Emilia taking a flute of champagne off a passing tray and handing it to Adrián, who looked stiff and awkward, adjusting and readjusting his tie, as Beatrice tried to get her attention—most likely to gossip about me. We lingered there, Mistress and I, seeing everything but not yet being seen. "I'd just like to know if—"

"I know, Grace. I know. All in good time."

As we descended the stairs together the conversation quieted and several heads turned our way. Emilia started clapping and then everyone was clapping and I wasn't sure what the applause was for because it couldn't be for me, only for me, not here in this room where I hadn't done anything but enter it, and as soon as I reached the bottom step I diverged from Mistress and walked straight toward my friend, focusing on her, only her, and the glass of champagne she held out to me, her smile like morning, like sunrise, so bright I could feel it on my skin.

"Oh, God, why are they looking at me?" I said as I took the glass from her but I don't think she heard me, and anyway, Mistress was calling for silence so she could make a proper toast. Behind me Adrián patted my shoulder in what I supposed was a gesture of congratulations, though it just as easily could have been consolation. Soon he would take my Emilia away. I sipped my champagne and turned to face Mistress where she stood in the center of the room, my hip pressed to Emilia's, no space between us. She was still mine, for now.

Honestly, I didn't hear a word Mistress said. I wasn't listening and I was aware I wasn't listening but I was too tired to tune in and hadn't I done enough for today? Mistress's monologue was not a battle cry or a lullaby, failing either to rouse me or to soothe me. When she said my name it felt like it belonged to someone else; when she raised a glass to me I looked down at my feet.

"There are fewer people here than I thought." Emilia rose on tiptoe and glanced around, biting her lip as she scanned the crowd. "But still, a very good turnout."

Mistress was still speaking, her words met with raucous laughter at intervals. I couldn't think of a single time Mistress had ever said something I found particularly funny. She was different here, in front of all these people, glossy with exuberance. *She's performing*, I thought, with something of a start—though I didn't know why this should shock me. I knew very little of Mistress's past, but just then I could imagine her on a stage, playacting as a magician's assistant, pointing her toes and raising her arms and shouting, *Ta-da!*

The toast ended and a line formed, a line of people who wanted to meet me. Abruptly Mistress appeared at my side, making introductions, small talk, graciously accepting well wishes. Low lighting and soft music and champagne bubbles popping in my stomach. I smiled and shook hands, and every pair of eyes I looked into I thought, *Could it be you?* The tall man with a gold ring on every finger; the muscular man whose shoulders strained against his suit. The older, yellow-haired man with cigarettes on his breath; the man with dirt under his fingernails who held my hand a little too long, who stared at me without blinking.

Could it be you?

I chatted more freely with the women who came to congratulate me, complimenting them on their dresses or their jewelry or the way they'd done their hair. They were much more affectionate and fawning with me than they might have been without the champagne, giggling and caressing my cheeks, calling me *little bird, little bird* the way Mistress must have done in her toast. The smiles I gave them were genuine.

At last there was no one left to greet, and I found myself standing in the center of the room, oddly alone. Mistress was engaged with a group of black-tied men, their heads bent together, and Emilia was swaying slowly with Adrián near the string quartet, clutching their empty glasses of champagne. Beatrice, standing with Anna, stared at me from across the room; she frowned when our eyes met, but didn't look away. Well past midnight, it was that blurry, yawning time in a party when everyone is exhausted but no one wants to be the first to leave. I drifted to the side of the space, intending to tiptoe around the corner and behind a ridiculously tall potted plant so I could slip my shoes off and lean against the wall for a minute or two, but halfway there a man with short black hair and the shadow of a beard intercepted me, holding an impeccably wrapped box in his gloved hands. Tall and elegantly thin, he looked like a sacrifice, like a tragic hero they'd lock into the labyrinth thinking, *Here at last is the one to best the Minotaur*, believing it fiercely up until the moment his bones were oiled for burial.

"Miss Dragotta?" he said in a voice that surprised me, deep and rasping, less like an ill-fated champion and more like the childhood monster you had long ceased to believe in suddenly whispering from the shadows. I nodded. The box he held was much smaller than the one containing my gown but larger than the heavy collection of Shakespeare's plays that I kept in my room, and I eyed it warily, wondering what it could be. "Master La Rosa was sorry he could not be here for the reception tonight, but he wished me to leave you with this gift. He also wished for me to impress upon you how fervently he awaits your inimitable performance again tomorrow evening."

"I'm sorry," I said, smiling to hide my confusion. He proffered the box, but I made no move to take it from him. "I don't know anyone by that name."

"Don't you?" His face was impassive, but there was a sly note in his rich voice, slippery like a secret. "He is your patron, after all. He picked you especially to dance the Firebird role."

My heart went cold—with frost, with winter, with the end of everything, inside me and around me. It is not enough to say I was frozen; no, it was like I had never been made of anything other than ice.

"*Mistress* picked me," I said, crossing my arms over my chest, a shield between him and my heart. "I *earned* this."

"I've no doubt you earned your place in this company; however, it was not the ballet mistress who picked you but Master La Rosa." The man's eyes suddenly narrowed, and his breath caught, an audible stop, a sharp sliver of silence; but then he exhaled, and his features settled back into that mask of careful dispassion. "That's a beautiful dress, Miss Dragotta. I am sorry again that the Master isn't here to see you in it."

"I think there's been a mistake," I said, but the man made no reply, only held out the box a second time. Like one in a dream, I took it. The man bowed to me, oddly formal, and began walking away before I could even say thank you. But it didn't matter anyway—I didn't have breath enough to speak, or will enough to make my mouth form the words. And I *wasn't* thankful; I was confused, and lost, and numb. Numb like I had sat outside in the snow for hours, and could no longer feel my knees or my fingers. Numb, as if I had been touched on the back of the neck by a hand in the dark.

All this time I had believed—had wanted to believe—that I'd been plucked from the corps because I truly was a little bird, a shooting star—*unique*. Not as technically clean as Emilia or Beatrice, perhaps, but adept nonetheless and with artistry unmatched. Seven years I had danced, early mornings with Mistress and late nights with Emilia, pushed myself until I thought I would collapse, until I thought I had gone and danced myself to death. Seven years of waiting and wondering and wishing, of losing hope and finding it again. Seven years, and I had thought it had all come true, that I had not needed to run but to *fly*, to fly higher and faster than ever before.

And now, in an instant—a mad, terrible instant—it was revealed that I had only been given the prima position at the behest of someone I had never heard of, someone I did not know.

Why? Why had I been chosen? Why was I here? Why had I agreed to this?

Why hadn't I fled long ago?

And why didn't Mistress tell me? Why didn't she think I deserved to know?

I was cold, it was true, but there was still fire in me somewhere, guttering but bright. With the package from Master La Rosa—*my patron*—under my arm, I pushed through the crowd, heading straight for Mistress, who stood in a group at the base of the stairs. She didn't see me coming; I raised my voice to be heard.

"Why didn't you tell me?" Not quite a shout but loud enough that it turned heads. I stood beside Mistress, looking down at her. "Why didn't you tell me about Master La Rosa?"

Mistress was calm; she merely waved me off. She smiled at the men she'd been speaking with, an apologetic glance. "Colombina, please, I'll be with you in a minute."

"No. We're going to talk *now*."

"Excuse me, gentlemen," Mistress said, the skin around her eyes tightening as her smile strained and widened. "You know how these dancers can be—prima donnas, one and all."

The men chuckled as Mistress grabbed my arm and pulled me away, steering me near the potted plant I'd wanted to hide behind before. There was no sign of the man who'd delivered the gift, no sign but the box itself that he'd ever been there at all.

"What is it?" Mistress hissed. "Those were very important—"

"Master La Rosa." Ice, frost, snow, winter. It is easier to feel nothing than everything all at once. "My *patron*."

At last the name registered; Mistress went rigid, as if the cold were seizing her too, her eyes wide and her jaw clenched tight. But like a spell breaking, she blinked and looked around, as if seeing the room for the very first time.

"He was here?" she said with an urgency that made my heart pound. "Now?"

"No. He sent a man on his behalf." I had begun to sweat, even as I shivered. "Some kind of assistant, or . . ."

"Russo," Mistress breathed, and the way she said the name was curi-

ous, with a note of fondness as well as distaste. "And, oh, good God—
you're wearing that dress."

I looked down at myself, at this dress that had enchanted me when I
first put it on, but that now I couldn't wait to rip away from my skin.

Mistress touched my hair, the sudden movement of her hand startling me. She tucked a curl behind my ear, all urgency gone. "I had
thought I would have more time. To tell you, that is. Until the closing-
night gala, at least."

I wanted to slap her hand away. I didn't. "What closing-night gala?"

"It's to be held at the Adler Planetarium. In honor of you, hosted by
your patron." She sighed, and for the first time I saw the depth of her
exhaustion, the hunch of her shoulders, the sagging skin beneath her
eyes. "You were supposed to meet him then."

This was all too much. Too much and too little, a labyrinth of questions with only dead-ended answers. "But why would you keep this
from me? I don't understand."

"I thought I told you not to fret," Mistress said lightly, but dropped
her false buoyancy at my hard, unwavering stare. "Oh, colombina, I simply didn't want you to be afraid. Forgive me, please, for only trying to
keep you at ease."

"Why should I be afraid?" I whispered it.

"It's quite a lot of pressure for one young girl, isn't it? Declaring she
must please her patron so that the company can continue to exist? I
didn't want to tie a weight to your ankle before you'd even begun." She
shrugged, and took a step back. She was tiring of this conversation, tiring of me and of this night. "Why don't you have another glass of champagne? My treat. The party is almost over—let's enjoy what's left."

I watched her walk away with a feeling like melting, like falling very
slowly. Every face in the room blurred into one face, and it was not
really a face at all but a blank space, a pit, a mouth opening to scream or
to sing or to swallow me whole.

I DID NOT want to open the gift from my patron where anyone could
see, so I tucked the box under my arm and held my gown with my other
hand so I wouldn't trip on the hem, and then—I ran. Quick, silent. The

music and the shuffling and the laughter like light on glass fell away as I went deeper into the theater, twisting as if in a labyrinth. The dressing room was dark, empty, but I couldn't bear to turn on the lights and see myself in the mirror, illuminated like a saint, like an angel, a feverish halo. The window, the small, high window on the other side of the room—I went to it, shivering, the glass thin as a knife and crusted with ice, snow falling slowly on the other side. A nearby streetlamp glowed through the thick white flakes and fell across the box and my hands gripping it.

The bow, the paper, the lid—all of this I untied, tore, lifted. And then there was only a layer of tissue paper. I parted it slowly, like skin.

It was a violin.

A cold sweat broke out on my forehead and the nape of my neck. My hands began to shake so violently it was difficult to fit the lid back on the box, but I wanted the violin gone, wanted it out of my sight. I felt eyes on me in the dark even though I was alone in the room. I *knew* I was alone, and yet, here was proof that perhaps I had never been alone for a moment in my life.

Who *was* Master La Rosa, and how had he known? Had he been watching me, following me?

And for how long?

I returned to the reception but spoke no more that night; I don't think anyone noticed. At that point I had done all that was required of me. When it was finally over and I was allowed to leave, Emilia and I walked home together, the violin box held securely under my arm. Emilia asked me what was in it, but I told her that I didn't know—that I hadn't opened it yet—and she was still too dizzy with champagne and the high of a good party to notice how my voice trembled just a little as I lied. We held hands as we walked, both for comfort and to steady ourselves as we slid over the icy cement.

At home, my gown was wet to the knees from the snow; in my room with the door closed, I peeled it off and let it fall to the floor before nudging the sodden heap with my foot into the corner, where I wouldn't have to look at it. Then I knelt in the center of the bed and said my prayers with barely a breath.

And in the dark and in the quiet and in the stillness of the long, frigid night, when everyone else in the boardinghouse, and the city, and perhaps the whole world, was asleep, I lifted the violin from the box slowly, reverently, like a broken thing. It wasn't broken at all, but I was not entirely convinced that it was real, as if it might crumble to dust in my hands. The varnish was dark, so dark it was almost black, and I held my breath as I turned the violin over, to see the back. *It can't be, it can't be*, I thought, for Sig. Picataggi's violin had been buried with him—I'd seen it, tucked beside him in the coffin. *It can't be!* I screamed, somewhere inside me, my hands shaking so badly that I nearly dropped the instrument as I brushed my fingertips over the carving below the tailpiece, as I touched the clear, clean shape of the initials set into the wood just as I remembered them.

GP

My heart swooped like a sparrow in a heavy wind, pushed down, down, down. Was it only my imagination, or was the violin much lighter than it should have been? There was no real heft to it, no certainty of solidity, and I wondered then if objects, like people, could come back to haunt us. If somehow the soul of the instrument had been resurrected while the original remained in the ground as intended. *A phantom violin.*

Did I dare to play it, this impossible, terrifying, miraculous gift? Here, now, when most everyone in the boardinghouse was already asleep? Would it even make a proper sound if I did, or only a grotesque, otherworldly wail? *No*, I decided. *I will not play it, not now.* I put the violin back in its box and slipped it beneath the bed to rest beside the one Lorenzo had given me, ignoring the tiny voice in the back of my head pleading with me to throw it out the window, drown it in the lake, smash it underfoot—whatever I had to do to be well rid of it. How had Master La Rosa even obtained it? And what did it *mean*?

I know you, Grace, the violin seemed to say as I put it away and climbed, trembling, into bed. *I know who you are, and I know where you've been.*

Was it a cruel message, a reminder of a time I'd rather forget? Or was it kind, an offering made in good faith? I could not decide. *You are not alone* felt like both a comfort and a threat.

Five

TWELVE PERFORMANCES OVER THREE WEEKS. SEVEN PAIRS OF pointe shoes, hundreds of hairpins. Three blisters, a rolled ankle, countless aching muscles. But onstage I hardly noticed how much it all hurt, like a dream when your brain knows but your body doesn't feel a thing. It was worse when it was over, the pain pushing through the protective layer of fantasy. When I stopped dancing I was mortal again.

"Can you see him?" Emilia whispered as we stood in the wings on the night of the second performance, leaning as far forward as she dared, peering not at the stage but beyond it into the audience. From our vantage we could see only a sliver of it, only the private boxes along the far wall, here and there a pair of eyes glowing in the dim. My patron sat in box number one, so close to the stage that he could almost reach out his arm and cross the barrier between the observers and the dancers, between dark and light, between stillness and motion. Were those his eyes swiveling toward me now? I drew back until I was firmly cloaked in shadow and tugged Emilia with me.

"I can't see anything in the dark," I said quietly, even though—the eyes. Now that I wasn't looking, I was sure there had been only one pair, not dozens, and that they were green, unnaturally so. And that whoever it was they belonged to had been staring right at me.

"Oh, well." Emilia chewed her cheek. "You know, I still think it was rude of him not to deliver the violin to you himself."

Emilia was the only one who knew about the Master's gift. She might have forgotten all about the box I'd carried home from the reception if

I hadn't left it partially sticking out from beneath my bed after I'd woken in the night for the thousandth time to check that it was still there, still real, still mine. She'd accidentally kicked it with her toe the morning after the reception when she came to eat breakfast with me.

"What's this?" she said, stooping down to pick it up. "A gift?"

I tried to snatch it from her, but that only made her more suspicious. She swatted my reaching hands away, quickly lifting the lid and pushing aside the tissue paper with a decisive crinkling sound.

"From my patron," I said as she stared into the box. By then, everyone knew of Master La Rosa; the news had traveled so quickly, it was almost as if every dancer in the company had dreamed of him overnight, and woke fully aware of what was now no longer a secret. In the morning there had been a great knock on my door, gossipers gathering around to hear more.

"Tell us about your patron," they said, almost as one, in low, giddy voices. Mostly it was the apprentices who had come, girls a few years younger than me, wide-eyed and stubborn in their insistence that the world was still a safe place. Beatrice lurked among them, listening silently. "Is he handsome, tall, young, old?"

I answered in evasions and riddles, smiling so they would not see how my hands trembled, or notice how my throat went dry.

"He is as handsome as a handful of snow melting in your hands, cold and shimmering, and as tall as a dream that goes on and on until morning. As old as laughter and as young as a breath."

"That's all well and good," said Beatrice, her voice rising above the others' delighted murmurs, "but why did he pick *you*?"

Again I answered in evasions and riddles, because I didn't know.

Eventually the gossipers had dispersed, disappointed in my rejoinders, leaving Emilia and me alone, consternated over the Master's gift.

"Was there a note?" Emilia had said after a pause. She closed the lid of the box and sighed as if she'd been holding her breath. I was grateful she hadn't lifted it, hadn't turned it over and seen the initials. I didn't have the will, just then, to explain.

I shook my head.

"But, Grace. A *violin*?" Her voice rose to little more than a squeak on the last word. "Do you think . . . ?"

I nodded, wrapping my arms tightly around my waist. Neither of us wanted to say it aloud, the implications of the gift: Master La Rosa had been watching me, following me, since my days performing on the streets for scraps seven years ago. And by giving me the violin, he wanted me to know.

Hearing again the tender tremble of my old violin, I tried to picture the people who had swirled around me as I played on the close, clogged streets. But all I could recall was a blurry procession of brown coats, knit scarves, and muddy boots. The clink of falling coins, distant trains rumbling, the slosh of puddles beneath shuffling feet. The hushed hysteria of winter, choking wind and screaming cold. I never once looked into anyone's eyes as they watched me or passed by. That way they were never quite real. And neither, truly, was I.

Emilia began to pace. "Let's just—*think* about this. On the surface it seems—"

"Eerie."

"Yes." She sat down heavily on the bed. Emilia was the only one I'd ever told about my past. She was the only one I'd ever trusted with it. "But, when you *really* think about it—I mean, if you consider it from another angle—it's actually, kind of, romantic."

I dropped my arms. "Romantic?"

"Don't you see?" she said with rising enthusiasm, warming to her theory. "He's been in love with you all this time! Imagine it: A prince passing in secret through the alleyways, the only time he felt he could truly be alone, where no one would know who he really was, where no one would recognize him as royalty."

"That's silly," I said, and though my tone was light, all I wanted was for her to stop, *please* stop. If Emilia believed that I was only promoted because Master La Rosa had demanded it in exchange for his patronage, because he was somehow a prince and the wishes of princes were not to be refused, I didn't want to know. I didn't want her to believe anything but the best of me. "There are no such things as princes anymore."

"There are in some places," she insisted, her eyes shiny in the dim lighting. "Royalty left over from a lost time. I bet he saw you once and was smitten, returning every day after to hear you play. He wanted to tell you how he felt but he was shy and didn't know how. By the time he'd worked up the courage to declare his love, you had already disappeared off the streets and joined the company. Now he's found you again at last, and this time he won't let you get away. Grace, he essentially bought the company for you."

A flush of pink stained her cheeks. I stared at her and she nodded once, firmly, as if to punctuate a magic trick shown to a skeptic. *And there you have it. How can you ever doubt again that magic is real?* Behind her, my little window was fogged from the snow falling incessantly outside, white tinged gold in the streetlamp glow. If I were to run right now my footprints would fill with flakes so fast I would never leave a trail. The clouds above like a great gray shield—no sunlight, no moonlight, no stars. No one would ever find me.

Years ago, when we had spun our fairy tales of the men we might someday marry, Emilia had often filled in the blanks for me when I came up empty. *For you, maybe a sailor,* she'd say, *someone who has journeyed to the end of the world and back.* Or, *Oh, I know—a radio newscaster! Someone with a lovely, deep voice to whisper you to sleep at night.* I would laugh, clutching my pillow to my chest, and agree that she was probably right, even while privately struggling to imagine it, seeing only the same bright-eyed shadow. But could *this* be him, a wandering prince who had come to know me before I knew him, who had listened to my music and now watched me dance while I had only just discovered his existence, who was still as distant to me as the sun from the earth?

"You must be right." I repacked the violin and slid it under the bed. "It's like a fairy tale."

I SPOKE HIS name in secret.

To my faint reflection in the glass of my little bedroom window; between my clasped palms as I knelt in church; into the softness of my pillow at night. As if I were feeding his name to a fire that must not, must never, go out, because the fire was my heart and the blood burning within.

Master La Rosa, La Rosa, La Rosa, La Rosa, La Rosa.

I built him with my breath, in whispers and sighs—his thick hair, his soft hands, his shoulders muscled and broad. Tender throat, the curve of a clenched jaw. Carefully, carefully, I carved him in the dark, every piece of a prince who reigned over silence. Intoned into existence, I couldn't see him but I could feel him, and each night before bed I said his name three times again; I closed my eyes and ran my fingertips over his face in my mind, desperate to know this thing I had made. Always I saved his lips for last, and always it was the only feature missing from my sculpture, a smooth strip of stone right where a mouth should be.

Master La Rosa.

His mouth mattered more than any other part of him. The rest I could live without ever knowing—but his smile, *his smile.*

Was it cruel, or was it kind?

THERE WERE NO more gifts.

None so striking as the violin, at least. Every performance thereafter I was given a rose; Mistress handed it to me as she came onstage at the end, before she clasped her hands to her heart and took a bow with the cast. I held it with two hands, brought the petals to my lips. Each was a slightly different shade of red: fresh blood, dried blood, apple skin, sunset. Mistress did not need to tell me whom the rose was from. All the thorns had been carefully snipped off.

The applause rang on and on, and as the cast took a final reverence, I lifted my gaze to the left and imagined I was looking right at him, a dark shape in the greater darkness of the audience. When the curtains were closed I lowered my eyes but not the rose. I breathed it in until I feared I couldn't breathe without it near.

"By closing night you'll have a whole bouquet," Emilia said on Monday afternoon, smiling at me over her shoulder before she turned to where I had put them on the nightstand in a glass cup I'd stolen from the kitchen, keeping them close while I slept so their fragrance could flavor my dreams. "That is, if they last three weeks." She brought her face to the flowers—a long inhale that turned into a soft gasp at the end. Across the room I stood in the doorway, adjusting my hat as I watched her. "They smell like . . . like . . . well, like roses."

She laughed and I didn't; it was time to go but she didn't move. Mistress was taking us all to a café downtown for coffee and pastries in celebration of the first week's performances done. We were late, but only by a minute—a minute or two—and there was more she wanted to say, her shoulders stiff as she paused.

"It's only . . ." she said slowly, wringing her gloves in her hands, her fingers long and pale. "There's something strange underneath the sweetness, almost as if they smell . . . well, *rotten*." She looked down, shook her head. Her cheeks flushed as she fumbled with her gloves, tugging them on. "But that's silly. They look perfectly—"

"No, you're right," I said, and swallowed hard, because I had thought I was only imagining it. The roses smelled like roses, but beneath that there seemed to be something *more*. "It's like they're dead, but they don't know it yet."

Emilia took a breath to reply but just then Beatrice knocked once on the doorframe behind me, even though the door was wide open, making me jump.

"Are you coming, or what?" she said, and left before we answered, simply expecting us to follow.

"Well," said Emilia, giving the roses one final sniff before coming across the room and hooking her arm through mine. "I wonder what kind of fertilizer he uses."

Fog obscured the tips of the tallest towers around us, and I couldn't remember the last time I'd seen their windows shining. Always, always the sky was gray. Snow like crumpled papers in the gutters, the El rumbling on its high steel tracks over our heads; a pinched frozen skin on the surface of the river. In the café on State Street, most of the company gathered at long tables along the wall, but Emilia and I sat by the window and sipped our espressos, picked at our scones. Lulling chatter, artwork on the walls that would sell for more than my soul. A world so far removed from Little Sicily, with its cracked windows and laundry lines suspended between the two-flats, and yet it was all the same city, smothered by the same smoke. We didn't quite belong there, our clothes threadbare and our shoes worn. This splurge was only possible because of my patron.

Still, I let myself relax as Emilia went over wedding details. It would be a small wedding, intimate, with the ceremony held in the afternoon at St. Francis of Assisi, the same church where we'd attended Mass together every Sunday since she'd first asked me to accompany her many years ago.

In my early days at Near North Ballet the other dancers didn't talk to me. It wasn't entirely their fault; I made no effort to talk to them either. I blushed under their curious and scrutinizing gazes, and turned my face away. Sweetly chiding, Mistress lavished her attention on me—her colombina, her new pet—and I knew I didn't deserve it. I was nowhere near as strong as the others, as technical and precise or as graceful and lithe, separated from them by years and years of training. But I was determined that one day I would match them, and maybe even grow beyond them. Until then, I was merely the girl who had wandered in. An orphan, a charity case.

In the evenings at the boardinghouse, I would eat my meal very fast and then I would leave the table, leave the laughter and the light and the conversations that were not meant for me. I would hide in my room, a sanctuary the size of a tomb. There I would play my violin, and it was like running away: While I played, I would imagine myself floating in space, stars congealing into courtly ladies dancing, their skirts glistening as they twirled and giggled and kissed the round cheeks of the moon until it blushed. Asteroids like pearls, stardust like lace.

Only a stampede could splinter the fantasy, only the raucous jostling of the other girls coming up the stairs when dinner was done, talking and teasing and complaining about their sore feet. But a single set of footsteps, careful not to let the stairs creak, did not attract my notice. Not until, three weeks after my arrival, those light footsteps were accompanied by a sneeze.

I stopped playing at once, a screech of strings. The sneeze had come from somewhere very close, right outside my door. I waited a full minute, but there were no other sounds. At last I laid down my violin and opened the door.

A tall girl with dark hair and light brown skin stood on the other side, her face turned as if she'd had her ear pressed to the wood only a moment before. Calmly she took a step back, tucked a piece of her hair behind her listening ear, and said, "Your music is so pretty, Grace. I hope you don't mind me eavesdropping, but it calms me before bed. I've never slept so well in my life than in the weeks since you arrived."

I'd never spoken to her, but I knew who she was: Emilia Menendez, two years older than me, and one of the best dancers Near North had ever seen, on track to take over as prima when the current one retired. I had often heard others whispering about her, citing her dark skin and working-class background as reasons she didn't belong, reasons she shouldn't be promoted. *We'll never get a patron with* her *in the lead. A dancing rat would have a better chance.*

But the corps is full of dancing rats, I'd said when I heard them talking this way in the dressing room, looking each girl in the corps in the face, *so what difference would one more make?* (This was, possibly, another reason why the other girls wouldn't talk to me.) Emilia was far better than all of them, enchanting and technically impeccable, and it was only the declining economy that had hindered our hopes for a patron. Hearing her say my name was like a slap of cold water across my cheeks. I hadn't heard it in months.

Emilia Menendez has heard my music. Emilia Menendez knows my name.

I panicked; I shut the door in her face.

All night I agonized over it, picking the moment apart—was she offended? Upset? Would she tell Mistress of my rudeness? Would she still leave dinner early to listen to my music, or would I be alone again? I had not even known I wasn't alone, but now that I knew, the loss of her companionship felt monumental, the potential for something greater, something deeper, choked at the throat before I could even take a breath.

In the morning I was awake but still in bed when there was a knock on the door. I slipped out from beneath the thin covers, my old socks so worn and stretched that they pooled around my ankles. I opened the door a crack.

Emilia stood there, her face washed and her hair curled, dressed in her Sunday best.

"Hello, I'm going to church," she said cheerfully. "St. Francis of Assisi. It's a bit of a trek all the way to Pilsen, but personally I find the bus ride relaxing. Would you like to go with me?"

I didn't really register the question; I had stopped going to church after Mamma died. But in that moment Emilia could have asked me if I wanted to go with her to my own hanging at the gallows and I would have said yes. I nodded, once, and she smiled.

Hers is the smile I use to measure kindness in others. It's not fair, but I do. And no one else has ever come close.

I still remember, so clearly, the long bus ride to East Pilsen that day. It had been early spring: puddles, rain, water droplets on the window, the clouds glazed like unfocused eyes. But I felt warmer than I had since summer, sitting on that crowded bus in the quiet that was not really quiet, the rush of the wheels and the chatter of the other passengers, the hiss of the doors letting people on and off. For the most part Emilia and I didn't talk, though every once in a while she would lean close, pointing at something. "That's where I had the best meatball sandwich of my life," she said, or "There's a woman who works at that tailor shop who can mend *anything*," and finally, "My family owns that bakery, just there around the corner. We'll stop in after church, if you don't mind."

I didn't, and I told her so, and it was settled.

But first, church.

The interior was more marvelous than my old church, with a triumphal arch over the altar, which itself was flourished with shining gold details and a painted mural of the Virgin Mary. But it had the same air of tension that I remembered, like the sun, full, bright, shining behind a thick cloud. A closed mouth, filling with blood. Vibrations, a scream felt but not heard. Silent peril, violent beauty; falling snow, falling stars, falling angels.

We slid into a pew near the back, to the right of the altar, just as Mass began. I bowed my head and let the old familiarity of the psalms and prayers comfort me—a comfort I had not known I'd craved until then. When it came time for Communion I took the wafer, even though I hadn't been to confession first. If Mamma were here she would not have let me take it, not without reconciliation, and as I made the sign of the cross I prayed she would forgive me.

Outside it was drizzling, and Emilia slipped her arm through mine as we walked. The bakery was only a few blocks away.

"I want to tell you a secret," she said with a slyly gleeful smile. "Would you like to hear it?"

I nodded, trying not to seem too eager. Secrets were binding; secrets meant trust, and trust meant friendship.

"All right, here it goes," she said, taking a breath and lowering her voice. "I fear the wrath of Mistress more than I fear the wrath of God."

I didn't expect this—it was less a secret, and more of a confession. I smiled, laughing a little.

"I do too," I said, and Emilia laughed with me.

"You're still shiny new, and she has yet to find a flaw she can pick to death in you," Emilia said as we waited for a streetlight to change so we could cross. Soon we came to a glass-fronted shop with a sign on the door that read La Estrellita Panadería. "But just you wait. It's something of a rite of passage, the first time you feel the full force of her fury."

The bakery was warm and bright, and the smells of flour and sugar confections immediately set my stomach to roiling greedily. Emilia introduced me to her mother and father and her older brothers. (Hector, the younger of the two, had been the first boy to ever make me blush.) They welcomed me like a long-lost member of their family, with hugs and smiles to rival the kindness in Emilia's. That day we ate apple empanadas for lunch, and they gave me delectable brown sugar coyotas to take home. I tried to pay but they refused my money. It was still raining when we left, much harder than before, but I didn't mind so much now, as if I were carrying the sun inside me.

And so every Sunday we went to church and afterward we ate conchas and pan dulce and banderas in the panadería, and I spent Christmas with the Menendez family and Easter too. Emilia and I stood together at the barre during ballet, and after class we stayed in the studio together so she could instruct me in a private lesson for another hour or two. Every night at the boardinghouse we left dinner early and she lay on my bed while I sat by the window and played my violin.

Much later, when we were more comfortable together, I asked why she didn't tell me she liked my music and was listening at the door.

"Because," she said, "if you knew I was there, you wouldn't have played."

And I knew that she was right.

Now, in the café with the sun setting in the window at our backs, Emilia leaned forward, an almost shy smile on her face.

"Grace, I want you to have a special role in the ceremony, if you'll agree."

"Of course," I said at once, and she laughed.

"Don't you want to know what it is first?"

"Oh, no, is it Adrián?" I pressed my palms to my cheeks in consternation. I affected a low, arch accent, like Katharine Hepburn in the talkies. "Do you want me to kill him the night before and make it look like an accident so we can run off together with the insurance money?"

"How dare you!" Emilia opened her mouth in imitation of scandalized shock, laying a hand over her heart. "I'm perfectly capable of committing my own murders. I was only going to ask that you help me hide the body."

We laughed, and it felt so good to forget for a little while—*princes and violins and roses that smelled rotten but appeared perfect*—and to pretend that I was just a girl sitting with her dearest friend, discussing what was sure to be the happiest day of her life. Once we'd settled down a bit, Emilia took a last sip of her espresso and set the little cup down on the saucer with a delicate clink.

"I'd like you to play your violin for me," she said, and I felt a shadow crawling over me at the request. I fought to keep my smile from waning. "I'd be honored if you would play while I walk down the aisle."

Even now I can't quite explain my reservations in that moment—I had played for Mamma, and for Signor Picataggi, and for countless strangers, and even for Emilia herself. And of course I would do anything to please her, my sister by covenant if not by blood. All I can say is that a heavy air of fate seemed to hover over the request like a long black veil. As if I already knew, somehow, that I would break my promise.

"Yes," I said firmly, because what else was there to say? "I would love to play at your wedding."

DUSK HAD CLAIMED the streets by the time we walked home. Emilia walked slightly ahead of me as she talked to Richard, our friend who danced the ageless Koschei this season. I nodded along to their conversation, but I wasn't really listening. I could smell my roses even though they were nowhere near, safe in my room. For several blocks we passed almost no one moving in the opposite direction, but then a young man with dark hair stepped into a spill of light.

At once I stopped. And stepped in front of him.

He hadn't been paying attention to me, and almost tripped as I blocked his path. He opened his mouth, either to apologize or to curse me, but something in my gaze must have caught his curiosity because his voice curled back on his lips, a stuttering exhale.

His lips.

Was his smile cruel, or was it kind?

Slowly, slowly, I slipped off my glove and raised my hand.

The man stood absolutely still, mesmerized, our fogged breath tangling between us. With the streetlamp shining overhead it was almost like we were onstage, like nothing existed outside of the light.

I raised my fingertips toward his face.

"Grace, what are you doing?"

I glanced away from the man and quickly back again. Emilia and Richard were staring at me, Emilia's black hair glittering with snow. (When had it started to snow?) My palm hovered near the man's jaw, close but not quite touching, my gloveless fingers already frozen and craving the warmth radiating from his skin. The man blinked once, twice, and I noticed then that his eyes were brown.

I dropped my hand.

"Sorry," I murmured, careful not to brush against his shoulder as I moved around him, out of the light. "I thought you were someone else."

Don't look back, don't look back, don't look back.

Richard went on ahead of us, catching up to the others, while Emilia clung tightly to my arm. For the rest of the walk home, neither of us spoke.

Back in my room, with my book of Shakespeare's plays shoved against the door to block anyone from entering, I lifted the roses from their cup, the stems dripping water onto the floor. I still only wore one glove, the other hand bare, numb, and stiff from the cold. One by one I fed the petals out the window, a feast for whatever monster waited to devour them in the alley below.

A WEEK LATER there were four more roses on my nightstand, and these I kept because the clouds had lifted from the sky like the lid of an empty coffin and the sun made all things bearable, for a little while at least. At the end of every performance, I allowed myself one glance toward the Master's box, and he was there every time, a shadow among shadows, remaining in his seat at least until the curtains closed and I could see no more. Was that his voice calling *"Brava!"* above the clamor? Were those his eyes on me, startlingly green, or was it only a trick of the light?

On Wednesday, Mistress took us to the Art Institute, wearing her new fur coat, and I gazed at paintings that looked like miracles, no trace of the sweat or strain that went into their creation. Wandering from room to room, I longed to reach out and touch each work with my fingertips, to feel the tension of the canvas and the swirls of paint. But of course the signs said no, so I stood behind the cordons with everyone else, and wondered if I looked like that when I danced.

Like a miracle.

"Who is he?" I said as Mistress came silently to stand beside me, the room suddenly empty except for the two of us. I didn't take my gaze off the Degas on the wall in front of me, a pastel painting depicting a dancer with dark hair standing at the edge of the stage. One arm hung at her side, the other bent near her face, and her head was tilted to the side at an odd angle, her feet in a rather sloppy third position. Almost it appeared as if she was in a moment of upright repose, a pause, a breath, even as the dancers of the corps pranced behind her, obviously in motion. It was titled *The Star*. "Won't you tell me at least one thing about him? I deserve to know more than a name."

I had asked Mistress so many times already for information about my patron—*Is he young or old, born in the city or come from away? What color is his hair, what color are his eyes? Please, Mistress, it is only a color*—and every time she told me to be patient, that I would know him when he was ready for me to know him. As we lingered in the quiet and the coolness of the museum, I expected her to repeat her usual line, but she surprised me with a long and acquiescent sigh.

"The truth is, I haven't yet met your patron, or even spoken to him. Not directly, at least. I'm as anxious to meet him as you are."

In the painting, the ballerina's dark hair was loose, rippling all the way to her waist, a black band across her pale throat, jewels glinting at her wrists. "What?"

"He sent an assistant to make the arrangements for his patronage. The same man that delivered the gift to you the night of the reception." Mistress shuffled her feet, heels scuffing the floor. "What was the gift, by the way?"

"Oh—a beautiful felt hat with a red feather," I lied. I stayed there with *The Star* long after she'd left my side.

On Saturday night, during the second to last performance, I stumbled. It happened in the first act, when Ivan corners the Firebird in the dark side of the forest, and the Firebird pleads with him. But as I bourréed and temps levéd I couldn't remember what I was begging *for*, and I paused en pointe, my legs crossed in fifth position and my arms raised over my head. *Arabesque*, I thought, already a beat behind the music, *the next step is a piqué arabesque.* But when I moved, my right foot slipped out from under me and I fell off my pointes to flat feet.

My life, I remembered then, as I skipped the arabesque and slid into the piqué turn manèges that came next, setting myself back on track. *I am begging for my life.*

The whole thing lasted only a moment, one second, really, and I doubted anyone who did not intimately know the choreography noticed or cared.

But I was sure the other dancers watching in the wings had seen my mistake, and certainly Mistress too. Maybe even my patron, who came to every show.

Worst of all, *I* knew. I replayed that stumble in my mind for the rest of the act, during intermission, for the rest of the evening. Though I didn't fumble or fall again, didn't even come close, my hands never stopped shaking; my heart never stopped squeezing, hard and fast, a warning in my ears. But a warning of what?

Later, much later, alone in my room while everyone else slept, I covered my face with my hands and cried quietly into my palms, sobs that shook me like a tree in a storm. I picked up my hairbrush and threw it as hard as I could at my little window—the glass didn't even have the decency to break. I ripped the pages of *Romeo and Juliet* from my Shake-speare collection—a tragedy that could have been a fairy tale if only it had ended a little sooner, before Death came and ruined everything—and shredded them into pieces that fluttered beneath my feet as I prowled and paced the tiny space, a girl caught in a cage of her own making. For the first time since the night it was given to me, I brought forth the Master's violin from beneath my bed and lifted it to my neck. I didn't care that it was somewhere around midnight, didn't care that everyone in the boardinghouse was asleep, didn't care that I too should have been resting, restoring my energy for the next performance. With a surprisingly steady hand, I raised the bow to the strings, and began to play.

It was the song Sig. Picataggi had taught me on the evening of my tenth birthday, an adagio in G minor that I was fairly certain he had composed himself, for never had I heard it before or since. But I remem-bered every note as if he had instructed me only a moment ago, as if he were there with me now, guiding my hand as I played on his own violin, music as a language for conversing with the dead. It was sorrow tinged with madness, the story of true love that had been thwarted by death. A throat splitting open, a scream at the volume of a sigh, the edges of a beloved memory yellowing like lace. It was lovely and terrible, more deeply piercing even than I remembered it, though I didn't know if it was the wretched state of my heart or the instrument in my grasp that rendered it so. The bow ran as smoothly as water over the strings, the sound as thick and rich as blood.

I shuddered when I was done, a full and cathartic release, certain that the entire boardinghouse had heard me—maybe the entire city. But no one knocked and told me to stop; no one shouted through the walls or the ceiling. I set the violin on my bed and crept from my room, tiptoe-ing through the hall and down the stairs to the kitchen for a glass of water. No one stirred, not a single sound behind any of the closed doors, and I had the sudden strange conviction that I was the only one left alive in a dead and decaying world. I drained my glass of water quickly, the cramped kitchen still warm from the heat of the stove, the lingering smell of creamed chipped beef for dinner, and hurried back to the sec-ond floor, where I let myself inside Emilia's room, the door unlocked as if she'd known I would come. Her eyes fluttered open as I knelt beside the bed, the floor creaking beneath me.

"Oh, Grace," she said with a sigh, her breath soft as it touched my cheek. "I was having the saddest of dreams."

"What happened?"

She closed her eyes as she spoke. "I was dancing with Adrián, very slow and very close, but when I looked up into his face it wasn't him at all. It was—it was no one, a blank space, like the night itself had taken a human shape, and I tried to get free of his arms but he wouldn't let me go, he held me until I couldn't breathe, until he strangled me . . ." She sighed again, a heavy exhale. "And there was music, like nothing I've ever heard before. It made me feel as if . . . as if the sun would never rise again. As if . . ."

My throat closed like a fist around empty air. Why hadn't my music woken her, woken anyone? They should have felt it like a cut, but instead it had been a bruise, spreading slowly under the skin.

Emilia was quiet, and I thought she'd fallen back asleep, but then she blinked and lifted her head, just a little.

"And you?" she said, her voice rough with the crust of deep sleep. "What's happened to you, Grace?"

"I have to see him, Em, I have to." I leaned a bit closer, resting my cheek against the side of the bed. She smelled like my roses—or maybe that was me. Maybe I would never be exorcised of their aroma, and maybe I didn't want to be.

"See who?"

"The Master. What if he's not a prince, Em? What if he's—" But I couldn't say it. *Some kind of monster, a beast.* Like Psyche raising her candle to Cupid's face, I had to *know*, even if his smile might open and devour me whole.

"I know, Grace," she said. "And you will. I promise."

She was right—I was set to meet him in a room full of people at the Adler Planetarium. Tomorrow.

"But what if he—*transforms* somehow?" I said, thinking of Mistress at the opening night reception, the speech she had given. The way she had performed in front of her audience, wearing her smile like clothing to cover the nakedness—the cruelty, the kindness—beneath. I understood it, even though it had surprised me in the moment: Rarely do we show our true selves in front of a large and appraising crowd.

"I'd rather meet him alone," I added, but Emilia's eyes had closed, and I knew that she would not open them again until morning. Her breathing was deep and even.

"I'm sorry I disturbed you," I whispered as I stood, and I wasn't sure if I meant for the music that had saddened her, or for coming into her room. Perhaps both. "*Sogni d'oro,* Emilia. Good night."

When I returned to my room, I picked up my brush and set it back on the nightstand by my cup of roses. I put the violin back into its box and slid it under the bed. In the fog on the window I drew a pair of perfect lips with my fingertip, and I fell asleep with them smiling at me in the dark.

Six

THE FIRST TIME I THOUGHT I HEARD THE VOICE OF THE DEVIL it was really just the sound of someone chewing. Slurping, ripping, almost hissing. Like a mortal trying to speak the language of stars, or maybe the other way around. An animal, I thought as I sat still on my old bed in the dark, awoken at midnight by the noise. Small, gaunt, a raccoon or a cat, a fox. I kicked back the blankets and went to the window, expecting to see a furred creature wrestling with the trash in the alley. But the alley was empty, and when I turned back to the room I realized Mamma's bed was too.

I opened the door and the chewing became louder, closer. One hand on the wall, I crept down the hallway, past Lorenzo's empty room, unopened since his death. Shivering in my thin nightgown, eyes blinking rapidly in the dim, I peeked around the corner and into the kitchen.

Mamma in the moonlight, Mamma eating meat. Ribs, I think, the bones slick and garish and glistening as she gnawed on them, juice dripping down her chin. Her hair was falling out of its braid, black frizz, and her robe was slipping off one shoulder. She faced the hallway, her back to the window with her face all in shadow, but still I could see her eyes, bright as a revelation, locked on mine. She didn't glance away, or flinch, or call out to me—she just kept chewing and swallowing and chewing and swallowing. And the *smell* of it—charred and almost rotten but still sort of sweet, sweet like redemption—I wanted to scream, it was there in my chest, but I would have collapsed from the effort of making even the smallest sound, I would have folded in on myself. I hadn't had any protein for months, just pasta and dandelion greens, tomato sauce. I watched her for a good long while, my mamma eating meat, until she was biting on nothing but bone, licking it. Until she was retching it all back up in the sink, her stomach empty for so long that her body now rejected the sustenance needed to save her. As quietly as I'd come, I tiptoed back to bed. I lay awake, waiting for her, for one hour, for two. But the chewing, the licking, the tearing, had resumed, and eventually I fell asleep. Restless and sweating, I dreamed myself celestial.

The second time it was fire, a house around the block from our flat crackling and spitting as it burned to the ground. Rushing out to the sidewalk to join with the neighbors, their eyes wide and reverent, some on their knees in the withering grass. The clasping of hands, cries, and tinny tears like rain dripping into a bucket. Mamma and I pushed to the front of the crowd, as close to the scene as the police would allow, the flames consuming wood like ghosts preying upon dread. Black and red. And the heat of it, wavering in the air—I breathed the smoke and felt hell in my throat; I held it there for as long as I could. *Breathe out, breathe out.* No one was hurt in the fire, and only knowing that—only in retrospect—did I acknowledge that I had enjoyed the spectacle, the dazzling relief of destruction. Yes, I enjoyed it, and I wanted to watch it again and again.

I wanted to be the one to light the match.

The third time I thought I heard the voice of the Devil was the day of the final *Firebird*.

The three weeks of the run were up and it was well below freezing. A wind that had seen every happiness and every horror in the world kept blowing, but really the sun itself could have burned out for all that it mattered inside the theater, where seasons and storms were rendered irrelevant.

"I'll be waiting in the wings," Emilia assured me in a quiet corner down the hallway from the dressing room as she helped me slip my long winter coat on over my leotard and tights so that it would look as though I had just come in from the cold. Although if anyone looked at my feet they would see my pointe shoes, the tips gray and frayed, the ribbons tacked in place at the ankle. It couldn't be helped—Emilia and I had a plan, but the plan did not allow any extra time for my shoes, or my hair, already slicked back into a high bun and which would be well concealed beneath my hood. I had to be as ready as possible so that when I hurried backstage just as the show started, all I would have to do was step into my tutu while Emilia did up the hooks in the back and pinned the red feather headpiece into my hair.

"Behind the old set on the right," I said, buttoning my coat and pulling on my leather gloves. I had risen before the sun that morning to attend an early Mass with Emilia, but now, as my fingers trembled with exhaustion as well as nerves, I wished I had slept in. "The gray one, with the—"

"I know, I know." Emilia laid a hand on my arm. "Everything is all set. Trust me, Grace—this will work."

I nodded. This was all my idea but Emilia seemed to think it was a good one, or else she wouldn't have gone along with it. Even if it didn't work, it was better than waiting, possibly forever. A question never answered was like a cut never closed, tender to the touch.

Cruel or kind?

I went out the back door reserved for performers and made my way around the theater, head down against the whipping wind. At the front doors I entered with the other guests, stamping my feet in the foyer, willing no one to notice me. I kept my hood up as I wound through the crowd and made my way to the second floor, to the private box nearest the stage on the left. A uniformed attendant stopped me as I pulled aside the curtain.

"I'm a guest of Master La Rosa," I murmured, and the name must have meant something to him because he nodded and fell back, allowing me to pass. Below in the orchestra circle, I'd expected to find ladies in long dresses and men in suits settling into their seats, conversing as they flipped through their programs, occasionally turning around to shake the hands of the people sitting behind them, old friends or new acquaintances. The reality was far grimmer: Despite Emilia's predictions of sold-out shows, we hadn't even managed to come close. A great number of seats were left empty now, and the ones that were filled saw their occupants dressed only modestly, no fine silks or furs, no jewels or pompous hats. It was not the glamorous tableau we would have wished, but at least I had secured a patron. A patron that would arrive imminently, and I would see his face for the very first time.

The minutes ticked by and no one came. I forced my gaze to the ceiling, to the mural of angels painted on the dome, white wings and vacant stares. So benign, I could barely fathom the artist's vision. Were angels not instruments of the divine, terrible and true? Where were their fury and splendor, their bold eyes, and their teeth? I straightened my spine and waited as the auditorium filled a little more but not fully, my heart rising like a moon inside me.

Overhead the lights flashed twice, signaling that the show would start in a minute. Pushing back my hood, I sat on the edge of the upholstered chair in the center of the small box and looked over the curved railing at the stage.

Master La Rosa.

I whispered his name, once. I imagined him watching me: In a suit so dark it was as if it were cut out of cloth made of pure night, sharp and showing his angles, his hair combed neatly away from his face. Leaning forward, his bent elbow on his thigh, chin balanced on his fist. His cheeks, still red from the cold. His eyes, blinking slowly. His lips, stretching. Stretching into a smile like dying, like death. A smile to stop your heart.

"What are you doing here?"

A voice at my back, dry and deep, like a black patch of soil where a rosebush once thrived but then died in an unexpected drought, and now nothing will grow there again. Stripped of softness, shorn of beauty, abandoned by light and life.

I stood so quickly I hit my knee against the railing and the blood drained from my head, leaving me dizzy.

The lights began to dim.

The theater went quiet.

I turned toward the voice.

A man stood behind me. He was tall, almost a foot taller than me, with the hood of his cloak—yes, a cloak, like something from the medieval age, falling to his calves and fastened with a silver clasp—pulled low over his forehead. But still I could see his eyes, just as green as I had imagined them, and, faintly, his mouth.

He was not smiling.

"Master La Rosa." I brought one hand to my chest and curtsied. I had never curtsied to anyone outside of the studio and the stage, but it didn't seem strange or out of place here, standing before him, his chest rising and falling as if he'd run a great distance to reach the theater. To reach *me*. "It's a pleasure to meet you at last."

A lie, a little one. Forgive me, God, whoever you are. A pleasure? No. His voice, his stature, his shadowed countenance—it felt like every terror in the dark was about to be illuminated at once and I would know the true face of the world at last. Oh, but I wasn't meant to know—I was only mortal, and flawed, a girl kneeling in a dark room within arm's reach of the light switch but believing herself to be in communion with the night, whose secrets weighed no more than the discarded clippings of her fingernails, every eyelash that had ever fallen out.

I was wrong to come here, but I couldn't look away.

The overture began to play, and Master La Rosa turned his head toward the stage, his cloak concealing the near side of his face. He looked younger than I thought he would by the sound of his voice—as young as I was, but ageless too. Not immortal, precisely; the word didn't feel right.

It came to me a moment later: *eternal*.

"Go now," he said, and his voice was quieter than it had been before, but no less bare or blunt. *"Now,"* he said again when I didn't move, and this time I jumped, my throat so numb I couldn't be sure I was still breathing, my heart a sacred sound, steady and fast and loud. But still I didn't move, I didn't go, because I hadn't seen what I came for, I had to know. *His smile—*

The overture ended and the curtains parted, a velvety swish. Emilia was waiting for me, waiting in the wings with my tutu and the feather for my hair. Red and orange and yellow, sparkling, magnificent. I was the Golden Firebird.

I couldn't stay here.

My heart falling, I stepped past my patron. As I pushed the curtain aside he gripped my upper arm, not hard, but enough to stop me. Poised on the tips of my toes to run, I looked down at his hand, ungloved, his fingers so long they made a complete circle around my arm.

At the end of his fingers were claws, dark gray and curling under at the tips, sharp as they sliced through the fabric of my coat and grazed my skin. I stared, his breath hot on my cheek.

It was like a hand you'd imagine reaching out of a nightmare, from underneath the bed, around a dark corner. My mind went blank. It didn't make sense—*and yet*. *Was* he the Devil? Maybe—oh God, maybe.

Certainly, he was a beast.

In the next moment he released me and I was running—through the lobby, out the front door, around the theater to the cast entrance. Down the hallway, into the wings, behind the old set piece that acted as a cover. I dove into my costume, Emilia's quick, cold hands at my back, fastening the feather hairpiece into my bun, scraping my scalp as she slid it into place.

"Well?" she whispered, following me from out behind the set and edging as close to the stage as we could get without being seen. "Was he— Oh, Grace, what happened to your arm?"

Startled, I looked down.

Five marks, in a ring around my biceps, red as raw meat.

It didn't hurt until I looked at it. And then there it was, pain like an incomplete apotheosis, new bones only half-grown.

"I must have bumped into something." I looked straight ahead, inviting no further questions, watching the dancers onstage as they reveled in the hunt, the prince and his companions. My pulse was a bird, trapped under my skin. I smiled, at nothing and no one, putting my performing face in place. I only had time to whisper one last false confession before I flew into the light.

"He wasn't there," I said to Emilia. "He never came."

Seven

I REMEMBER LITTLE FROM THAT FINAL ACT OF *FIREBIRD* EXCEPT that I didn't stumble, not once. I danced as if in a dream, watching myself from just above and behind, hovering over my own shoulder. All eyes—*his* eyes—were on me.

My memories come in gasps after that: a standing ovation that went on and on; clutching the eleventh rose—wine dark—to my heart; laughter and tears and Emilia throwing her arms around me, crushing my rose between us; Mistress, coming over and patting my cheek, saying only "Good girl," so that I felt like a child again, like only yesterday I had flown through her window, trembling and mute. Then she looked down at the rose near my chest. "Tonight, colombina," she said with a smile, and I watched her disappear into the wings to shake hands with the crew. I didn't see her again. I walked back to the boardinghouse with Emilia and the others to get ready for the closing gala, the cold scraping me clean.

At home I waited my turn for the bathroom, and then I shut myself inside.

Alone, for the first time all night.

The narrow room was overly warm, the lighting dim. It smelled like half a dozen different fruity perfumes, a scented haze hanging over my head. I twisted off the top of the lipstick tube I'd stolen from the dressing room and brought it to my lips, the shade an immaculate match for the rose now pinned behind my ear, my hair falling in loose curls over my shoulders. (It was Sunday, after all, the only day I wore my hair down.) Slowly, slowly, I painted it on, my hands shaking ever so slightly, short breaths puffing through parted lips. I paused several times, my fingertips tingling, almost numb. When it was done I sighed and dropped the tube onto the sink with a clatter, uncapped. It rolled over the edge and to the floor but I didn't reach for it.

Long ago—so long ago it almost seems like a dream—Mamma and I used to put on our best clothes and walk around Marshall Field's. Window-shopping, she said, because with the exception of a box of Frango mints, rarely did we buy anything. We looked and pretended and picked out gifts for each other and gifts for ourselves. Each trip I stared so longingly at the lipsticks behind the glass of the makeup counter that eventually the saleswoman gave me a sample tube to keep. *For the fancy lady*, she whispered, handing it over, her eyes up to make sure no one was watching. I took it, too breathless even to thank her. The color was called Ancient Brick, and when Mamma helped me paint it on at home in front of our water-stained mirror she said it was like I wore the streets of Rome. Caesars and palazzi, temples and gladiators, an empire ended in fire.

"Have you been there?" I had asked Mamma, twisting around to smile at myself in the mirror, at my burnt sienna mouth. "To Rome?"

Mamma put her chin on my shoulder. "I've never been anywhere but here. Here, and Cefalù."

"But aren't we always *here*? If I went to Rome right now I would call it *here*, and Chicago *there*. And if I went to the moon, I would call both Rome and Chicago *there*, while the moon dust beneath my feet would be *here*," I said, smacking my lips together. "So really we're always here, no matter where we go."

It was nonsense and I knew it; I only wanted to make her laugh. But she seemed distracted. With long, thin fingers she brushed my hair away from my face. When she spoke, soft and close, it was with an urgency I did not understand.

"Listen, Grazia. This lipstick is *magic*. It will take you anywhere. Anywhere on earth. Or even beyond the earth, to some other star far, far away. Wherever you want to go, without restraint. All you have to do is put it on, close your eyes—and you're there." She kissed my temple, quick. "Come on, let's try."

She wrapped her arms around my waist, my spine to her chest, and closed her eyes. I didn't. Instead I watched her in the mirror, a smile on her face that I had never seen before—clandestine, like she knew forever was only a moment, and that moment would soon end. She was so very young, but I had no concept of that then. When at last she opened her eyes, she gave me a gentle squeeze.

"Did it work?" she asked, her cheek pressed to mine.

"Yes," I said, clasping the lipstick tube tightly in my hand. Wherever she was, that was where I wanted to be.

Mamma never wore my Ancient Brick lipstick, not even when I offered it to her. *It's yours*, she insisted with a shake of her head, *a gift for you alone*. She didn't wear it until she died. I painted it carefully on her cold, open mouth, then slid the tube into the circle of her loose fist.

I hoped it would take her wherever she wanted to go.

ANOTHER GIFT FROM Master La Rosa, and though I had grown wary of him and his gifts after the violin, this one was not *entirely* unwelcome: a black A-line gown to wear to the gala. With a full skirt and high neckline, it would have been stunning in its simplicity if it weren't for the embroidered lines on the bodice that resembled a golden rib cage stitched precisely over my own bones, elevating it to uncanny. Emilia helped me into the dress, marveling at the cut, the quality, how it complemented my slender form perfectly, but I didn't hear a word she said. The satin was cool against my skin, and even after a minute, after ten, the heat of my body did nothing to warm it, to soften the edges of the chill. When I looked behind me, my shadow was dark enough to eclipse the sun.

As Beatrice and others from the boardinghouse waited for the bus, Adrián drove Emilia and me to the South Loop in a black Ford V-8 he'd borrowed from an uncle or a cousin or someone for the night, past Grant Park and to the planetarium perched on Lake Michigan's shore. Its dome rose against the dirty clouds like a swollen bone, a bent kneecap, the water beyond quiet and still, less like a lake and more like a stain, a cup of dark wine spilled carelessly by some drunken god. We climbed the steps to the doors, the warmth of the entrance hall welcome, but I froze as a porter came to collect our coats, our scarves and gloves and hats. The cap sleeves of the Master's dress weren't long enough to hide the marks on my arm, still glistening like a fresh burn, and I was reluctant to shed the only bit of protection I had. But it would have been conspicuously strange to keep my coat, and so I surrendered my effects and scraped up a few pennies from my clutch to tip the porter, coveted shiny coins glinting from one hand to another. Anyway, it turned out not to matter much; inside the planetarium's colossal dome, everyone's eyes were directed up.

"*Lovely*," Emilia breathed beside me, and as I tilted my chin and beheld the stars above us, those pinpricks of light projected onto the dome by the machine whirring in the center of the wide room, I envied my friend, truly envied her for the first time. More stars than I had ever imagined, like the tips of tiny teeth in a mouth the size of forever, the whole galaxy rendered accurately over our heads, and yet, I wished I could feel what Emilia felt when she looked at them, because I only felt small, and finite, and afraid.

"Em, listen," I said, tearing my eyes away. We were among the first to arrive, though more and more guests were filtering in behind us, gazes going up and then to the tables set along the far wall where a feast had been set, so much food that it made me dizzy to look at, dizzy to imagine eating any of it. I was hungry, I was hollow, but in that moment I knew that nothing could change that, nothing could fill me full again. "What if we—what if we skipped the gala and went home? I'm not feeling very well. I'm so tired, and you must be too. If we tell Mistress—"

"Grace, stop. Stop," she said, taking my hands in hers, and I adored her as much as I envied her. She would never imagine running away because she already knew there was nowhere to run *to*. Like the sun, she brightened the sky wherever she went. I was always trying to outrun the night. "What are you saying? You can't miss the gala, and besides, we're already here. Aren't you eager to meet your patron?"

"No," I said as Adrián returned to us with drinks in both hands, a third glass balanced in between. I hadn't even noticed that he'd left to fetch them. "I mean, I *am*, but—"

"Do you think he's here already?" Emilia took a sip of martini, her gaze sweeping the room. I gripped the stem of my glass in a sweating hand, afraid it might slip and shatter. "Or does he plan to make a grand entrance?"

"A grand entrance," I said, though naturally I had no idea. He could've been there already, among the steadily increasing crowd, and we'd have no way of knowing unless he announced himself.

Unless he was close enough for me to see his bright eyes, his claws unsheathed.

"Odd," Emilia said, still scanning the crowd. "I don't see Mistress either. It's not like her to be late."

The stars glittered, tilted above us as the earth turned on its axis. The planetarium was so full now that the room had grown hot, loud. I wished everyone would speak a little bit softer, just as if we were all about to go to sleep.

"Em, listen," I said, resolving to try one more time. Emilia's eyes had drifted back to the sky, and she wouldn't look at me, wouldn't look. How could I compete with stars? "I have to tell you something. About Master La Rosa. I *did* see him today, in his box. I didn't mean to lie to you, but I was so frightened. Emilia, he's—"

"There she is," said a voice at my shoulder, and though the voice was wrong, I still expected to find Mistress, scolding me for not mingling. Instead it was an older woman with gray hair and a strand of pearls around her thin neck, a face shrunken with age but still elegant, fine wrinkles around her mouth. I recognized her vaguely from the opening night reception, a personal friend of Mistress's, though Mistress had introduced everyone that way—*Come, you must meet my dear friend so-and-so, my dearest friend in all the world*—until I couldn't tell what was sincere and what was only flattery. A young girl of about twelve or thirteen stood just behind her, gawking at me as if I were made of smoke and might uncoil at any moment.

"The lady of the hour, at last," said the woman, and the young girl inched closer with a small, timid smile. "Betty here is a most ardent admirer of yours, Miss Dragotta. Made me take her to see the show twice! I tell you, my granddaughter is going to run me straight into bankruptcy, what with all the dolls and frocks and other frivolities she begs me for, but how can I resist that sweet little face?"

The young girl with the blond curls didn't look like she had ever begged for anything a day in her life. I smiled at her, and I hoped my smile was kind. "Thank you, Betty. I'm glad you enjoyed the show."

Emilia had drifted away with Adrián—not far, but far enough. Every time I took a step toward her I was intercepted: *Miss Dragotta, what ballet are you hoping to conquer next? Miss Dragotta, will you sign my program? Miss Dragotta, is it true that you and Miss Menendez are the closest of friends? Won't you miss her terribly now that she's retired? Is it true that you were an orphan with no previous training, and she helped you rise to where you are now?*

I put on the grin that I employed onstage. *I am still an orphan, and yes. Yes, I will miss her; yes, we are friends. Yes, I will sign your program—do you have a pen? Oh, I don't know, perhaps* The Sleeping Beauty, *I've always loved that one . . .*

And all the while I was aware of every body in the room, every face and every smile, and none of them were his, I was sure of it. When I had intruded on his box at the theater, I'd felt him behind me, like a sudden change in the wind, from cold to hot, from north to south, like a pivot of seasons, winter sleet to summer rain. I would have sensed his presence but I didn't, not here. I didn't even see Mistress, and I wasn't sure if the tightening in my chest was a sign of despair—or relief. Had he changed his mind about me? What would happen to the company if he had?

After an hour under the glimmering light of the false and radiant stars, my cheeks hurting from grinning, from cheer that was not forced but not natural either, I finally made it to Emilia's side, who all this time had been ringed by her own set of admirers.

"Emilia," I began, intending to ask her if she wanted to slip away for a moment, somewhere quiet, when there was another voice at my shoulder, summoning me. I turned rigidly.

"Mistress wants to see you." It was Beatrice, wearing a gold dress with a petal bodice and full skirt, her hair set in pin curls around her face. "She's just outside the building, smoking a cigarette."

I looked at Emilia a little desperately, knowing that when it came to Mistress it was best not to delay.

"I'll be here when you get back," she said, and though the last thing I wanted to do in that moment was leave her again, I nodded and followed Beatrice out of the dome, the stars winking at my back.

"Your dress is divine," Beatrice said as we shuffled down the hallway that led to the narrow foyer where we'd left our coats and hats with the porter. "I suppose it was a gift from your patron?"

I nodded. Beatrice led me to the front doors but stopped before pushing through. It was cold here, so close to the outside, and the skin of my bare arms crinkled with goosebumps. Would I ever be warm again, truly?

"You did well, orphan girl. Honestly, I didn't think you had it in you." Beatrice laughed humorlessly and stepped aside so I could finish the journey alone. Her eyes were so blue, bright and sharpened to a point. "Every girl in the company wishes she were you right now."

"Do you?" I wasn't sure what possessed me to ask, but once it was out there, I couldn't take it back. For so long I had wished I were more like *her*, wished I had begun my training as a small child instead of as a floundering thirteen-year-old trying desperately to catch up; wished I had the security of a privileged family, wished I didn't absolutely need this job to survive. Heat flared suddenly, vehemently, in my chest, in my cheeks, and it took me a second to recognize it as *resentment*, twisted and burning, clouds of black smoke. Why couldn't Beatrice simply be grateful for what she had instead of wishing for more, more, more?

Why couldn't I?

"Oh, sure." Beatrice shrugged, bringing me back to the moment. "I mean, who *doesn't* want to be prima?"

The fire in me faded to a simmer, but didn't extinguish entirely. "Do you know why Mistress wants me?"

"No idea." She smiled, thin and without warmth. "Anyway, be careful on the ice. Wouldn't want our little bird to slip and break a wing."

With a frown I turned my back on her and stepped into the frigid night just as Mistress stamped out her spent cigarette. Her face was grave when she looked up and saw me.

"Come," she said and started down the concrete steps to the street, where an old blue car I'd never seen before was parked by the curb. The roof was flat, out of date, and the headlights bulged from the front like eyes in a startled face. It took me a moment to realize that the car belonged to Mistress. "Hurry up. We're leaving."

"But—my coat," I said, glancing back toward the building. I hadn't thought this would take long enough to need my outerwear.

"Don't worry about it."

"But—"

"Come."

I marched down the planetarium's steps and climbed into the car with a held and aching breath. The interior was cool, but at least it was out of the wind. Sliding in beside me, Mistress ignited the engine, the car shaking forcefully on its frame.

"Where are we going?" I asked, but Mistress didn't answer. She was dressed for the party in a lilac gown with a silver belt at the waist, and I thought the color was wrong for her, too soft, too much like spring. I watched her face in the rearview mirror as we puttered through the city, shadowy buildings on one side and the lake on the other.

"Your patron has paid a dizzying sum."

The towers grew taller around us as we passed through the Loop and cut right through the center of the city. It appeared that we were going back to the boardinghouse, though I couldn't fathom why. The gala had been in full swing, much of the food still untouched. At the thought, my belly rumbled low and long; I hadn't eaten a thing.

"With this much money, the company can do incredible things," Mistress continued, and there was a dark echo to her words I did not understand, or maybe I just didn't want to. This was wonderful news—and yet. There was something more, somewhere a severed vein diverting blood from the heart of the matter. "Tour the world, perform on the very best stages."

I looked down at my hands so that I didn't have to see the El tracks arching like great metal ribs over our heads, the regurgitated snow in the gutters, men in checkered suits strolling home from the bars, laughing women on their arms. If I kept my eyes on my hands, we could have been anywhere, driving through any city in the world, another place at another time that was not marked by the scars of my grief.

"What role will I be playing next season?" I said, trying to project an aura of detachment. The bodice of my dress was overly tight, but I suspected it was the only thing keeping me from sagging against the door, my cheek pressed to the window glass. I had never been so tired, the kind of tired that even sleep couldn't fix.

"Oh, colombina. This will be your greatest role yet."

I waited for her to elaborate, but instead she reached across the space between us and took my hand. The gesture was so sudden, so startling, that I snatched my hand back and tucked it under my thigh.

Mistress placed her rejected hand back on the steering wheel. We stopped at a red light, waiting to cross the river. "He will give you a life I never could. Comfort, luxury. Warmth. Every girl here longs to be so lucky."

I wish I were you.

"I don't understand," I said, my insides quietly turning to ice.

"You will stay in his house. Eat his food. Wear the clothes he provides you. There will be servants to dress you and draw your bath, to clean and cook for you. You will have access to his library, his gardens and galleries. In return, he asks only that you dance with him. One waltz, every Sunday at midnight."

The stoplight changed and I was jostled in my seat as Mistress navigated the car over the steel bridge, the seam in the center where it often parted to let boats pass unheeded, the entire structure splitting, lifting like arms in exaltation toward the sky.

"You *sold* me?"

Mistress lifted her chin, kept her eyes squarely on the road. Traffic was thin; we were almost home.

"No need for such dramatics," she said. "*Sold*, as if you were a piece of meat. No, during the day you'll return here, and all will be as it was. At your patron's request I am choreographing an original ballet—one he has commissioned just for you. You will play a girl caught between brothers, whose names are Sleep and Death. Sleep has fallen in love with you, but you are dying already—too young, too soon. And though Sleep pleads for your life, Death makes no exceptions."

There was a trembling in my throat so violent I nearly couldn't speak. *A warm weight on my shoulder, a hand. Death has come to take me too.* But no, it was only fiction, a fairy tale on the stage.

"And Emilia?" I asked, my voice sounding very far away.

"Always with you and that girl." Mistress scowled. I stared at her until she went on. "Miss Menendez is leaving. Have you forgotten?"

For a moment, yes, I had. The prospect of her absence hit me hard all over again.

"Beatrice will dance the Queen of the Shades in the second act, ruler of the ghosts who welcome you to the afterlife. Girls similar in that they died too soon and yearn still for those dreams that have gone unfulfilled."

"And me?" The plot wasn't important now, I knew that—but as long as Mistress was talking, then I did not have to go. "The girl who loved Sleep? What happens to her in the end?"

"Well, she's dead—and Death will not give her up. But Sleep cannot die, and so they cannot be together, not truly. To be near her, he follows her through the Land of Shades for eternity, always two steps behind."

My mouth was dry, my scalp tingling. Coarse, shallow breath. "And what is the title of this ballet?"

"I'm not sure yet." Mistress glanced at me in the rearview mirror with a sallow grin. "Perhaps I'll call it *Little Bird*."

I almost retched, right there all over her car. But there was nothing inside of me but ice, cold and getting colder, winter settling in the spaces between my joints.

"Enough of this now." Mistress pulled to the curb in front of the boardinghouse, its windows dim. "You leave tonight for your patron's house. At once."

I stayed seated. Stared straight ahead.

"Come, dear." Her voice softened, startling me. I could not remember her ever speaking with me this way, even when I was a child of thirteen. Her mouth, though, was still hard, a pressed line. "Come. You must go inside and pack your belongings—I have an old suitcase you can use. His assistant will be here soon to fetch you."

I peered up and out the window as Mistress got out and came around to my side of the car, but between the buildings blocking the view and the thickness of the clouds I couldn't see much of anything. I imagined the moon, bright beyond the gloom like a bell atop the dark sanctuary of night. Ringing and ringing and ringing.

"*Colombina*." Mistress opened my door and grabbed my arm. Not hard, but her fingers pressed against the five little claw marks on my skin and it stung. "Stand up, girl. He's expecting you. We don't have a lot of time."

I allowed her to pull me to my feet so that we were eye to eye.

"He's not human," I said, my voice rising at the end. Gunshots like birds smacking glass, the slow chewing of thunder. The voice of God, the voice of the Devil. Maybe they're one and the same.

"I assure you, he's only a man." She released my arm and sighed, her breath a sour cigarette stream. "You've built him up in your mind, made a monster out of him. Like a child fumbling in the dark."

"*No.* I saw him."

"I know." With another sigh, Mistress let her head loll back. "Ah, little bird. You should not have done that."

I tried to run; I got as far as the corner. When I rounded the side of the boardinghouse, there stood the assistant who'd given me the box with the violin, his hands folded calmly in front of him as if he'd been waiting very patiently. He was not much older than me, I realized, only three, maybe four years my senior, though he held himself with an assured grace that lent him an air of agelessness. And of lithe strength, I noted, despite the dark and sleepless red of his lower eyelids. Snowflakes clung to the lapel of his long, trim coat.

I had not noticed that it had started to snow.

"Go on and pack your things, Miss Dragotta." He stepped toward me and I stepped back. "I'll give you ten minutes."

Holding my skirts aloft so I wouldn't trip, I hurried into the house and up to the third floor, encountering no one on the way. When I reached my room, it was empty. I went straight to the window and turned the lock. I tried to lift it but it wouldn't budge, my arms straining, the tendons on my neck tensed to aching. *Please, please*—just last week I had opened it; I had tossed rose petals into the alley below. Why should it be stuck now? Oh, it was too cold, too icy, too much snow, I don't know—the world conspiring against me. I tugged and pleaded and made promises—*I'll be good, so good, a good, good girl who never dreams of magic and the things she cannot have, never dreams at all,* I said, even though I didn't know what being good meant anymore—but still it wouldn't budge. Finally I stepped back, pressing the heels of my hands against my eyes. Darkness, take me. My window, sealed shut—had it ever been a way out?

"Grace, are you all right?"

Emilia stood in the open doorway. I didn't understand how that could be, but she rushed to explain that when I failed to return to the gala, she'd had Adrián drive her to the boardinghouse right away. She couldn't think of where else we might have gone.

"Grace, tell me what's happening."

"They're taking me away," I whispered, turning from the window.

"Who is?"

"Mistress. Master La Rosa." I tore the flower out of my hair. Threw it to the ground and stepped on it. "He paid her a *dizzying* sum and he . . . he bought me."

"What? Slow down—"

"I'm to go and live with him, eat his food and wear whatever clothes he gives me, like a little dress-up doll, and in exchange I have to dance with him, one waltz at midnight every Sunday."

The Master's assistant appeared behind Emilia, the snow on his shoulders turned to quivering water drops. "Time is running short," he said, and Emilia jumped, his approach so silent she had not known he was there.

"It hasn't been ten minutes," I snapped, but the man didn't move, only clasped his hands and bowed his head.

Emilia looked from him to me. "I'll help you pack," she said quietly, and went to fetch Mistress's suitcase.

While she was gone I began tearing clothes out of my dresser drawers: mostly old dresses and skirts, a few threadbare sweaters, leotards and tights and dead pointe shoes. The wedding dress that had been Mamma's last project. I wouldn't need any of it, but it was all I had. Emilia returned and began folding my clothes with concentrated precision, so efficiently I almost missed that her hands were shaking, violently. From its hiding place under the bed, I carefully lifted my treasured violin from Lorenzo and hugged it to my chest before setting it on top of the clothes in the suitcase, along with my book of Shakespeare and my pillow. The other, newer violin I left under the bed.

Let the next girl find it.

When the packing was done, Emilia and I reached for each other. I wanted to cry, for the feeling of release it would bring, to break the pressure building and building behind my eyes, but no tears would come. If it wasn't for the incessant screaming of my heart in my ears I would have thought I was dead, or just nearly. I felt like a shadow, darkness created by light. Thin, flat, swept away with the night.

Emilia spoke first.

"If you can't leave your new home, then I'll come visit you there."

She nodded, firm, and I remembered how, on the feast day of Sant'Agata after we had first met, she had brought me to the panadería for a surprise celebration of Mamma's namesake, and I had wept hard enough to break my bones, bruising all my memories. And we wrapped our arms around each other and I thought, perhaps, I could make new memories, each more luminous than the last.

"I'll come," she said.

I shook my head. I hadn't explained very well—it was coming out all wrong and she didn't understand. "No, no, I—I'll be back during the day. To rehearse for the next ballet. I'm only to live with him and—and—"

I couldn't finish the rest. I didn't *know* the rest.

"Oh, Grace, I won't be in the next ballet. But I promise I'll be there in the front row for every show, watching you." Emilia leaned close and kissed my cheek. She lingered a moment, and whispered low: "He's your prince, remember? You're going to rule a kingdom."

I squeezed her hand for what felt like a very long time. And then I smiled, so she would not be afraid for me. "See you soon," I said, and it was a plea as much as a declaration.

In the downstairs hallway I touched the wallpaper and it felt like skin—smooth, warm. Perhaps a girl did die here. Perhaps she never left.

Mistress waited for me by the door, running her hands through her hair. Master La Rosa's assistant took my suitcase out to the sleek black car across the street, giving us a moment alone. She reached to embrace me, but I stepped back.

"What have I done to deserve this?" Half whisper, half cry.

"Colombina, no." A rush of wind brought a sweep of fresh snow blowing across the threshold toward us. Mistress shivered. I didn't. "No, no, no. This is not a punishment. Don't you see? This is your salvation."

Again she reached for me, and again I stepped away, an odd little dance. Once, coming *here* had meant deliverance. How many times did I need to be saved?

"Won't you give me a kiss?" she said, with a smile that went nowhere, and I looked at her, her wavy hair and the fine wrinkles around her eyes, and I thought, *You could have been my mother.* But she was only a witch from a fairy tale so standard it was barely even a fairy tale anymore—a woman neither cruel nor kind as she peeled meat from bone, as she chewed and swallowed, too hungry to savor, doing only what she must to survive. Like me, like anyone. A kiss, she wanted, but a kiss I could not give her. I was too cold to let her touch me, to let anyone touch me ever again. Whosoever did would freeze, a sculpture of solid ice, translucent and sparkling in the sun.

Another surge of wind and snow. Mistress bowed her head.

"Fly away, little bird," she said.

I walked out of the boardinghouse.

The sky was low with wrinkled clouds. Through the fog the streetlamps glowed like eyes, and every one of them was watching me. In my gown with the golden ribs, I made my way down the slick steps and over the sidewalk to the curb, where the Master's assistant was holding the car door open.

"I don't know your name," I said over the hissing wind as I approached, tilting my chin to look up at him.

The tips of his ears were red. He wore no hat. "John Russo."

"Thank you, Mr. Russo," I said, seized by an eerie calm, and slid into the backseat.

BING CROSBY PLAYED on the radio, the volume turned so low I almost couldn't hear it at all. The streets seemed unfamiliar to me, the brick buildings and the sickly trees, even though I'd lived in this neighborhood for years, even though I'd just passed through it with Mistress, only minutes ago when everything was different. Whenever I had envisioned the Master's surroundings in the careful, obsessive sculpting of him, he stubbornly remained before a blank backdrop, a hazy gray that could have been the clouds of Heaven or smoke from the fires of Hell. A no-where land, the soft padding of my imagination. But now that I was about to face the reality of his home, I tried to imagine him in a pent-house suite looking down at the smudgy streets, or bent over a desk in a dark study in a decades-old house that appeared gutted from the out-side but opened like a treasure box on the inside, dumbwaiters and ten-foot ceilings. I tried, but panic had excised any hint of near and far, here and there, past and future—suppressing everything but the present, ev-erything but the bumpy tread of the tires, the streets like black veins pumping through the city, the entirely too upbeat music and the dull streetlamps and the back of Mr. Russo's head, his long, thin hands steady on the wheel. There was nothing before or beyond this. Nothing but now and now and now, never-ending.

I brought a hand to my throat and clenched my nails into the skin on the side of my neck, over the vein throbbing there. I dug them so deeply I almost cried out. This was a dangerous precedent to set—pain as an-chor, pain as relief from the fear flapping like failing wings, telling my-self the only way to conquer it was to kill it, to bury it deep. But what else was I supposed to do? I was firmly ensconced in a motorcar moving down Lake Shore Drive, easing in and out and around the other, slower cars, the lake as blank as the edge of the world and twice as wide, twice as steep, a sheer drop down into the tender devotion of nothingness. I couldn't scream, I couldn't sing to myself without Mr. Russo hearing, and this terror was *mine*, mine to keep.

But terror takes energy to sustain, and I didn't have much of it left.

The car was oddly warm—from the heat of our bodies, maybe, or the engine working away—and against all odds, I began to grow sleepy. I fought it, keeping my jaw hard and my head held high, feeding on the cold spot in my chest—an endless, delicious frost. I remembered how sometimes the pipes would freeze in our flat when I was little, and Mamma, Lorenzo, and I packed snow into buckets and bowls to heat over the stove, water to drink and to cook with and to wash our faces and hands. How even in my gloves my fingers would stiffen, solid and heavy as gold. How I would shiver for hours after, even with every blanket we had wrapped tight around us. A coldness that never truly left me.

"You can ask me," Mr. Russo said suddenly, and our eyes connected in the rearview mirror. His were light brown, like tea left too long unattended, too cool to enjoy properly. He looked away first, his gaze settling back on the road. "You must have many questions. I'll answer those I can, if you'd like to ask."

I leaned forward, feeling like a sinner in a confessional, peering at the priest through the grate.

Where are we going? What will I endure?

Why me, why me, why me?

"Will he eat me?" I said, and my voice didn't shake.

Slush under the wheels, whisper of the engine, heat pumping through the vents. I thought Mr. Russo would lie to me, dismiss me, call me hysterical. *There is no such thing as monsters.* Or maybe he wouldn't answer at all. I sat back in my seat, raising a hand to wipe the condensation from the window glass.

But then he lifted his chin and smiled at me in the mirror.

His smile was kind, even as his words were not . . . quite.

"Miss Dragotta," he said, and I pulled my hand away from the window. "He is not that kind of beast."

Part Two

Eight

"Not much farther, Miss Dragotta."

Slowly, heavily, I opened my eyes. When had I fallen asleep? I saw foliage through a fogged window, twisting trees with heavy leaves, a smear of green as the car slid silently along. I didn't think there was any green left in the world and it stopped my heart. Where was my winter and ice? I blinked and the trees were dead again, old again, brown and bare. I closed my eyes.

"Miss Dragotta? Miss?"

The car had stopped, the engine cut. Radio off. I lifted my head as the driver's door thudded shut, and, shortly after, another one opened. My door. The cold kissed me awake. Mr. Russo leaned down, extending a hand. His palms were callused, his fingernails short.

"Can I help you out? Careful—it's slippery."

It was, and I huffed in frustration, and continued to cling to him as we moved away from the car, my eyes on my feet, wary of black ice. After several tiny, well-placed steps we made it to a thoroughly salted cement path and only then did I look up.

A house, a mansion, a castle—I didn't know what to call it. Surrounded on both sides by similar—though smaller—houses, separated from them by narrow gated alleys, it rose three stories high, the white-washed stones in its façade seeming somehow too tightly packed together, clenched like teeth. There were two rows of arched windows, and each window had a wrought-iron grate guarding the glass. The whole structure had an air of perpetual rigor mortis; stiff, impermeable, preserved forever against a sky scabbed over with clouds.

And I could have sworn, just then, that I had seen it before. Once, yes, in a dream.

"Where are we?" I knew I had spoken due to the vibrations of it in my throat, but it took a long while for the sound to reach me, and then my voice was tinny, wobbling, as if recorded and played back on a phonograph.

"Hyde Park," said Mr. Russo, and I blinked. *Hyde Park*. That was only thirty minutes away from River North and Near North Ballet. I knew where it was, though I'd never been; it wasn't terribly far from Club DeLisa, only a little farther east, hugging the lake. *We're still in the city*, I thought with relief. *Still close*.

But then why did I feel as if I had entered another world entirely?

My breath billowed in the air, and I could feel my lips turning purple, blue. Overhead a crow cawed, once, twice, and went silent, and I could feel the silence stroking my hair, or maybe that was the wind; it whispered, telling me how pretty I was, how soft, how much it wanted to eat me all up. A face appeared in one of the many windows on the second floor—an indistinct pale shape. I stared at it until my focus blurred and I couldn't be sure it was a face at all.

I fell to my knees in the snow.

"*Emilia?*" I murmured, but she wasn't there. I had come somewhere she couldn't find me, and since I hadn't seen the path we took to get here, how would I ever find my way back?

"*Mistress?*"

But she was gone too.

A hand on my arm, gentle until it wasn't anymore, trying to tug me back to my feet. I ignored it, slumping sideways, resting my cheek on the snow as if it were a pillow. I could decay right there, and in spring flowers would spring from my ribs, enriched by the remains of arterial blood. It didn't seem so sad a fate. Life after death, beauty from sacrifice. My eyes fluttered, half-closed.

"Grace Dragotta, you are welcome here. But . . . what is wrong?"

A voice like midnight, like the ending of an hour and the beginning of another, darker than the last. Distantly familiar, it was colder than the cold around me and I shivered, but I did not get up from the ground—no, I burrowed deeper. And then there were footsteps lurching over the snow, cracking its frozen crystalline surface with each step, and I thought of Mistress proclaiming my salvation, and I thought maybe she was right but not in the way she had meant it. Sometimes lies are truth in disguise, like stories. I breathed out, and my breath was the only warm thing left in the world, and even that, when it passed my lips, was taken too, and given over to winter as a quiet offering.

"What happened to her?" The midnight voice was close. It belonged to the Master; I knew it for certain now, the same cadence to his words as when he'd ordered me away from him in the theater.

Mr. Russo's voice didn't shake as mine might have as he lied. "She said she wanted to pray."

A hooded figure loomed over me then. Arms slid beneath me, rolling me over. *No.* I kicked, thrashed, but the arms were strong and lifted me, one behind my back and the other under my knees. I opened my eyes and all I saw was darkness, shadows, snow and tears crusted in the corners, but I didn't have to see to know where they were taking me: to the house like a dead thing resurrected, where I would live and eat and dance and waste silently away.

I was too numb, too frozen to fight, so I went limp instead, dead weight. The Master only shifted me closer.

"Shush, little dove," he said, and now there were stars in his voice, a hidden constellation that could only be seen on the darkest of nights. "You are safe now."

I smiled a little because I didn't believe it but, oh, I wanted to. Tilting my chin, I tried to focus on him, on the long shape of his face half-hidden by his hood. I reached up with a shaking hand and touched my fingertip to the corner of his mouth.

Across the lawn, up the hill, my cradled body rocked with his movements. I caught a last glimpse of gray sky and then we were inside. I couldn't even scream. There was only one escape, and so I closed my eyes and kept them that way.

Swaying, winding, climbing up stairs—eventually we came to a bedroom, what was to be *my* room for the rest of my eternity, and he set me down on a bed. It was so warm, I was already melting, a fire crackling somewhere but it didn't smell like burning. It smelled like roses, old ones but not rotten, nauseatingly sweet, and though the roses demanded to be admired, to be seen, I kept my eyes closed tight, squeezing, squeezing. As long as I couldn't see the walls that bounded me, I could have been anywhere, far away and free—in an open field, in a forest near the sea—and soon I fell asleep, like falling to the bottom of a dark, abandoned well, a sublime, if temporary, retreat.

I OPENED MY eyes three times before they stayed open, and even then it felt like some part of me was still asleep.

The black gala dress was gone, and in its place I wore a white nightgown with puffed sleeves, one I only vaguely remembered changing into. I was warm, too warm, sweat gathering at my temples, and I kicked off the sheets—a soft cotton of richest red. Across the wide room a fire simmered in the grate, casting prickly shadows across the Persian rug in the direction of the bed where I lay—the biggest bed I had ever beheld, so wide I could stretch my arms straight out to the sides and my fingertips wouldn't even come close to either edge. On the wall nearby stood an enormous wardrobe made of the same oak wood as the bedposts, and the size of it almost made me laugh—my meager trousseau couldn't hope to fill more than a quarter of it. The room was dark except for the secretive glow around the fireplace and the dull-edged rectangle of diluted late afternoon sunlight falling on me as if through a narrow keyhole. The light came through a set of windowed doors, high and arched, beyond which jutted a shallow balcony, untouched snow glittering on the railing.

A knock on the door startled me, my heart turning over. I went to the door and cracked it just enough to see who was on the other side.

It was Mr. Russo. I began to open the door wider to admit him before remembering I was in a nightgown as thin as a whisper, and though I had seen that he had a kind smile, he was still a man and a stranger, and we were alone.

"Miss Dragotta," he said, his voice deep and moving over me like the shadow of a tree swaying wildly in the wind. Beyond him the hallway was a dim tunnel, and if not for the doors and the light at my back, I would have thought we were underground, buried like corpses only mistaken for dead. "It's nearly time for dinner. You must be starving after sleeping like that, like a cursed princess."

I hadn't thought of myself as cursed until he said it. Only *unfortunate*, to have attracted the attention of someone so rich and so enigmatic that he could whisk me away from everything and everyone I had ever known with very little fanfare or resistance. But maybe I *was* cursed in some way, like a girl in a fairy tale stumbling upon a box she should not open or striding deep into a glimmering forest where she should not go. Instead of choking me with dread, this revelation gave me hope: All curses could be broken. A curse that couldn't be broken was called fate, or destiny, and I could not—would not—believe that this was mine.

"How long have I slept?" Surely I couldn't have been in repose for more than a few hours; I didn't feel particularly rested. But his comment made me wonder.

"Three days."

I leaned against the doorframe, dizzy. *Three days*. Was that even possible? No wonder he'd likened my sleep to a spell.

"Where is the Master?" I said, crossing my arms over my chest. I longed for a robe, something thicker and warmer to wear. "I wish to speak to him."

I hadn't quite worked out what I was going to say when I saw him except to demand to know why he had chosen *me* to bring to his estate as a lavished-upon prisoner, to eat his food and dance with him once upon a midnight. He'd put me in his cage; how long was I expected to sing? And to what end? Was I expected to die here, as well as to live?

"You'll see him tonight. He asks that you change into the dress laid out for you in the wardrobe."

"I thought I was only to dance with the Master on Sunday midnights. Like going to church."

"Yes, but you slept through the last one, and he is still owed a dance."

I frowned at his use of the word *owed*—why did I owe anyone anything? I didn't ask for any of this. I wanted out of this house, out of his sight. "When do rehearsals for the new ballet begin?"

"I'll drive you to the studio tomorrow morning." Mr. Russo smiled, and it was not quite the same kind smile of three days ago. "In the meantime, please get dressed. I'll be waiting out here to escort you to the dining hall when you're ready."

Shutting the door, I went to the wardrobe, and yes—hanging there was a dress of dark green, forest green, with a full skirt, a tight bodice, and butterfly sleeves. A dress more suited to a queen than a captive, with a necklace of emeralds and matching teardrop earrings lying beside it. I peeled off my nightgown and stepped into the dress, almost tripping over the petticoats. I tightened the laces as best I could on my own, and when the dress was secure I re-pinned my hair, licking my fingertips and smoothing back the wisps. By this time the sky through the window was as black and still as a deep pool of water, and I almost felt I could fall right into it and sink, down and down forever, my lungs filling so that I'd never need breath again.

There was a scream inside me somewhere. I sighed instead.

As promised, Mr. Russo waited for me outside my bedroom, dressed in a dark suit with a crisp white shirt beneath. The hallway was otherwise empty, dark and cold, and I could not see either end of it, stretching both ways into shadow. Candles were lit in rusted sconces but their quivering flames did not cast far, only enough to illuminate patches of fleur-de-lis wallpaper and a crooked row of mirrors of various shapes and sizes hanging on the wall at eye level. I didn't see myself reflected in a single one.

"This way," Mr. Russo said, holding an arm out to me. After a moment of hesitation, I took it. *Remember his smile. His smile was kind.*

"Why can't I see myself in any of these mirrors?" I asked, deeply unnerved by the blank glass where our images should have appeared walking quietly beside us.

"They only reflect the dead."

"The dead?" I made to stop but Mr. Russo swept me along. I looked again to the mirrors and still saw nothing there. "You can't be serious."

"I can, and I am." Then, before I could ask any further questions, of which I suddenly had many, he said, "You look lovely, Miss Dragotta. I knew green would be your color."

"You picked this out?" My grip on him tightened in surprise as we started down a staircase to the second story.

"Who did you think had chosen it?"

"I don't know," I said after a long pause. "Doesn't the Master have servants?"

We were on the second floor now, about to descend the curving staircase into the foyer. The chandelier cast crystal petals of light on the marble floor. Thankfully there were no mirrors here. "What do you consider *me*, if not a servant?" he replied.

"Mistress called you the Master's assistant."

"And so I assist," he said, and the bitterness in his tone made me want to sink my nails into his skin until I scraped a nerve. Why should he complain? He wasn't trapped here like me. "I also serve, when the need arises."

It seemed an irrelevant distinction. As long as he was paid to be here, what did it matter if he served or assisted?

"Are there any women here? Women servants, I mean?"

"There is no one here but myself and the Master. And you, of course."

We entered a small, dark chamber, a set of closed doors framed by heavy drapes at the other end. Distracted by our conversation, Mr. Russo had steered me so confidently through the house and around pieces of withering furniture that I could not now remember exactly the path we had taken to arrive here. The walls were close, the ceiling low, and I felt exposed, despite the lack of light.

"No one else?" I asked, alarmed. Was I truly expected to live in this house with only two strange men for company?

"You are as safe here as you are anywhere else," he said, and gently slipped his arm out of my grasp. I was not convinced in the slightest, but I let the conversation stall as he pushed open the double doors behind the drapes and I was confronted with what seemed like another world entirely.

Before me in a long, narrow room, was a long, narrow table, whose surface I couldn't see for the piles and piles of food. I couldn't smell any of it, as if it were false food, fairy food, one bite meant to truly trap me here until the end of an endless winter. There was fruit and bread and meat, colors upon colors, brightly shining, heaped in large bowls and overflowing on tiered servers rising halfway to the ceiling; steaming vegetables and a crystal decanter of red wine. A tall glass vase of roses rested in the center, their lurid red petals stretched like mouths with too many tongues. It was a feast for forty people, at least—with a place set for only one.

"Where is the Master?" I said, lingering on the threshold. I had the sudden and certain feeling that if I stepped fully into the room I would not be allowed to leave the same way I had come in. There were no windows, only the doors Mr. Russo held open for me and an identical set at the opposite end, silver sconces along the walls holding scentless candles already burning down to black.

"He'll meet you in the ballroom," said Mr. Russo, pointing toward the other end of the room. "Those doors will open at midnight."

"I'm to eat alone?"

He thought about what he wanted to say before he said it. I waited, curling my toes inside my shoes. Finally, "The Master does not dine on this type of fare," he said, and I felt the world spin out from under me, like falling though I stayed on my feet, like drowning though I continued to breathe. Like breaking though my heart continued to beat. Very, very fast.

"I thought you said he was not that kind of beast," I said, taking a tiny step back and then another. Mr. Russo moved closer to me, laying a gentle hand on my arm. If I ran, he would catch me; if I screamed, who would hear?

"And so he is not. Human flesh isn't on the menu. Human blood however . . ."

I stiffened under his touch.

"I'm kidding," he said, giving me the same smile he had in the rear-view mirror of the car as he drove me away from my old life. I took a tentative step into the room, his hand slipping off my arm.

"Please," he said, and I drifted toward the food almost as if in a dream, my stomach empty and aching. "Relax and enjoy. You've certainly earned it."

I turned back toward the doors, meaning to—to what? Thank him? Beg him not to leave me here alone? Swipe a butter knife off the table and hold it to his throat, demand that he drive me back to the beginning of this dragging nightmare so it could play out again, hoping for a different outcome this time?

But Mr. Russo was already gone, the doors closing soundlessly and latching with a click. The silence—it was in me, choking the scream that was all I had left to cling to from my life before.

I felt so claustrophobic then, all of a sudden—not of the room, or the house, or the city, but of the world in its entirety. I was stuck here, in this world, and there wasn't another one; there wasn't anywhere else I could go. There was nothing beyond this earth with its wonders, pyramids and waterfalls. With its horrors, war and poverty; with its art and cynicism; with its cathedrals and trenches.

Please, please, *there has to be more,* I thought, *I need there to be* more. I needed myth and mysticism. I needed a god who would burn the tragedy out of me and clear the guilt from my eyes, all my transgressions, real and imagined. The world could not be so finite, so closed. I pushed back against the silence, dispelling it with the thrashing of my heart. This can't be all there is.

This can't be all there is.

I ran my hands along the walls; I crawled beneath the table. Searching for a hatch, a latch, a way under, a way out. I did not try the doors through which I'd entered—I couldn't bear to, couldn't bear the handle refusing to twist, the lock refusing to part, the doors refusing to bow to my will. Surely my will was stronger than a bit of metal and wood, stronger than this house, these walls, this life.

But it wasn't, and there was no way out.

I blew out the nearest candle. It ignited again immediately, automatically, the wick bent like a broken finger. No matter how hard I breathed on the flame the candle refused to extinguish, and even seemed to burn brighter in spite of me. Finally, I gathered my skirts and sat down at the table. I poured myself some wine.

I ate with abandon. Like an animal, I guess, all hands and grinding teeth. Hunched over, elbows on the table, half-crouched with one knee tucked to my chest, foot on the chair. No one watched; no one cared. There were crumbs stuck in the ends of my hair, as I ripped and chewed and slurped and swallowed, hardly finishing one delicacy before moving on to the next, to the next, to the next. I ate like dusk eating light from the sky, like the tide coming in. I ate like I was praying the rosary, with terror and awe and *amen* hissed between bites. If this was fairy food, a glittering ruse, then so be it. *So be it.* A curse is not a curse if it cannot be broken.

My mouth was wet; it glistened. I intended to glut myself on juicy roast beef, but it had been so long since I'd had such rich and tender meat that I could only manage a thin cut before I began to retch. I reached for more fruit, more wine instead, apples and candied almonds, tiny sponge cakes dusted with sugar. I started laughing, or maybe I only heard laughter in my head. Mamma was watching me. I didn't offer her any food, any drink.

The wine was like the wine in church except I could have as much as I wanted. Black cherry and black currant. Drink a little bit of God and you'll know exactly how He created the world but never be able to do it yourself. I plucked the petals off a rose, the lightest one, the color of chapped lips, and I ate those too, two at a time.

There was still so much food, even with my mess, even with my rinds and crusts and puddles of apple juice, strawberry and watermelon juice. Spills of wine, an overturned candle still burning. Delicate carnage. I stretched my arm out long on the table and I laid my head on my arm. I closed my eyes and then it was midnight.

First, I heard music.

A string quartet played over a phonograph; the song sounded like a blush warming winter-touched cheeks, quiet but creeping, a pinkish glow around the notes. I lifted my head, listening, and saw the doors open outward, into a dark room beyond.

I was alert now, but only in the way you sometimes realize you are dreaming, and thereby gain some measure of control over the dream. Lucid, but no less strange.

I stood, and noticed a stain on my dress, down the front. It was dark; it could have been blood—not mine. Likely it was wine. I drifted toward the open doors, a cool wind at my back, though the doors behind me were still shut tight. *The only way out is through.* This was true of Hell too. I stepped over the threshold and into a crowded room.

Only not crowded, no. It was only me, a thousand times. The room was round and the walls were mirrors.

Long sheets of them, like in a ballet studio, stretching from the floor to more than halfway to the dome of the high glass ceiling. No candles, no lights; the only illumination was that of the moon, full and heavy and old, its rays refracting off the glass and lending an illusion of enhanced luster. The music played on—a waltz glowing with fever though I had no idea where it was coming from; the phonograph was somehow hidden. I spun in a slow circle, seeing myself from every angle: wide, wet eyes and a trembling mouth, a spoiled dress and silver pins losing their grip on my hair, the stark blue veins on the side of my neck. How could I feel so vicious inside but look only like a lost little girl?

I made a full revolution and stopped. The Master stood before me, a tall dark figure not three feet in front of me. I had not seen him in any of the mirrors, but he was in all of them now. He wore his dark cloak with the hood pulled low, a deep shadow falling across his face. That face I knew intimately, and yet not at all.

At the sight of him, my heart had bared its teeth. I had not known until then that it had any teeth, and that its beat could bite. Perhaps, in another situation, in another time and place, it might have thrilled me— this desire, this urge, this *will* to fight. But it didn't. This instinct only kicked in here, now, because I was a cornered animal.

Flight was not an option. There were no other doors but the ones I had come through, and those had closed as soon as I was clear of them. How had he gotten in?

How would I get out?

Silently, the Master held out his hand. What else could I do? I took it.

His was gloved and mine was bare, pale skin on black leather, and I was relieved I would not have to touch him, that there was this thin barrier between us, at least. He slid his other hand behind my back, resting just beneath my shoulder blade. I breathed a moment, I licked the wine from my lips, and then I looked up.

It was just as I suspected: Master La Rosa was a beast.

Oh, he looked human enough—strikingly so. Handsome, even: dark brown hair, high cheekbones, square jaw, his teeth straight and white. And his mouth, which had vexed me for weeks—was normal. There wasn't anything special about it, and maybe if he were just a man I might have wanted to kiss him. And his eyes: They were green, just as I'd seen from the stage, lurid in the dark. Green like lichen growing illicitly on the Tree of Knowledge in the Garden of Eden, blurring good and evil, breaking the boundaries between want and greed. Once I fixed on them they were all I could see, those eyes in an otherwise shadowed face. They pulled me in, soothing, convincing my frenzied heart to slow. They promised me all sorts of wonderful things, things I had yearned for and still continued to seek: sanctuary and compassion and acceptance and absolution. And love—yes, even love, romantic and true.

No fangs, no scales or horns or other devilish horrors, though with his gloves on I could not confirm the existence of the claws that had raked me in the theater. Classic in visage, the portrait of chivalry.

But I wasn't fooled. Not for a moment.

It was a trick; it had to be. He was only a mirror, no different really from the ones on the walls, reflecting what I so desperately needed to see: a prince in place of a monster, kindness challenging cruelty. An illusion; this was not his true skin. For only a monster would tear a young woman away from her home, flexing his wealth to exert his dominion over her. He did not have to smile for me to know it.

"Why?" I whispered, though I had not meant to whisper. I had come here intending to howl and scratch and demand. But the moonlight, the mirrors, the Master's gentle grip—it called for softness, for warmth. That was part of the deception, I supposed, lulling me into acquiescence. "Why did you choose *me*?"

He did not answer right away—to the point where I thought he would not answer at all. I had hardly noticed, but we were already dancing.

"Because you keep your death inside your heart," he said at last, and his voice was sky-deep, like something cold and endless, like something I could fall right through.

"My death?" He led me around the room, *one* two-three, *one* two-three, our many reflections spinning with us, a dizzying whirl of color and light. "Don't you mean my life? Last time I checked, my heart was still beating."

"No," he said. "Your death."

It was like the answer to a riddle in a fairy tale, like Koschei the Deathless in *The Firebird*, who kept his death where he thought no one would ever discover it. Inside of an egg inside of a casket. But I was no sorcerer, no demon or god, possessed of no deep magic to keep my death hidden and safe. Just a girl, mortal and alone, clinging to life where I could.

"What do *you* know of my death?" I said, trying to hold on to the cold spot melting in my chest, melting against my will. Cold all over except where he touched me, burning even through his gloves, and the fabric of my fine dress. "Mine, or yours, or anyone's?"

Did his grip on my hand and high on my waist tighten ever so incrementally, or did I imagine it? His voice, as ever, was steady.

"Because I have seen it. Because it is *all* I see when I look at a mortal, when I walk through the world." There, no, I did not imagine it—he held me like something that cannot break. His eyes brightened as if there were glass behind them, and light flashing on the glass. "Death is all I know."

I breathed quietly, I don't know why; suddenly I didn't want him to hear. Still we swept around and around, and the mirrors made the room look infinite. Suddenly there seemed to be so many of him but only one of me. "You say *mortal* as if you are not one."

"I am not."

My heart stopped—but only for a moment. Was I truly so far from the world I had known, a world in which everything in it must one day die, that I could accept his immortality—*his beastliness*—at a word? Perhaps it would have been harder to bear had I not seen it once, his claws and his great glowing eyes. But more than anything it was his claim that he understood the kind of grief that only a human could carry that set every muscle in my jaw to trembling as I held back a scream.

Immortal? Then you know nothing of death! I wanted to cry, but something—some instinct, of self-preservation perhaps—stayed my tongue. Wasn't it I who had lost a mother, a brother, a father, a beloved neighbor and violin instructor? Yes, my heart *was* full of death—it was home to everyone I had loved who was now gone, home to memory and to endless longing. What could some immortal beast know of human grief?

"How would you know what is in my heart?" I asked, when at last I felt I could speak without an excess of vehemence. "You know nothing about me."

The Master's gaze was so earnest on mine, wide-eyed and calm, that

I had to look away. "I heard it in your music," he said. "And I saw it in your dance."

So he *had* been following me, watching me—closely. For seven years, at least, and maybe even longer than that.

"You picked me because my death was in my heart," I said into the air between us. "But I do not see how that makes me different from any other mortal on earth. There is nowhere else in the body to keep our grief."

"Some do," he conceded, and I felt the frost in my chest creeping, blooming again. It didn't have to be me here; it could have been anyone. I was only an Ivan; he with a bow for his arrows and me with a bow for my violin, stumbling upon a story we didn't belong in and making ourselves the center of it anyway, whether we wanted to be there or not.

But the Master wasn't done.

"Others keep it in their belly, an ache like hunger," he said, and maybe he *was* a beast, but he was also solid and warm, and I leaned toward him as we spun, ever so slightly. "Some keep it in their throat, holding on to it like silence, like words they are too afraid to say. And still others keep their death behind their eyes, in their mind. They think about death constantly, whether they are afraid or resigned."

"What does it look like, my death?" I asked, wanting desperately to talk of something, anything, else, but I was also curious. And it was better to know, wasn't it? To study the face of the demon under my bed, so that when it smiled at last, I wouldn't flinch. "How can you see inside of me?"

"I do not see *inside* you. It shines *out* of you, not like a star but like a diamond when the light hits it just right. I am the light; it ignites when I am near." He slowed our steps until we came to a stop. With his hands on my shoulders he gently turned me around so that I faced the nearest mirror, his breath grazing the back of my neck. "Look, little bird. *Look*."

I saw it then, beneath my skin: a glow like lamplight through a thick mist, pure and colorless, radiant in the place where my heart beat like wings in water, like a bird on the surface of a sea that was too deep, too dark, to fathom. There, brighter than dawn, and in the next moment— gone. Though my death had shone, it had brought with it no warmth, no blaze like the sun, and no chill when it had faded either. No feeling at all but the blood rushing, the heart pumping, the shock of seeing it there, so stark but still intangible, a terrible, secret thing.

Hands shaking, I turned away from the mirror. I held out my arms toward the Master to keep dancing, and he stepped into me, but once we were in position neither of us moved. I stared at his chest, my eyes level with his collarbone, while the music swelled like a blister about to rupture. How could he have seen my death in the very thing that made me feel most alive? Unless life and death have always lived close, side by side.

"And where do you keep yours?" I asked. "Where is your death?"

He smiled, I think. I blinked, and missed it. "Hidden safely."

My head spun even though we still had not moved. The Master had not let go of me and I did not let go of him.

"Why have you brought me here?" A whisper on a sigh. "To die?"

"No," he said, and I wondered how he could speak so softly with all those sharp teeth. Except he didn't have sharp teeth, only normal ones, and it was all so confusing because he looked exactly the way I had hoped he would look and yet he was a beast, I knew he was a beast. His claws—they had raked and pierced my skin. "To dance. To dance forever."

"I don't understand," I said, and dropped my arms, too tired to hold them up. Our dance tonight was done.

"I can show you." A hint of fever crept into his voice, and he lifted his hand from my back to tentatively touch my cheek. "Only you must come away with me. Away with me until morning. To a place far from here, where the moon casts no shadow and the night comes alive inside of you. Little bird"—my eyes rose to his—"will you come?"

How could I give an answer when I could barely breathe? Away from here—with a beast?

"No," I said, almost reverent. Could he truly have believed I would give any other answer? I felt compelled to offer a reason for my refusal: I don't know you, I don't trust you, I am human and you are not. Any of those would be true. But really I was afraid—of him, of this place, of being taken from the world and hidden away like his death, a kind of quiet devouring.

"No," I said again. "I will not go anywhere with you."

The Master nodded and stepped away. I swayed.

"Good night, little bird," he said.

And then he was gone.

I wish I could explain it, but even now when I picture that moment it is muzzy in my mind. He stood there, in front of me, and I was looking past him, at his back in the mirror, because I had a thought that maybe his cloak was hiding a pair of folded wings, some ineludible proof of his monstrousness. And as I inspected his reflection he stepped sideways, out of the panel I gazed into, and vanished from view. A trick, I thought, another illusion, like a magician disappearing in a puff of smoke. I was disoriented, my head heavy, my belly heavy, my hands like little metal weights forcing my shoulders to sag. The moonlight had dimmed; it was dark. The music played on but the song was now a sorrowful one, speaking of heroes mortally wounded and graves dug too soon and storms that washed the blood away and memories too.

The Master was gone from the mirror, and gone from the room entirely.

EXHAUSTION, COLD SWEAT. Something inside me collapsed and went to sleep, but the rest of me walked out of the ballroom the way I had come. The doors were unlocked and they did not lead back into the dining hall but rather into a corridor I had never seen before, long and without mirrors of any kind. I kept one hand on the wall, scraping, reminding the house that I was here, that I was at its mercy. *Please be kind to me. You are my prison and my sanctuary.* At the end of the corridor I was back in the foyer, the chandelier lit low. I went up the stairs to the third floor, peeking into every room I passed in pursuit of my own, only to find abandoned rooms with gray sheets draped over the furniture, or storage rooms piled high with boxes and trinkets and lamps without shades, dusty portraits leaning against the walls. Old junk, a tainted perfume of mold and moths. Frayed drapes, ice on the windows. In some places the wall was stripped away to reveal the wood framing behind it, the gaps long and thin like marks made by sharp claws.

It was a relief when I finally found the right room, and a relief too to lock the door behind me. I would never grow tired of the sound of it clicking.

The nightgown was laid out neatly on the bed, not where I'd left it, and I was beginning to suspect that what Mr. Russo had said was correct—that there were no servants except him, *assisting* the Master in whatever manner or capacity he required. Maybe this was the first time they'd ever had a guest, and hadn't realized what a burden it would be. Maybe the Master would hire more servants—or *any* servants—now that I was here.

It wasn't until after I had changed and brushed my hair that I noticed the letter on the nightstand, a thin piece of paper folded in half. My heartbeat quickened as I lunged for it.

Grace, it said at the top, and that alone almost made me cry. Even if I hadn't recognized the handwriting at once, shaky and cramped as it was, I would know who had written this letter. Emilia never called me colombina, little bird, little dove, or any derivation thereof. Only Grace, always. Sitting lightly on the edge of the bed, I read the rest:

> *I tried to see you this morning, but they wouldn't let me in—a man, the same one who came to fetch you from the boardinghouse—said you were sleeping and not to be disturbed. This disturbed me, because I've never known you to sleep late, except when you're sick. I tried ex- plaining to him that I am your very best friend in the world, practically a sister, and that we do, in fact, share blood—a glass of it, every night before bed. Good for the skin, I said, but the man at the door didn't even laugh at my joke! Rude. Anyway, I told him you wouldn't mind me waking you up but he refused to let me pass the threshold. At least let me write her a letter, I said, and he grudgingly obliged, pulling out this little scrap of paper from his pocket and a pen. I'm writing this on the front porch, huddled in the cold, using my knees as a table. I hope they are treating you better inside the house than they are treating me out here. I assume so, or else you would have run by now and found your way back to me. Still, I feel uneasy, and I won't be able to rest well until I hear back from you.*
>
> *It is strange, but Mistress could not provide an address for Master*

La Rosa. Even now I don't know it—there is no number on the house,
and no street name on the corner. And of course the man at the
door won't tell me a thing, only watches me with his arms crossed
while I write, waiting for me to leave. Needless to say I am furious
with Mistress for this entire situation and I will never forgive her.
I've already moved out of the boardinghouse and am staying with my
cousin Eliana until the wedding (only two months away now!).
Rumors abounded after you left and I tried to set the record straight,
but it was difficult when even I had no idea of your true whereabouts,
other than that you went to live with Master La Rosa. I was in despair
of ever finding you, until early this morning, on my way to the pana-
dería. A white dove flew down and landed on the sidewalk at my feet.
It stared at me for a long moment, and then took to the air again, land-
ing just a few yards ahead of me. It looked back, as if waiting for me to
follow. And I did follow, all the way here. Not on foot. At some point
I jumped in a taxicab and instructed the driver to follow the dove.
He didn't even look at me strangely—I suppose he would follow a
fire-breathing demon into Hell as long as I paid him handsomely for
the trouble. I know this sounds absurd, especially in writing, but it's
God's honest truth. A dove led me here, and I can see her even now at
the end of the walkway, waiting to lead me home again. I don't know
where we are—I think Hyde Park, but the street looks strange, almost
shimmery, and shrouded in fog even though when I set out it was a
perfectly sunny day. I don't think I'll be able to find my way back here
without Little Grace—I've named the dove Little Grace, you see,
it comforts me, like you sent her to me—so I hope she'll call on me
again soon that I may try again to visit you. If not, I hope you will find
your way to me. Eliana lives in Pilsen, at 1121 West 19th Street. At the
very least, write to me. I feel half dead without you, and dying more
every day that goes by without some news of you. And no amount
of blood consumed at the witching hour will revive me.

I read the letter so many times I lost count. It warmed me and chilled
me all at once, and the resulting sensation was the numbness of repeti-
tive prayer, expecting something to happen, to change immediately and
right before my eyes. But nothing did. I stood up, the letter fluttering to

the floor because I didn't have the strength to hold it up anymore, my wrists brittle enough to snap. With sweating hands I went to the window and opened it. There I whispered into the soft curve of night, into the fog and ice: I said Emilia's name, three times. A summoning.

Come back to me. This time I'll be ready.

I believed her about the bird. I believed her about everything.

With the window open still, the cold warring with the fire crackling in the grate, I crawled into bed and went straight to sleep.

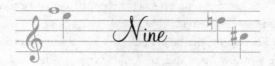

Nine

IN THE MORNING I HAD ONLY ONE THOUGHT IN MY HEAD AS I dressed in the black leotard and pink tights waiting in the wardrobe for me, as I ate a warm breakfast of eggs and sausage left on the nightstand, as I hummed to myself to banish the silence sticking like smoke in my chest: *Away.* Away from the Master, and away from this house. Even if it was only for a short while. Even if only to remind myself that I was still a girl on the ground and not a bird in the air about to be shot down.

I moved through the house without looking at a single mirror, still disturbed that I could not find my reflection there. When I opened the front door the air outside wasn't as chilly as I thought it would be, or perhaps I no longer felt the cold so keenly. A thick mist hung low over everything, obscuring the houses on the other side of the street entirely. The lawn was long and covered in a thin layer of snow like a burial shroud; the street was empty, save for a lone black car cleaving through the fog. At first I thought it wasn't real, conjured by my craving for escape, but as it drew closer I saw that it *was* real and it wasn't just any black car.

I stepped off the porch.

It was harder than it should have been, that single step. My body felt slow and my head oddly heavy, the tendons of my neck straining as I held my chin high. Another step, and another, each more of a struggle than the last, as if I were running headlong into a murderous wind, into a storm. The houses to either side of the Master's estate were dark and somehow distant, as if they belonged to some other world, impenetrable, though there was only a thin alley to separate one structure from another. I wondered who lived there, and if they knew the true nature of their neighbor, or if he kept out of their sight the way he seemed to keep out of mine. Showing his face only at night, dizzying me until his hard edges looked soft and luminous and like something I could care for.

My stomach tumbled, groaning, and I felt utterly sick, half-wasted away—but I was almost there, almost to the curb where the black car was just pulling to a stop. Sweat ran down the sides of my face as I reached for the door to the backseat and wrenched it open, throwing myself inside before Mr. Russo had even turned off the engine.

I put a hand over my heart, over my death, and I sighed.

A stench of cigarette smoke, stale and lingering. It reminded me of Mistress, of that night outside the planetarium, the last glimpse I'd had of stars, a projected galaxy I'd never actually see with my own eyes. Mr. Russo took off his flat cap and raised his gaze to mine in the rearview mirror.

"Everything all right?"

My breath came in gasps, and I glanced back briefly at the Master's house, the windows dark. At once there was an inexplicable yet undeniable tug, a promise that my torment would end if only I stepped through the doors and did not venture out again. The cold would return, and I could rest. It was a good promise, a true promise, but I turned away, doubling over as my ribs began to ache.

"This house," I said, wiping my clammy forehead with my wrist. "It—it doesn't want me to leave."

His long, thin fingers tapped the steering wheel. "You've heard of Persephone? The pomegranate seeds?"

Oh, yes, I had heard the myth—how Hades, king of the underworld, had captured the maiden of spring while she was out gathering flowers and brought her to his sunless world to rule over the shades as his queen. But when Persephone's mother, Demeter, goddess of the harvest, demanded her daughter be returned to earth lest nothing should grow there again, Hades offered his queen six pomegranate seeds to eat, which would guarantee her return to the underworld for six months of every year. Persephone accepted the seeds, swallowing them down quick, and that is why we have winter, the soil growing cold and barren without her here.

Now I thought of the fairy food, the feast. I had eaten at the Master's table; I had accepted my place in Hell. Not a curse, but a contract. I had signed my name in shining ink, and now I burned for the breaking of my vow. But I couldn't abstain—I would waste away.

"Will it be like this every time?" I asked.

Mr. Russo breathed deeply, and didn't answer right away. Then, "Sometimes the Master doesn't realize the cruelty he inflicts."

A prickling, all across my chest. "You'd have me forgive him?"

His gaze was steady on mine in the mirror. "It's not an excuse," he said, "Only a reason."

I looked away. The world was relentlessly gray, and I had a dizzying feeling then, like we were the last living beings left in an empty expanse. I sank into the seat cushion, letting my head tip back.

"Please, will you—will you take me to 1121 West 19th Street? It's in Pilsen."

It was a moment before he spoke. He cleared his throat. "I am only to take you to rehearsal, Miss Dragotta. Nowhere else. And your rehearsal isn't set to begin for another two hours."

I sat up so quickly the blood rushed from my head and my vision went spotty. "*Please*, I have to see her. I have to—"

"I would if I could. But those are my orders."

There was something in his voice—a note of fatigue, an unwillingness to fight, neither with me nor against me—that called to the cruelty in me. I imagined twining my fingers through his thick hair, pulling his head back, exposing his throat. An animal seizing on weakness, playing with a sore spot.

"And why must you follow the Master's orders so precisely? You work for him, but you don't *belong* to him." *Just like me*, I thought. Master La Rosa paid the company and I danced; he could tell me how to dance, and when, but the movements—the meaning I gleaned from them—would always be my own. "I won't tell him we took a detour if you won't."

I had thought I'd made a convincing point, but Mr. Russo wouldn't yield. "I am pledged to help the Master in any way he requires. It is part of a bargain we've made."

"What bargain?" I asked, but received no answer. I dug my nails into the skin of my wrist, all those veins. "Can you drive me around the city then? Anywhere, just—away from here."

Mr. Russo started the engine and pulled from the curb. Mist on the windows, headlights barely slicing the gloom, the gentle rocking of the car as we trundled away from the house. Slowly the pain in my chest loosened, my pulse dulled, and I had just begun to let my eyes drift shut when Mr. Russo spoke, his voice both near and far at once.

"It might help, Miss Dragotta, to sleep for a while," he said as I slipped into the haziness of a half-dream, when magic is as real and moving as a muscle and the sky is very close. "You'll feel better when you wake."

FINGERS IN MY hair, playing, pulling my head upright from where I had sagged heavily to the side, my neck stiff and sore, insisting that I open my eyes, that I *look*—but when I turned, no one was there. The car slid so slowly through the streets that if not for the tiny bumps and bounces as we jostled over potholes and cracks in the pavement, I wouldn't have thought we were moving at all. Every window was frosted, even the windshield, and the sunlight—*sunlight?*—was so bright that I couldn't discern anything beyond the interior, our warm little world of leather seats and spinning dials on the dashboard, the hum of the engine and murmur of the radio, faraway voices unintelligible. Lulled into a placid trance, it took me longer than it should have to realize that it was no longer Mr. Russo in the driver's seat—it was Lorenzo.

"Hey there, bearcat." Even with his back to me, I would have known him anywhere: his tall, lanky, sixteen-year-old frame, wrists so thin they looked likely to snap at the slightest provocation; slightly hunched shoulders, thick curling hair kept just a little too long, too shaggy, prompting Mamma to scold him that it was past time for a trim. And his voice—it had a melody, an ebb and flow like the waves of Lake Michigan, a lightness to it like morning, like the world always on the brink of beginning. I leaned forward, straining for a glimpse of his smile, but no matter how far I stretched from the backseat he angled his face away from me so that I couldn't see beyond the edge of his jaw, the side of his cheek. "Where to, Gracie girl?"

Where to? Did it matter where we went, so long as we were together?

"*Voglio . . .*" I said slowly, reaching for a language I hadn't spoken in an eternity, even though it wasn't necessary. It felt right to use it, more honest. True. "*Tornare indietro.*"

"You want to go *back?*" His hands drummed the steering wheel, completely out of tune with the music on the radio. "Back to the beginning? Or back to the end?"

I stared at the nape of his neck, wanting so badly to touch him, to tug on his hair. But I was afraid that if I did, he would disappear. "How can I return to the end when I haven't been there yet?"

"The end came and went a long time ago," he said, but now his voice wasn't his; it was no longer light. Instead it was Mr. Russo's voice, deep and measured like an anchor scraping along the bottom of the sea, dragging me along with it. "It came and went without you."

I sighed, sinking back into my seat. "I have to go to rehearsal."

"And then?"

I was so sleepy. I let my head loll to the side. "The Master's house."

"And then?"

I closed my eyes. "There is nowhere else."

And, quietly, as I drifted off again, Mr. Russo's low voice with Lorenzo's playful cadence: "*Oh, bearcat. You sure about that?*"

FROM THE OUTSIDE, the studio looked the same as always, an old crooked brownstone with fog on the window glass, and I could not fathom why, in the few seconds it took for me to emerge fully from sleep, I had thought it would appear different, transformed in some way I could not articulate. But nothing had changed—only me.

The engine idled as Mr. Russo waited for me to climb out. The skin beneath his eyes was blue like a moonless sky. He drummed the steering wheel with his thumb.

I leaned forward, between the seats, until we were nearly cheek to cheek. I could barely breathe around the knot in my throat, the tangled remains of my dream. Lorenzo asking me where in the world I wanted to go.

"Take me back," I whispered, my heart beating once hot, and then cold. Only a few hours ago I had been desperate for escape, but now I saw that there was none—the studio, the stage, I was no longer quite of that world. How could I go in there and act like everything was normal and good even though I had eaten fairy food and danced in a mirrored room with a beast mere hours ago? "Take me back to the Master's house."

Mr. Russo did not turn his head or look at me in the mirror. "Your rehearsal is about to start."

"Are you not a driver?" I said, and my voice was pitched so high that it came out more like a cry. *"Drive."*

But Mr. Russo said nothing and we went nowhere. It was too hot in the car, too hot in my skin, and I couldn't fathom the shape of myself anymore—long bones and tight muscles and my heart all bloody and sore. I reached for the door and jerked it open, climbing out. I collapsed on the curb behind the car, my knees pulled tight to my chest. The snow melted beneath me and soaked through my clothes. I was only vaguely aware of Mr. Russo getting out of the car. He crouched before me in the street, his elbows balanced on his knees and his cap back on his head.

"Miss Dragotta," he said, "you're panicking, and for no reason. It's only dancing, nothing more. And I'll be right out here, waiting for you when you finish."

"You won't leave me?"

He laid a hand over his heart, voice grave with some weight I did not understand. "Never."

I allowed him to take my arm and help me to my feet.

WORKING OUT OF order, we were to rehearse the second act, the dance of the shades, when the girl caught between brothers descends to the underworld and meets the queen of the girls taken by Death tragically before their times. It was perversely fitting, then, that a similar scene should ensue when I walked into the studio and was confronted with all the girls I had briefly left behind. I tried to enter quietly, without notice, but soon the room had gone silent and all heads had swiveled to look at me, a many-eyed monster, openly hungry. I stood in the doorway and lifted my chin, conscious of the clean, new dress I wore over my leotard and tights, of the crisp green ribbon wrapped in my hair, of the icy shine of my eyes. Out of the corner of my vision I saw my reflection in the mirror and somehow, strangely, it made me feel less alone.

For a moment the girls blinked at me and I at them, until finally Beatrice stalked forward, the others quickly surrounding us. And I wanted to cry that none of them were Emilia, that Emilia and I would never again sit in the corner alone and hold hands as we talked of angels and poetry and wondered when the weather would turn warm. Ordinary was gone.

"What happened?" Beatrice said. She tried to whisper but it was impossible to keep our voices a secret. Behind her stood Anna and a half-dozen other girls I had seen every day for years, all peering at me eagerly.

"I danced with him," I said quietly. "That's all."

"What is he like?" said Anna, a light in her eyes.

I had to give them something, I knew, or there would never be an end. But I could not tell them about the house, or the feast, or the mirrored room. Or the waltz and the music and the Master's large hands covering mine. "He's . . . tall," I said at last, and this remark was met with scowls.

"Tall?" Beatrice laughed, and while it wasn't exactly cruel, it certainly wasn't kind. "That's all you have for us? The foreign prince is *tall*?"

"He's not a prince," I snapped, and some of the girls stepped back.

"What is he then?" Beatrice asked, and a chill swept through the room. "I think we deserve to know. He could have picked any one of us."

Her words struck me to the bone. They called to something in my marrow, buried deep, something that stirred from a century-long slumber and gnashed its gleaming teeth.

"Is that so? Tell me then: Where do you keep your death?"

"My death? What does that mean?" Beatrice breathed hard and fast.

"In your belly, with all your bile?" I taunted, even though I knew I should stop, that we didn't come to the studio every day to think about death, and certainly not to talk about it. We came here to *live*, to keep our hearts beating, untouchable. But I couldn't stop, even as the looks on the other girls' faces grew frightened—frightened of *me*. "Or do you keep it in your head, a looming nightmare from which you can never escape?"

"I have no *idea* what you're talking about."

Before I could say anything more the door opened behind me, and the girls discreetly dispersed as Mistress came into the studio. Even Beatrice, until there was no one at my side.

"Oh, good, you're all on time." We watched, utterly still, as Mistress shed her coat and hung it on the rack in the corner. Even Elsie looked hunched and small behind the piano. There was a silence like a sparrow perched on a windowsill, head tilted to the sky. I waited for Mistress to look at me—*Look at me!*—but she never did. "Let's begin, shall we?"

I DIDN'T SPEAK for the rest of rehearsal; I don't think anyone noticed. Alone, I sat in the corner and stretched with my legs to either side, leaning forward so that my chest was nearly to the floor. The other girls didn't engage me again, though they continued to whisper behind cupped hands and throw furtive glances in my direction. Mostly, that first day, Mistress worked with Beatrice, the Queen of the Shades, choreographing the scene that took place before I would arrive in the underworld. My character didn't even have a name. Only *The Girl*. The Girl that was loved. The Girl that died too soon.

The very moment rehearsal was over and we curtsied in a reverence, I pulled my dress on over my leotard, the sturdy, floral fabric immaculate and unwrinkled even though it had been balled up in my bag, and made straight for the door. No one stopped me; no one said goodbye. Beatrice wordlessly waved a limp hand, but I pretended I didn't see.

Outside the sun was setting behind the clouds; there was snow on the ground and snow in the gutters and snow beginning to fall from an endless gray sky. I rounded the corner to where Mr. Russo had promised he'd be waiting for me. He eyed me in the rearview mirror as I slid into the backseat.

"Miss Dragotta," he said as he started the car, and his voice startled me—I don't know why. There was kindness in it, but no compassion. "Are you all right?"

I wanted to tell him he didn't have to call me Miss Dragotta anymore, that Grace would be fine, but I didn't have the energy or the will. What were we to each other, he and I? Both of us in service to a master I did not yet fully understand—did that make us friends? Associates? Or nothing, nothing at all?

"Just take me away from here," I said, the day sinking like a stone inside me, heavy. "Take me back."

Ten

ONE MORE DAY OF REHEARSAL BEFORE THE WEEKEND, AND IT was much the same as the first had been: I stretched in the corner, and every time I looked up I caught someone staring. I blinked back steadily, until they flushed and looked away. And still Mistress worked on a scene that I wasn't in, and I wondered what the point was in my being there at all.

That evening, as well as the next, Mr. Russo brought dinner to my room—the dining room was only open to me on Sundays—and I sat in front of the fire late into the night while I read from what remained of my book of Shakespeare, memorizing the words to *Antony and Cleopatra*, a love story doomed from the start. On Sunday morning, I thought about asking—well, more like *demanding*—that Mr. Russo take me to church, but even if I'd truly believed he'd agree, the idea of bowing my head in prayer, of kneeling before the altar, of submitting before God to say I was sorry for my sins—*me* and not *Him*, the all-knowing Almighty who had surely watched the Master whisk me away from the world and stuff me down a dark crevice, who had witnessed with no intervention, neither mundane nor divine—caused something to clench deep in my belly, a hard and unyielding resistance. I only hoped Emilia would forgive me for missing it—that she would not worry too much.

There was no clock in my room, no sense of time passing but the slow crawl of the shadows. I only knew when it was time for dinner on Sunday by the moon like a wound in the sky, a mortal blow bleeding light, and my hunger crying out like a lost thing wandering in the woods. I waited for Mr. Russo to return, opening the door a crack and peeking out into the hallway, but it was empty and stayed empty. Very well; the house wasn't so large that I couldn't find my own way. A gown hung in the wardrobe that hadn't been there earlier, and it was somehow love-lier than the last: royal violet satin, sleeveless, with a short train and a sweetheart neck. I struggled into it and tied the front locks of my hair away from my face with a matching ribbon resting on the vanity. Once again I looked like a princess, and I smiled at myself in the mirror. What harm could come of pretend?

I went to the balcony and stood a moment in the open doorway. Fall-ing snowflakes made a tiara in my hair, half-crushed and glistening like little bells. Then I shut the glass doors, reluctantly, and left my room for the first time all day.

The mirrors in the hallway still did not reflect me. I had thought, for a moment, that maybe they would. That they would see my dry, wilted parts, the rot. The parts of me that had begun to die. But no—nothing in me would decay as long as I kept to the cold, as long as the snow in my hair didn't melt, as long as my heart was packed in ice. I swept through the house and fogged the mirrors with my breath, the only part of me that still insisted on warmth. At the end of the hallway I turned the corner, and there was Mr. Russo.

"Ah," he said, and stepped back, allowing me to pass. I did, with hardly a glance at him. He wore his coat and cap, as if he'd just come from outside, and I wondered where he had been. He walked beside me and did not say anything, and I did not say anything, and the silence fell around us like rain.

Hunger pulsed in my throat.

"I'd like to know more about the mirrors, please," I said as we de-scended from the third floor to the second, gripping the railing with one hand and lifting the hem of my dress with the other.

"I'm sure you would."

I stopped on the stairs and he stopped also, two steps below. He turned and looked up at me, his face edged in shadow. Candlelight, dust in the air. I put my hands on his cheeks and held his gaze. A sigh escaped his lips.

"If I have to live in this house," I said, "then I deserve to know its secrets."

He clenched his jaw; I felt it under my palms. "It's just what I said—glass to see the dead. There is no deeper mystery or meaning."

Liar, I thought immediately, viciously—but no, I believed him. What choice did I have? There was no one else but the Master to ask, and I could hardly rely on the word of a beast, and my captor. Not that his accomplice was much better.

"Is the Master afraid?" I said very softly, as if there were someone—something—sleeping nearby that I did not want to wake.

"Of the dead?" he said, and my peripheral vision went blurry; there was only his face. But it was not him I was entranced by so much as the Master's secrets, the secrets this man before me must know.

"Of death itself," I said, and sensed right away it was the wrong thing to say. Mr. Russo stiffened under my touch.

"Death and the dead do not frighten La Rosa," he said, and the softness was gone now. The world had edges again. I dropped my hands but he didn't move, and neither did I. "Nothing frightens him. Though, if he were wise, there is one thing that should."

My bird-heart thrashed with wild wings. "And what is that?"

"Sleep."

The word carried an echo—a resonance of hands wet with holy water, of the disordered notes of a dark lullaby, of dreams poured into a chalice like wine. *Sleep*, I thought with awe. *What is there to fear from sleep?* It chilled me that I might be missing something, that there was a monster lurking close all my life and I only ever thought its breath on my skin was the wind.

Sleep.

"Sleep is a character in *Little Bird*, the ballet the Master commissioned," I said as we hovered on the stairs, and though I was above him, looming, I still felt small. "But I don't see any reason why Sleep should be feared—only Death, which takes and takes and gives nothing in return."

"That is true," Mr. Russo allowed, the tendons of his neck tightening. "But Sleep has dominion over dreams, does he not?"

"I suppose."

"Some dreams are terrifying, but those are likely to fade with time. It is the sweetest dreams that stay with us, that make us long for things that perhaps we can never really achieve. For places we can never go, and for people—people we love that are now gone."

I shivered because it was true, because there were dreams I had cried over, dreams that had inevitably met their ends even though I wasn't finished with them. Dreams like a tooth being torn from my gums, a raw, empty spot that I poked with my tongue, sore to the touch. Dreams I had wanted to turn inside out so that they were real and my reality only a dream. But always I woke; and always, more and more, I did not want to.

Where to, Gracie girl?

"It is a gift to dream," I said, even as my heartstrings stretched taut enough to snap, even as I wished with all my might that the dream had been real, that I could have my brother back. "We would go mad if we had to be awake every minute of the day and the night, with no escape at all from reality. I—well, *I'm* certainly not afraid of Sleep."

Shadow of a smile. "No, I shouldn't think so, Miss Dragotta. You've had no reason to be."

We walked the rest of the way to the dining room in silence, the house pinching around us. Lost in my longing, we arrived at the familiar double doors and I realized again I had not paid attention, that I did not know the way to find them on my own. Without a word, Mr. Russo pushed open the doors, and I stepped through them, no hesitation this time. But I did stop them from closing with my hands, one on each door. I turned to look at him over my shoulder.

"What do you suppose the Master dreams of?" I said as cavalierly as I could to conceal just how brightly my curiosity burned.

"The Master seems a lonely creature, does he not?" Mr. Russo said, his voice so quiet that it made mine seem loud in retrospect, still echoing around the room. *Dreams of, dreams of, dreams of.* "I am certain his dreams are of you."

At once my cheeks flushed, scarlet and hot; Mr. Russo saw, and laughed. I turned away quickly and let the doors close between us, sealing myself inside until the only sound was that of my quick-beating heart.

∞

THE DINING ROOM was utterly unchanged from the other evening: bread rolls torn open, grapes plucked from their clusters, an apple missing two bites, tiny crackers floating on the surface of the soup. Candle flames conquering the darkness as best they could, and long, stray hairs clinging to the curved arms of the low chandelier. My spills, my crumbs, my mess—still there, wine drizzling languidly off the end of the table as if I'd only just knocked over the glass. When I sat, the chair was still warm.

I ate more evenly this time, with a knife and fork, my back straight, my ankles crossed under the table, a napkin across my lap. "Thank you," I said graciously to no one as I helped myself to more. More of everything, seconds and thirds, and none of it quite filling me up. And, oh, how I despaired at the same time I savored, because if these jeweled fruits and juicy meats and crusty breads could not satisfy—if the rich wine did not slake and the luscious cakes did not appease—was there any feast anywhere in this world that would be enough? Or was this hunger like my heartbeat, and only death would bring its true end?

Was hungering the same as feeling alive?

I didn't realize the doors at the other end of the room had opened until I felt a shallow breeze and looked up to see the Master lingering in the shadows beyond the threshold, his hood and cloak obscuring the lean shape of him, a gentle scent of rain and roses. I sat very still as he walked into the room, his steps even and deliberate, faint piano music seeming to follow him and growing louder the closer he came. When he reached me I stared up at him, the bright eyes in the darkened face, and he put one hand behind his back and bowed deeply, at the waist. The other hand he held out to me. I put down my fork, a piece of pink steak still speared at the end of it, and took his hand.

I felt warm to be near him, and I did not shy away. The mirrors were not as disorienting as the last time, so long as I kept my gaze firmly on the Master and nowhere else. He led me in a light, slow waltz, round and round in a dance like daybreak, like ice melting, like your eyes opening while you are still in a dream.

"Are you a prince?" I whispered, and though out of the corner of my eye the world beyond his shoulders was a smear of silver and white, I was not dizzy. I looked at my beast and I was clearer than I had ever been.

Gently, he pulled me to a stop. The dance had ended, though the music played on. I thought, for a moment, that maybe I had angered him, but that wasn't it. There was no ire in his eyes as he let go of me, relaxing his stance, and pressed a gloved hand to my cheek before taking a step back. He pushed away his hood and on his head was a crown, a circlet of gold. His hair was mussed, a little, on one side, and it was this more than anything that made my heart soften, ever so slightly, toward him.

"No," he said, his voice like falling endlessly. "A king."

"Show me," I said, and I did not know if it was a request or a command, or what, exactly, I wanted to see. Only something, anything, to make me believe he was not a beast.

I saw it then, with the Master's face in full view—a smile. It was a secret thing, meant for me and me alone, and I did not see cruelty in it, nor pure kindness, but rather something new, something thrilling that made my heart thaw the slightest bit: *devotion*.

"As you like," he said, and the mirrors began to rise.

At first I could not believe it; I did not understand. I gasped—the sound rose from my lips like steam, soft and curling, and I spun in a slow circle, bewitched by this magic, familiar but not, the mirrors pulled upward on wires like the scenery of a stage, like the backdrops and the legs. Steadily they rose to reveal two long rows of tall marble columns, stark white against a black sky.

I pressed my hands to my heart and breathed, out-in. It was a temple, ravaged by time, by weather and war, ruins as ancient as human history. Uneven stone floor, creeping vines, weeds and bushes overgrown between the cracks. Half-crumbled friezes and a towering cult statue so eroded I could not discern whether it depicted a god or a beast. Abandoned but still wondrous, a cool breeze blowing over my feverish skin. The open air felt as if it sparkled inside me as I pulled it, fresh and clean, into my lungs. More and more; I couldn't get enough. The silence there was like the silence in church after a long prayer, taut with reverence, with holy awe that fills you up and leaves no space for guilt or blame or regret. I wanted to live there, to dream there, to curl into the cold and disappear there. I felt as if I had eaten the sky. Finally full, the tip of my tongue burned on a star.

"Will you dance?" the Master asked, as quiet and resolute as the ruins all around us. I turned and reached for him but he shook his head, took a tiny step back. Somehow he did not look as small as I felt standing in such a vast structure, as if this temple was dedicated to *him*, as if that was his likeness upon the altar.

Maybe it was. *Immortal*, he'd said. *Death is all I know.*

"You mean ballet?" I said, and he nodded. "Why?"

"There is magic in it. Power as well." He touched my hair, a little piece beside my ear. His knuckles barely brushed my cheek. "You'll see. Dance for me, little bird. Please?"

I looked down at myself and bunched my fists in the fabric of the dress I wore. "In these clothes? I can't."

He glanced away, toward the darkness, at something I couldn't see. I looked at the Master and at the temple and at the sky—not quite the same sky I had known all my life. It was more like a mouth, stretched wide with a scream or the long note in a song, the stars like little teeth. I closed my eyes, shutting them tight.

"Next time then," he said, and the disappointment heavy in his voice made me change my mind in an instant. *I'll try*, I thought, with the first flush of a fever in my heart. *I will dance in this cumbersome dress if it means you will not look so sad.* But before I could voice this he leaned very close. When I opened my eyes the ruins were gone and we stood once more in the mirrored room, crowded by our reflections.

"Little bird," said the Master, and stopped, biting his lip. It was the most human gesture I had ever seen on him. I waited, an ache in my ribs. "What can I do to make you less afraid of me?"

I brought my hands to my throat, as if to shield it. "Show me your true face," I said, my pulse shuddering beneath my palms. "Tell me why I'm here."

In the mirrors, I saw the Master clasp his gloved hands behind his back. His fingertips twitched, as if he was nervous.

But what could possibly enervate an immortal beast?

The answer came to me in Mr. Russo's voice, low and deep: *Sleep.*

Sleep, whose dominion was dreams. Dreams that could leave you breathless, choking with longing for things you could never have, places you might never see. For the loved ones you've lost, and for love that has only just begun to bloom.

I am certain his dreams are of you.

But that couldn't be true. Could it?

"My intention is to share with you all that you have seen tonight, and more." He bowed at the waist, keeping his eyes on mine. "I desire to marry you. To make you queen there."

My hands fell away from my throat. I looked up at the sky, but the sky wasn't there anymore. Only an indifferent ceiling, held aloft by walls that reflected one another endlessly, into infinity, creating an illusion that the world was wider than it was.

"You need not give an answer yet." The Master straightened, and I felt like I could breathe again. "I had not meant to ask until you had seen the whole of my kingdom. Only then will you understand the truth of what I desire."

He stepped away from me, back and back until he reached the mirror behind him and seemed almost to step inside it, becoming his reflection. "Good night, little bird."

"Wait," I whispered, but he didn't hear. He did his trick of stepping sideways and out of sight, which I still couldn't fathom even though I'd been staring right at him. My head had filled with more shadows than there were pillars to cast them, my cheeks stained pink from a rush of heat. He didn't want to peel me apart and watch my heart beating, didn't want to scatter my bones and read them like a prophecy. He didn't want to eat me like a beast.

He only wanted to marry me, like a man.

But the Master was not a man, he was something more—or less—than that, and maybe that was why, in all my discussions with Emilia, I had only ever imagined a shadow in the place where a husband would be, eyes like stars in a face like night, an abyss that was not meant to be feared but *explored,* not empty but ever-expanding, full of light. His bare hands, clawless and kind, not rending my flesh but skimming my skin, and his mouth, his lips, forming a new constellation with each and every kiss. An embrace as warm as the sun and as soft as the moon; love that did not seek to own or consume.

I could imagine it. God help me—I really could.

I smelled the open air of the temple and beyond long after the Master had gone, long after I had discarded the dress and crawled into bed in my underthings; I smelled it as I lay in the cold and dreamed with my eyes half-open.

I BARELY REMEMBER that week between Sundays. I dreaded the Master's midnight and longed for it in equal measure, vacillating between terror and desire like the highs and lows of a fever—one moment burning and sweating, the next chilled and shivering and begging for warmth. In the studio, Mistress continued to work with Beatrice while I sat to the side, watching her—watching her closely. If Beatrice was bitter about landing the second-best role—*again*—since the Master and his machinations had stolen the best from her in favor of me, she didn't show it in her dancing. Her movements were lithe and precise, no patron and his expectations to weigh her down, and for a moment I wished our roles were reversed, that the Master had cast me as the queen in the ballet so that I might get used to being queen as make-believe first. But then, perhaps he would not have wanted me to try it and decided firmly against it, to keep what was real and what was fairy tale separate. For now.

At the end of the week, Mistress finally began to set the choreography for my solo in the second act, and I felt like fate as I danced—like something inevitable, unavoidable. Cold, perhaps, but radiant. My shadow was long and touched every single person in that room as I piquéd and promenaded. "Good girl," Mistress said with a smile. No one asked me about "the prince" any longer. They spun their own stories about him and about me, and I let them, because their whispers felt like worship, even if what they were saying wasn't true.

In the car with Mr. Russo I slept, even when I tried to stay alert, and so I never quite saw the path we took from Hyde Park to River North and back again. On the mornings when the radio cut in and out he hummed a lullaby under his breath, almost as if he didn't know he was doing it. And as he did I drifted off and dreamed of a girl who used her voice to sing her enemies to sleep. The girl's voice was lovely, but no one near her could stay awake for long enough to hear it. As soon as she began to sing, those around her collapsed. But when she stopped, they woke at once. The song she sang in my dream was the same one that Mr. Russo hummed to me.

The girl's village was at the edge of a dark wood where a beast killed anyone who crossed its path. Over a weary age of a thousand years, soldiers and kings alike had tried and failed to slay it, but all who plunged between those accursed trees perished in the pursuit. Without hesitation she walked into those woods and sang for the beast, but the beast did not fall asleep. He bowed his great horned head and turned back into the prince he had been, so long ago now that he couldn't remember his name. Strong and shining he stood before her, and the beast was vanquished once and forevermore.

I wished I had a power like that.

There were so many questions I wanted to ask Mr. Russo, but when I woke I no longer remembered them—not until much later when I was alone. It was like a spell cast over me, one I was far too preoccupied to break.

On Saturday, the one day I did not dance—not for Mistress or with the Master—I played my violin.

Not the one the Master had given me, the one that both was and could not possibly be Sig. Picataggi's violin, the one that had been buried with him. I'd left that violin behind, for better or worse. I resolved not to think of it now as I took up the violin of my childhood; I thought instead of the signore frowning when I hit a wrong note and Mamma laughing from the kitchen as she made potato and onion soup—again— for dinner. While I played they were alive once more, and their love was too.

Outside the window the lifeless late winter earth lay in a shroud of fog, so that I could see nothing beyond my balcony. I sat in a chair by the open window, simultaneously sweating in the heat of the fire that never went out in the hearth and shivering in the frigid air that flowed in. Mr. Russo brought hot tea while I played but I let it go cold. I could not stand for anything else to burn inside me that day, and when he came back sometime later to collect the cup he listened for a while and then asked me a question. I didn't answer him the first time so he asked it a second time, slightly louder than before. I lowered my bow and twisted in the chair to face him, my back to the dark sky. The teacup looked so delicate in his long, elegant fingers. So different than the Master's.

"I wonder why you joined the ballet instead of an orchestra," he said, leaning against the doorframe.

"Oh," I said with a little shrug. "My playing is only adequate."

"I'd say it's more than that. I have a good ear for it, you know."

I blushed a little and shrugged again—perhaps he meant it or perhaps he was only being kind, but it pleased me to hear it, more than I wanted to let on.

"Do you love ballet?" he said then, and my reply was automatic.

"Of course I do."

"You love it?" He peered at me so intently that I began to flush despite the winter wind curling around me like a cat with its claws out. "Truly?"

"Yes," I said, defensive. "All I ever wanted was to be a ballerina."

He took a tiny step closer to me, his voice low as if he were telling me an old, forbidden story, of labyrinths and lips kissed and history written wrongly—of saints whose names burned in the fire along with their bodies. "But you longed to run away. Every morning, you imagined how you might manage it. *Out the window, down the alley, through the park.*"

I stood so fast I knocked over the chair. "How do you know that?"

"You thought you would find magic in the company, on the stage, but there was none," he pressed on, indifferent to my distress. "Only the same emptiness, the same hunger, the same gray clouds high over your head."

"How do you know that?"

"Miss Dragotta, you talk in your sleep," he said, as if it were obvious. "The night you arrived here? In the car, you fell asleep. You repeated it, like a prayer almost—*out the window, down the alley, through the park.* Forgive me, but it wasn't difficult to deduce the meaning of your mumblings. I too have known that hunger for escape. The way it consumes, so that even in sleep you find no relief, chewing all night on the raw meat of your dreams."

I swallowed hard, and didn't believe him. Had I ever talked in my sleep? I didn't think so. *Dead to the world*, Mamma used to say, *dead to the world even during a storm. A war could be going on around her, and she would lie amidst the spray of bullets and gore and dream that she was a star in the sky.* But, then again, Mamma had been gone a long time. Perhaps I started speaking in sleep after her death, when I slept with all my cousins on the floor in Zia Vita's house, or in my narrow room at the boardinghouse.

Out the window, down the alley, through the park.

There was no other way he could have known that.

"Can I not have even one secret left to myself?" I snapped, my heart twisting with dread. This man—still practically a stranger—knew about my heart's dream, my private wish and musings, and no matter how innocently he had learned of it, his possession of this raw piece of me felt like a hideous violation—almost, an *invasion*. As if he too had claws, and somehow I had not seen them, had not felt them sinking into my skin until they had burrowed halfway to my heart. And now that he had a firm hold of me, I could not rip them out.

Mr. Russo had the grace to hang his head.

"Apologies." He moved toward the door. "It was rude of me to pry."

After that I no longer felt like playing, and sat instead in weary silence.

As soon as the sun fell on Sunday I flung open the wardrobe and found a long-sleeved black leotard, pink tights, leather ballet slippers, and a short, chiffon wrap skirt, also black. I dressed and went to the foyer, where I sat on the stair with my chin in my hands and waited.

Half an hour passed before the front door opened and Mr. Russo came through, a whistled tune stalling on his lips. The snow in his dark hair melted so quickly that in another moment I couldn't be sure it had ever been there at all. I stood at once and he frowned to see me, ready and waiting for him.

"Where do you go during the day?" I asked, and my voice echoed against the high ceiling, a warbled response, as if we stood in an ancient holy place, our prayers refracted back to us.

"Somewhere you can't follow," Mr. Russo said, with a shrug and a small smirk that was not quite kind, though I dismissed it and replaced it in my mind with the smile he'd given me the night he'd taken me away, taken me here. How could I ever forget that?

"I see you are eager for your audience with the Master," he said, and oddly I felt chastised, my cheeks going warm. I followed him up the stairs to the dining room without another word.

The feast gleamed like polished jewels in the candlelight, and despite my hunger I was almost too nervous to eat. But still I drank a little wine, finished the bite of steak still speared on my fork, as warm and tender as if it had just been cooked, and stared at the glow beneath the doors on the other end, thin and lurid as a slit throat.

When at midnight the doors opened, I stood before them and met the Master at the threshold. His hood was thrown back. He smiled at me and my heart felt like clear water, like an ocean at rest.

"Hello," I said shyly, all too conscious that I wore only a leotard and tights, the fabric clinging to my body, the lines and curves of me displayed openly for him to see, and he was completely covered in his cloak. But he wasn't looking at my body—only my face, my eyes.

"Good evening," he said, and paused a moment. Then he leaned down, slowly, as though I might startle, and kissed my cheek. I stayed very still; his lips were so terribly soft, and his eyelashes brushed my skin.

Not a beast, I reminded myself fiercely, closing my eyes with a silent sigh. *A king.*

Master La Rosa took my hands and led me into the temple.

I danced—not with him, but for him. He stood between the columns like a shadow and watched, and at first I was timid, unsure, because there was no stage to separate the dancer from the audience, no lights and no music. The ground was rocky and uneven, and I could not pirouette or do any turns on one foot. But I could leap, if I was careful—tour jetés and saut de chats—and I could arabesque and promenade, an adagio. It was so strange, and so different than any dancing I had ever done, and soon I could hear that there *was* music, that the night had a rhythm and a tempo: the scratching of clawed feet, the coo of an owl, the rasp of the leaves on the vines in a silken wind. I never once forgot the Master's gaze on me, but it was welcome, and warm. It was a summer night; here I had no need of the cold.

There were blurs of white light between the columns. I became aware of them only gradually, and at first I thought it was just my eyes playing tricks on me. But when I stopped dancing to look at them, they retreated into the shadows, animal-like. The Master stared in the direction they had gone, and I felt a stab of resentment. *Look at* me, I thought, and resumed my peculiar ballet. But as soon as I began, the white lights appeared again, nictitating like frost in a sunrise. And I realized that the lights were watching me.

No—not lights, not exactly. I kept dancing and the creatures crept closer, and I saw that they gave off light, yes, but that was not what they *were*. They walked like humans, and their features were human, but they had no skin like my skin, no muscle and no bone—only the idea of these, the close memory of a body now gone.

I had always believed in ghosts; now, here they were, dozens of them. At last they stepped from the darkness and into the temple, surrounding me.

Though my hands trembled, I was not afraid. There was no air of benevolence to the ghosts, but neither did I sense any malice or ill intent. I stood still, my feet aching, but the lights did not retreat. They seemed to be waiting for something. Waiting for *me*. Somehow, I had summoned them here.

I felt a spark like strength in my fingertips, a hope in my heart. Was this magic my own, or did it belong to the Master?

Would his magic become mine if I married him?

Breathing hard, I turned to the Master.

He looked at me like one who has never seen snow, or the moon, and marvels at the sight.

"You asked to see my kingdom," he said, and the echo of his voice shook my bones. "Come with me now and you shall know it."

He led me out of the temple and into the night. I saw that the temple was in the dip between two steep hills, and the hillsides were spotted with trees, leaves of emerald so green they glowed in the dark. But there was a path through the brush and this was where he led me. At the mouth of the path I looked back, caught between my old hungers and the new. *Mamma*: I thought with longing of the lipstick I had left in her fist, the lipstick that could take me anywhere in the world I wished. How often had I longed to travel beyond the world, behind it, through the bloodstream to the heart? Even if it was messy, even if it meant clawing my way past sinew and bone. Some part of me had always known it was possible. I would not have made it this far if I had not believed I could.

The Master held his arm out to me and I took it. All was quiet, serene. We walked the path, and the ghosts followed behind us.

A century might have passed and I would not have known it. It didn't seem so very long a walk, but then, it all felt like a dream where everything makes perfect sense until you wake up. I thought I saw something through the thicket, running quickly, but not at all like the lights— something else, something darker than the dark around us, something stumbling. My eyes were not used to a night so unrestrained as this. Neither was my heart.

At last we reached the top of the hill, and below me was a city of light.

For a moment I was so blinded by the brightness that all I could do was stand there and blink, clutching the Master's arm. The ghosts that had followed us here streamed around us, attracted to the glow, and I stopped thinking of them as ghosts and instead as souls. Untethered, unbounded, no longer lingering over their old lives, but looking ahead to the new. I searched their faces as they passed, but none were familiar to me.

Soon my eyes adjusted, and the scintillating skyline sharpened. I had never been far enough away from Chicago to see it like this, its angles and edges made infinite in the surrounding dim and the illumination from within. Was my home even half so dazzling at a distance?

"What is this place?" I asked the Master, little stars bursting in my heart.

"This is Noctem," he said, and when I glanced back at the dark path we had traced, I saw that his shadow was in the shape of a bird behind him, wings stretched like a long breath. "The city of the dead."

Eleven

*I*T WAS NOT LIGHT FROM THE BUILDINGS THAT MADE THE CITY of Noctem gleam; indeed, there wasn't any electric light to be found there at all. Instead it was the souls themselves that brightened the night, the souls that glittered like gems in a jewelry box. Theirs was the glow of death I had seen in my own heart, secret and cold, but with their dying breath it had broken open, cracked like an egg, and filled them with a warm radiance to light the way through the ever-dwelling darkness of the afterlife. It called to the death in me, tugged on my heart as if tugging on my hand, and turned the heavy grayness of my grief to shining gold. On the Master's arm I followed the souls streaming toward the city, entranced.

Noctem was an old city, though not in the way Chicago was old: It was built solely of brick and mortar instead of glass and steel, medieval. Stone towers twelve stories tall, with brass bells at their peaks, narrow alleys and balconies brimming with flowers that bloomed even in the dark. And a great wall surrounding it all, so that as we came down the hill I could no longer see its sights. But still I could hear it, achingly loud—laughter and footsteps, the clinking of silverware, sidewalk magicians performing all kinds of tricks—and I could smell it, roasted coffee and sprigs of lavender, the earth after a long, hard rain.

How much of this was real, and how much in my head? Already my imagination ran away from me as I envisioned murals painted in the brick alleys, and parks lined with stalls selling all manner of delicacies and sweets. With a craving in your heart you could turn a corner and there it would be—a cannoli just like the ones Mamma used to make, or a bowl of almond granita. Operas and museums and cinemas, libraries whose laden shelves boasted every book that had ever been—and had *yet* to be—written.

But above all there was music, and it was music I recognized, played on a lone violin: the special song Sig. Picataggi had taught me on my tenth birthday, the piece I had played on the Master's violin in the boardinghouse. Only now it was played in a major key, a song like a soft hand to haul you from the depths when you'd been so very close to drowning. I imagined his wife sitting beside him as he played, a small smile on his face as the bow skimmed over the strings.

"Whose violin is he playing?" I wondered, more to myself than anything, wrapped in a daze, remembering that *I* now possessed the one he'd been buried with. I shook my head in response to my own question. What difference did it make if he played his own instrument or had borrowed one from someone else? All that mattered was his music, his song drawing me in—I had thought I would never hear him again. I held my breath, listening, as the Master led me right to the gate, the souls already far ahead of us, home at last; from here they knew the way. Trembling, I made to follow the souls, to follow the music that filled me like water, but the Master placed a hand on my arm, staying me.

"I hear him," I said, not yet realizing what that hand on my arm might mean. I smiled, so wide, dizzy with joy. "It's him—Signor Picataggi! My old friend and instructor. He's there; he's playing for me. I must go, I must—"

Again I tried to move forward, to pass through the city gates. And again the Master stopped me, his hand now gripping my arm. My smile faded, slowly like a sunset, and when I gazed into his face his eyes were cast down, away from me.

"I am sorry, little bird," he said, and still I did not quite understand. The music—it wrapped around me, familiar and as deep as the ocean. I felt as if I could float in it forever.

"I hear him," I repeated and tried to pull my arm away, but the Master only held me more firmly. His cloak billowed in the breeze. "His music, *please*—I have to go. Let me go?"

"Little bird." He sighed, and it seemed endless. "Noctem is not a place for mortal flesh."

"But the signore—and Mamma and Lorenzo! They might be with him. *Please*—"

I was just shy of begging on my knees, but the Master remained immovable.

"You hear it, though? It's not just me?"

"I hear it," he said, and it was a relief to know it was not only in my head. "But if you go there now, the blood will spill from your body; your heart will burn to ash. It will be worse than death—you will disappear. Is that what a song is worth?"

He released me, letting me make a choice. I hovered, taking neither a step forward nor back.

"The living cannot step foot in the city of the dead," he said. "But if you were to marry me, become queen . . ."

The music had filled me up like water, and now it had turned to ice.

"It is a lot to ask of you," the Master continued, and though his voice pulled at me, I couldn't look at him. "I am not alive, not in the way you are; I never will be. That is why, if you are to be mine, you must die. Through death, through a heart given to me willingly, I will anchor you to my side. Then, and only then, you may walk freely in the city among the dead."

Now I did look at him, sharply. "But not among the living as you do?"

"I need you here. You saw how the souls followed you, how they came when you danced. Marry me, little bird, and dance for them—for me—forever."

"You are cruel, Master La Rosa," I said, "to bring me here and no farther, unless you get what you want." Abruptly, my throat closing, I turned my back on Noctem.

How much steeper the hill seemed then than it had going down; how much faster my breath, coming in little gasps almost like sobs. And not a single thought in my head—only a roiling tide of emotion, black as the sea at night, salt and open wounds. Its current swept me up the hill, seething and storming, but when I finally reached the top and the rush receded I only felt empty, nearly numb and wan with exhaustion. Below was the temple, its columns and stelae with a luster like bones in the moonlight, half-hidden in creeping vegetation, a fairy-enchanted place. And beyond the temple was another hill, and beyond that another, and another, with secret wonders nestled there, and above it all a long breath of stars.

Not once had I looked behind to see if the Master followed me, but all the same I'd felt him there, a dark and steady presence, and when I stopped on the hill's crest he settled beside me. The warm wind tangled the ends of my hair.

"Little bird, I did not mean to . . . I only wanted . . ." The Master paused, struggling for the right words, and I waited, holding my breath. "I should have explained before we reached the gates, before you heard . . . but it is too late now. I am sorry."

I gazed out over Noctem, the bright city barred to me, and decided I had been unfair to him. He was only showing his kingdom to me, as I had asked. It was not his fault, after all, that I was still in possession of a beating heart, and that the only way to enter Noctem was to give it up.

"I'm sorry I called you cruel. Thank you for showing me your kingdom." I didn't see any lights in the distant hills, in the dark and the underbrush. Where had the souls come from? And were there more of them?

"I have been called far worse than cruel, and cursed with many a dying breath," he said with a small self-deprecating smile that made me turn away. *Beast*, I had called him in the privacy of my heart, and a beast I feared him to be still.

But yet, as the Master bade me follow him back down the path the way we had come, I stayed very close to his side—perhaps a little more close than was necessary. When we reached the temple, I put a hand on his arm.

"Will you bring me here again?" I asked as the world around us darkened, and the temple faded as though it were no more than a set on a stage.

"If you wish," said the Master, and between one blink and the next we were standing once more in the mirrored room. There was my face reflected a dozen times, open and eager as I gazed up at the Master, and it was a wood floor now beneath my feet, not stone and dirt. But when I breathed I could still smell the wildflowers with petals that opened like the pages of an old storybook hidden in the long grasses on the hill, and I could still hear the signore's music rising above the walls of Noctem, calling to me like birdsong after a storm. Half of me was still there, dancing in the land of lost souls, and I suspected that from this day on, half of me always would be.

I smiled at the Master, and there was no fear in it. "I do."

YOU WERE RIGHT, I wrote to Emilia. *Master La Rosa is royalty.*

Across several sheets of creamy white paper I told Emilia of Noctem, of the inner city with its music and colors and lights. I spoke of it as if I had been beyond the wall, as if I went there every night. A lie, all of it, but if I could not go then I would content myself with dreams.

The temple, though, I kept a secret.

The way my heart opened wide as I stepped inside, the first breath of air so clean it clawed my throat raw, shadows anointing the stone beneath my feet. Dancing in the dim, dancing for the souls edging nearer to see. *Be not afraid*, I said through my movement, through my rhythm and my grace. *Another world awaits thee.* Dancing for the Master, my skin tingling, knowing his gaze was ever upon me, unwavering.

I forgot ice; I forgot snow. There they did not exist, not even the idea of them. Sweat and a pleasant soreness in my limbs, leading the gathered souls over the hill to Noctem, the darkness a revelation. The wind slipping through the marble columns, the skitter of unseen animals in the underbrush—something long asleep in me yearned and ached to join them, to leave the temple, to eat my piece of the night and become a wandering dream.

But no—there were beasts crouched in the damp and the dim and their hunger was deeper than mine, older and arcane. So said the Master—and besides, the souls required us as their guides.

"There are those who go straight to Noctem, lured by its light and the promise of eternity," the Master said when I had asked him why the souls came forth from the shadows on the hillside when I danced, and why they did not make their way to the city on their own. It was our third evening spent together in the sparkling land of the dead, a tentative trust settling between us as we walked back through the hills to the temple just before the morning light that would grip the mortal world.

"But then there are souls that are lost, stubborn, or despairing. They wander through the hills between the ephemeral and the everlasting, slowly becoming a blank space, and not even the wind can find them. During the day it is my duty to traverse these wild lands and draw them out. But often my presence frightens them, and I lose more souls than I can save. That is why I need you, little bird. Your kindness—your *light*—draws them near, while mine only turns them away."

The path ended. We stopped, standing for a moment before the temple under a clear and bloodless sky.

"But why are they afraid of you?" I whispered it, because part of me did not want to know.

"Because I have held their death in my hands." His crown looked like pieces of sharp glass in the starlight. The columns of the temple around us shone the color of bone. "Because in the end, it was I who seized their death and cracked it open."

"Cracked it open?" I went very still. Like a sculpture of myself, like a thing with no breath and no heart. Memories of a warm weight on my shoulder, the hand I had been trying to shake ever since I'd first felt it on the sidewalk while my brother bled his life into the cracks of the concrete, food for the worms and the weeds. The hand that had touched me at Sig. Picataggi's burial, and standing by Mamma's sickbed, and forever after when I thought of them, when I wore Mamma's dress or played the songs the signore had taught me. When I woke from a dream of Lorenzo, or saw the echo of his face in another's.

I reached for the Master's wrist.

He let me, his bright eyes on my face. Holding it with the veins facing up toward the sky, I peeled the glove slowly from his skin, revealing the hand beneath. An ordinary hand, large and soft, the nails rounded, no claws. It was so warm, and the weight of it familiar, solid and sure. I traced the lines of the palm, the bones of every finger, and then flipped it over, feeling the ridge of the knuckles, the smoothness of each nail. Lifting my gaze to his, I brought his hand to my cheek, pressing his palm to the coolness of my flesh. I sighed, and he did too, leaning toward me, close.

"You are not King of the Dead, or not *only* king," I said, and somewhere a bird let out a low and tremulous cry. "You are Death. Death itself."

Hades, I had thought him, and here he was Thanatos all along. *Death*—the name, his true name, rang in my ears. Echoed in my bones.

He did not deny it.

I kept his hand on my cheek, and I was seized not with terror but with calm, a deep and steady peace like I had never known before. I had been born into this world as Death ravaged my city through sickness and strife; in my childhood I had watched him consume the three people who had meant everything to me, who had meant laughter and love—who had meant light. All my life Death had been with me, and I'd believed if only I kept dancing, kept moving, kept running, he wouldn't be able to touch me long enough to take me too. Through movement I'd thought I could escape, could slip beneath the skin of the world where I would be free, unseen.

This can't be all there is.

Well, I *had* fallen through a gap in the world, hadn't I? A hole like a wound, past muscle and severed tendon, and Death was here, he was warm and he was with me, and I was still afraid, but not *only* afraid.

"You have held my death as well?" I whispered, and the Master brought his other hand—still gloved—to my uncovered cheek.

"Have you forgotten? Your death is in your still-beating heart. And unless you agree to marry me, I will not take it from you."

There was a word unspoken, and that word was *yet*. Everyone must die, eventually.

"Does it hurt?"

The Master was quiet, and it was like a dark curtain fell over the ruins; there was only sky, and him, and me. My time in the temple had ended . . . for now. Slowly the curtain turned silver, and then it was not a curtain at all but mirrors. Reflections—I saw how small I was before the Master, a maiden trembling before the monster. Except—except I didn't *feel* small. Or I *did*, but it wasn't a bad feeling, nor belittling, it was—it was safe. His tall, broad frame, his large hands, his alertness to the world and his softness toward me. I felt oddly protected. Protected by *Death*, of all things. Death, who would make me his queen.

"I can promise that it will take only a moment," he said at last. The room was so terribly small. "Just one moment—and then, forever."

Forever. The word sunk deep inside me, down to the cold bottom where sunlight could not reach. Forever, where there was no true summer because there was no winter, and no true night because there was no day. Those things I had loved about this place only a minute ago now seemed hollow and strange. Irreversible, unchanging—there was no running away from forever.

Out the window, down the alley, through the park.

I had already discovered more to the world than I had dreamed—who was to say there wasn't *more* beyond even this?

The Master took one step toward me. "Will you marry me, little bird? Will you give your heart to me now, freely?"

Marry him. Then all that was his—the temple, the city, the souls—could be mine, and his magic too. I could fly without wings, I could dance without strings, and always it would be night in my soul and I would sleep buried in stars. I would guide the souls to Noctem, a safe and glittering place, where death could not touch them twice. It dizzied me that both peace and purpose were right within reach.

Until I remembered that the price was my life.

"No," I said, remembering ice, remembering snow. "Good night. Good—"

I did not even finish my farewell. I was already walking, running down the hallway, leaving Death and the dead behind.

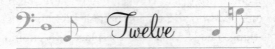

Twelve

I SLEPT FOR ONLY A FEW HOURS IN THE MORNINGS, DREAMING of magic that stained my hands like blood. There was tea waiting for me when I woke, sugared and steaming, and I drank it greedily as I sat on my bedroom's balcony, wrapped in layers of blankets pulled up to my chin. It was late March by then, my least favorite month; always it felt to me as if we should be nearing the end of the long labyrinth of winter, only to round another corner and another, relentless snow extinguishing any hope of spring. In just one month *Little Bird* would premiere, and a week before that Emilia would be married. I tried not to panic as I wondered how I would get to St. Francis of Assisi if Mr. Russo refused to take me, as he had refused to drive me to Pilsen to see if I might find Emilia there, somewhere. Already I had begun scheming how I might trick him, how I might lie and say there was a special preview of *Little Bird* in the church. An act of charity, a godly deed, a taste of the arts for those who couldn't afford a ticket. If that didn't work, I would beg on my knees. I would do anything, anything to reach her.

As the days slipped by, I settled into a routine: After finishing my tea in the lingering hours before rehearsal, I bathed and played my violin. I sat with the window wide open and the fire crackling merrily—I could not have one without the other; I had tried. In the car with Mr. Russo I slept again—a last gathering of energy that would carry me through the afternoon.

"Do you still wish you were me?" I said to Beatrice between scenes, the sweat on her forehead glistening like jewels. Quickly she bit her lip and looked past me, behind me at Mistress, who clapped her hands once and ordered us—ordered *me*—to focus. The other girls drifted away from me as I pressed my cool palms to my cheeks and sighed.

For the rest of rehearsal I watched her, the way she floated en pointe as she bourréed with her arms crossed over her chest, ghostlike, her face a mask of mercilessness, and I wanted to scream at her, to tell her she was doing it all wrong. Death wasn't cold—he was warm, and his queen needed to convey that warmth in a way he could not to the souls that still feared his touch.

In the temple on Sunday, my fourth visit to the temple in the land of the dead, I put aside forever and thought only of *now:* Now I am dancing, now the souls are gathering, now it is dark; now the Master is beside me (so close), and now we are walking in the penumbral place where breath becomes wind and shadow becomes skin and at any moment you might cross over into a dream without knowing it.

Now I am standing before the city of light.

"I'd like to show you something," said the Master as we rested a moment on the hill above Noctem. I turned and followed him, not back to the temple but to a narrow path between the low and tangled trees on the hillside that I would not have noticed on my own. A rich scent of dirt, of wet loam and new moss; a choking sound like birds with their throats torn, like animals scrambling for a place to hide.

"Stay at my side," the Master said. Gently, but it was still a command. And I had that feeling again—of smallness, but only in the way a star is small from far away.

"Tell me again of the beasts in this land," I said, when what I meant was *Assure me you are not one of them.*

There was a little moonlight to see by, slices between the branches, but his hood was pulled low and I could not see his face. He had told me a bit about the beasts on my third night in the temple, but I was tired of imagining and wanted to know more—to know everything. When he answered it was in a whisper, clear but quiet.

"Some souls wander too deeply into the dark, and for too long," he said, and his gloved hand brushed my bare arm, making me jump. "They sink inside themselves, forgetting who they are, where they've been, what came before. It is like drowning, and they fight it, thrashing and clinging to the one thing humans, even dead ones, are slow to forget—their hunger, and their thirst."

Overhead, clouds began to gather, thin and flat, like ash from a cigarette. The path narrowed, and the Master gestured for me to walk ahead. The air cooled suddenly and my skin became gooseflesh; my breath seemed to stick in my throat. The Master continued, speaking over my shoulder.

"And so they hunt other lost souls to feed on, to tear apart and chew, swallowing their dreams, their memories, their identities, until the prey too becomes a husk and must seek the life energy of others in order to remain tethered here. Else they will truly die, and disappear for good."

The path opened, and there in the dim was an old stone church, with chimeras crouched on its bell tower, rising only two stories tall. The stained glass windows cut into its worn façade were aglow from the inside, casting colored shadows on the ground. It was not a particularly stunning church, but still the sight of it filled me with a rapturous dread. Was I about to encounter my Catholic God? Since beholding Noctem I had let go of my dichotomous notion of Heaven and Hell, but God Himself I could not quite forsake, nor the angels either. I turned back to the Master, my teeth clenched so tightly my jaw ached.

"What do you look like, really?" I asked him, and, straining, I thought I could hear the church's bells ringing, the tolling of faded brass ghosts. "I must know."

He looked down at me. "I do not *look* like anything. I am a force, like gravity. I am energy, like light."

"Yet you wear the face I crafted for you in my dreams."

"To please you," he said, and my heart twisted. "I have many forms, but this is now my human one."

I thought of the claws on my skin, cutting me open, and touched that place on my arm where there were now five little scars.

"If no part of you is truly human," I said, "then why do you want one for a wife?"

"Not just anyone." Was that a blush creeping over his cheeks? Pink warmth, a faint glow. *"You."*

God, how could one word carry so much weight? *You.* It echoed like a pulse in my throat. It moved, sinuous, through my veins. Wringing my hands over my heart, I turned away from him. Took a step. Turned back.

"But *why*? I don't—"

"Shall I compose you a poem extolling your most shining qualities?" he said, and though his voice was perfectly serious there was a hint of warmth to it, a lightness that I'd never heard there before. "Shall I sing a song of your kindness and beauty that will endure for all the ages?"

"Well," I said, as carelessly as I could manage, even though, of course, I cared very much and didn't appreciate being mocked. "It might help."

He laughed, and it was a kind laugh, a bright laugh, like the moon rising above a dark cloud. I was mesmerized by it, and didn't flinch or fall back when he crossed the short distance between us and took my hands. He cleared his throat, and I could see that he was really going to do it; he was really going to recite a sonnet for me, or croon some love-lorn melody. I shook my head, embarrassed. A sudden swell of memory, a flicker from the week before: his skin on my skin, his palm pressed to my cheek, endless warmth.

"All right," he said softly, though there was still laughter in his eyes. "Not an epic then. Perhaps a jewel for your throat as a token of my favor? Or a strand of pearls that sparkle like the stars? Crystals to dangle from your ears?"

Teasing still—I think he knew that none of that would please me, none of that would satisfy. I looked down at our hands entwined.

"Only tell me this," I said. "Why should *I* want an immortal king?"

"Look to your heart, little songbird. You have immortal longings in you."

Give me my robe, put on my crown; I have immortal longings in me. I thought of my collection of Shakespeare, the one I'd spent so many sleepless nights in the boardinghouse reading and rereading until my eyes blurred and my head felt as heavy as the earth. *Antony and Cleopatra*—how had he known?

The Master held my gaze a moment, then let go of my hands. And, oh, how desperately I wanted to turn back; how fiercely I longed to go on. How can one crave contradicting actions and still hope that some-how both might happen? He was a beast, but not a beast; I was a girl, but not the girl I was or would ever be again. His claws, imagined, raking my skin. His hand, soft, on my hand. My death, hidden, in my heart. Now that I was aware of it, I felt it like a stone, a jewel rattling within me, as small and heavy as a diamond but one whose edges were as fragile as an eggshell, shuddering with every tick, every pulse, every beat. He would take it from me, not cracking it open like the deaths of the souls around me, but extracting it and keeping it safe, enshrining it in the place where he kept his own death. (Where, where? Still he had not told me where.) He would make me immortal, a queen. If I let go of my fear and my anger my hands would be empty, and what then?

Then I could reach out and touch him, truly. Nothing between us but trust—and maybe even love.

I lifted my chin, and went with the Master into the church.

ROSES.

Red ones and white, pink and yellow and orange. Even impossible hues, blue and sea green and pale violet. Hundreds and hundreds of them. They wrapped around the pews, spilled over the altar, and climbed the walls toward the vaulted ceiling. Even the floor was half-covered in vines, and I kept a distracted eye on where I stepped as I walked down the aisle. The Master stood to the side, watching as I bent to touch the velvety petals, to press my nose to their lips and breathe in. They smelled . . . like stories: biblical and mythical and fairy tale. When I smelled them these stories flashed through my head: *Here is La Befana, and there Pippina the Serpent, and there Catherine the Wise. Nick Fish, and the Dove Girl, and Gràttula-Beddàttula*, and—oh! one I did not have a name for, a story I had yet to hear.

"This is your garden?" I asked the Master, dizzied by so many scents. I had a strong urge to lie among the petals and thorns, to let these tales twist my dreams into shapes my waking mind could not imagine.

"It is not mine." His voice echoed like a glimpse of spring in the open jaw of winter. "It belongs to all who wander here."

"It's—" *Beautiful, exquisite, overwhelming, unnatural, enchanting, eerie.*

"I know," said the Master, so that I did not have to find the right word. "I have found peace here. I thought you might too."

I smiled at him shyly, swaying pleasantly on my feet. *Peace*. Yes, there was that. Though it could not last forever, even here.

"Little bird," he said, as I bent to inhale another rose, "I ask you again—will you give your heart to me? Will you marry me?"

I straightened and glanced by chance to the front of the nave, away from him. And I saw them then—bones, large ones and small, piled in the far corner of the church beyond the altar, half-buried beneath the leaves and the vines. A grim collection, shining dully in the low light.

Only animal bones, I thought, licking my dry lips and turning away. Even Death is not without hunger.

"Ask something else instead." I brought my hands to my throat, to the sudden tightness choking me there. "Ask me my favorite season, or the last wish I made in a well. Only—not that."

The Master's gaze was steady on me. "I must have your answer."

Slowly, slowly, I shook my head.

"Aloud," he said.

I set my jaw and looked away, angry that I must say it, angry that I must hurt him. I wasn't ready to die, even for a kingdom. Even for a king. "No."

In silence we walked back across the hillside to the temple and to the mirrored room. But it wasn't an angry silence, only the tension between two people trying to connect with the other and missing, mired in loneliness and misunderstanding. In the clouds there was a ripple of lightning, like a twinge of pain in a sore muscle, followed by thunder. Just before we parted the Master turned and pushed back his hood. It was almost a shock all over again to see his face so clearly, and so like the prince I had spent hours crafting out of the clay of a daydream.

"What is your favorite season?" he said, and a warm drizzle began to fall. I tipped my face to the clouds because I had never minded the rain. Only the snow that could bury me.

"Summer," I said, "when it storms."

"And the last wish you made in a well?"

I looked up at the glowing gray sky, my cheeks wet from rain or sweat or tears—it was all the same. "Honestly, I don't remember the last time I made a wish. Not a formal one, anyway."

He paused a moment. Then, "If you could have one wish right this moment, what would it be?"

I froze.

Freedom.

It was my first thought but it wasn't a true one, not quite. To choose freedom would be to lose Noctem, and to choose Noctem—and the Master—would be to lose my freedom, my mortal life and my mortal loves. Two cities, shining, and between them stones and stars and stories. And me.

"To sleep a little," I said at last, and the rain stopped as abruptly as it had begun. The Master bowed his head and turned from me so that I would not see his disappointment—but I wasn't done yet. There was more that I wanted, and this was the most important. "And to see you again tomorrow."

His eyes lifted. There was a hunger in them as naked as I had ever seen, and I knew in that moment that he wanted to eat me, truly—soul as well as bone, all-consuming—and I think I would have let him. I would not have flinched at the sinking of his teeth into my flesh because I knew he wouldn't hurt me, even as he tore and rent and unmade me. We took a step toward each other in tandem, a maiden and her monster, and very slowly he raised his hand to my face, seized my chin, and tipped it up toward him.

"Your wish is granted then," he said, and pressed his lips to mine so softly it was like the dream of a kiss, or the *memory* of a dream of a kiss, and when he pulled away all I wanted was to pull him back, to keep him there within my grasp. But he was already beyond reach, slipping through the shadows. I followed at a distance, my heart beating like an angel falling, its wings pierced full of arrows, and the Master's kiss lingering like a stain on my lips.

Thirteen

*I*N THE STUDIO, AWAY FROM THE MASTER, I DANCED AS IF THE sky were melting and soon I'd dance no more; I danced as if my heart were beating outside my body, as if it were all I had left to give. And still Mistress only said, "Good," and turned away. With less than four weeks before the first performance of *Little Bird*, I spent my days waiting for night, and my nights wishing that daylight would never arrive. For so long I had been desperate to escape Death, but maybe I'd been mistaken—what I'd really wanted to defy was *time*.

But the Master had granted my wish, a wondrous gift: No longer did I have to wait so long to see him, or the lost souls of Noctem. I began to visit the temple every midnight.

In the church among the roses the Master told me stories, all the ones I did not know. Names I repeated like a magic spell—Lilith and Kali and Marya Morevna. Joan of Arc, warrior queens, girls trapped in towers. His voice was like an old, yellowed lullaby, so that sometimes I fell asleep there in the garden and woke in my bed, a bright petal or two caught in my hair. I imagined the Master carrying me back through the mirrored room and up the stairs, asleep but safe in his arms, and with this picture in my head I stood outside on my balcony until I was blushing from the cold and not from heat that had risen within me, my hands trembling from the blighting touch of the wind, and only the wind.

I learned to see in the dark. Or rather to sense what was there, hidden in the night: a hunting fox, a puddle between two pines, a dying patch of wildflowers. Three ravens sitting silent on the temple's crumbled cult statue, a spider completing its web. Farther, and farther still, to where the shadows clawed and hissed. I sensed the souls, coming from that moonless place, their steps like the steady beat of a heart.

It was awareness, not prophecy, though I reveled in the steep magic of it—a mad fever rush of dancing, sweating, and believing myself nearly divine. Flushed with a dark euphoria, I snuck glances at the Master, watching him watching me. Above were stars like snow, never melting. I danced, and I wanted to stay in the moment forever, when no questions were asked and no answers were given.

Some of the souls, when they stepped into the temple, at first looked familiar to me—but then I would glance again and realize I was mistaken. Once I had thought I caught the demeanor of Emilia and my heart dropped to the center of the earth; another time it was Lorenzo in profile, his long nose and messy hair. But it was only my mind playing tricks on me—dread in one case and yearning in the other. Two people dear to me I so longed to see, but not here. *Not here.*

Sometimes I encountered the souls of children. The littlest of them, a girl no more than six, held my hand as I led her to Noctem, and after I had bid her farewell with a kiss on her shining cheek I turned my face from the Master and wept. He saw, of course—I couldn't hide it entirely and didn't want to—but he let me cry in peace.

Once, mid-pirouette, the sky split apart, quite suddenly and with the violence of make-believe—one moment all was calm, and the next there was lightning in the cloudless night, bruising rain that seemed to fall from nowhere at all. The approaching souls dispersed into the dark, startled, though the rain couldn't harm them, and I ached to keep dancing, to coax them all back, but the rain was too heavy; it fell too hard and fast.

"He is trying to enter the city again." Eyes to the sky, the Master swept me to his side and shielded me with his cloak as the rain blotted out everything in the world around me—except him.

"Who is?"

"My brother," he said in a voice, truly, like death.

A trespasser, mysterious to me. I suppose it was natural he should have a brother—some kind of family, somewhere—but despite my fervent and often ghoulish imagination I could no more picture it than I could will the moon to fall like a feather and land in my outstretched hands.

"What does he want?" I whispered it, but the Master heard.

"Someone who was lost to him not so very long ago."

Thunder like grinding teeth. I trembled beneath the Master's cloak.

"A mortal?" I asked, thinking of the nameless girl I played in the ballet, the one that Sleep had loved so dearly he'd try anything—like breaking into the forbidden city of the dead—to get her back. I'd had no reason until now to assume that *Little Bird* was anything other than a fantasy, but why not suppose it was a true story? Since the Master had entered my life, anything felt possible. Anything at all, no matter how strange. No matter how sad. "She died?"

"As all things must."

"Except you."

He looked at me then and said nothing. I flushed but did not look away.

"Why can't he come here?" I pressed, as we huddled beneath his cloak and waited for the storm to pass. We were not face-to-face but side by side, and suddenly I did not feel warm enough, dry enough, close enough; I curled into him, wrapping my arms around his waist and burying my face in the place between his shoulder and chest. For a moment the Master tensed, hard muscle and bone, held breath; then he sighed, and the sigh was picked up by the wind, echoed across the skies. We held each other, my head tucked under his chin.

"His realm is sleep," he said, all but confirming that the tale of *Little Bird* was real, that there was a soul somewhere in Noctem so beloved by the Master's brother that he would risk his own life to reverse death itself. "He walks through dreams, and the dead do not dream."

I clenched my jaw to keep from shivering. The rain was relentless.

"I'm sorry for you, that you must always be parted," I said, the wind swirling, howling around us like the cry of a lonesome creature, so desperate and desolate that I edged even closer to the Master, pressing my ear to his chest where all was calm and quiet. I had never thought to have anything in common with Death, but here it was then: that my family and his should reside in realms separate from our own; his in dreams, and mine in death. "I miss my brother terribly."

"I may meet my brother in the mortal realm, though I do not walk it in this form as comfortably as he. Sleep comes to mortals every night of their lives, while death only comes but once."

I looked up at him. "But you've been with me all my life."

"So I have, little bird." The Master smiled his secret smile just for me. "For you, it was easy. You imagined me there, and I took care of the rest."

The Master and I held on to each other long after the rain slowed, even after it stopped.

"DID YOU KNOW the Master has a brother?" I asked in the car with Mr. Russo, delivering me to rehearsal the next morning. A touch of feverish exhaustion, an ache behind my eyes. Frost on the window, and in my fingertips. The city lights here seemed dimmer to me now, flat and ordinary.

Mr. Russo turned up the radio. "Never mentioned him to me."

"Do you think he's a king in his realm too?" I said, but Mr. Russo never answered, so there is a chance I only wondered it in my head.

I BROUGHT MY violin. Not to play for the souls but to play for the Master in the church among the roses. He had given me so many stories that I thought it only right to give him one of my own. But the words of my story often tangled on the tip of my tongue, and so I weaved it into a song.

The Master watched me attentively, just as he must have when I made my music on the streets, not a hand on my shoulder but a shadow stopping to absorb my offering for an all too brief moment in between where he was going and where he had been. If only I had paid attention, if only I had looked up, just once—might I have seen him there, standing tall and broad and resolute in his dark cloak? Might I have known that his presence would peel the skin off the face of the world so that I would glimpse the twisted veins and pitted bone beneath? If I had looked up and seen this, and known what would come, would I have run?

Or would I have reached out and taken his hand?

Take me away. Take me away now.

Perhaps neither. Perhaps I simply would have dropped my gaze and kept playing away at my old instrument, even as my heart went quick and sharp.

My song then was like snow falling, like bones grinding, like the earth. Soft and hard and soft again, slow and quick and slow again. It was truer than any cry my throat could produce, longer than any breath. My music wasn't perfect, but it was just that—*mine*. Music like a heart-flutter, music like wings.

When I was finished I looked to the Master, hoping for some word of praise or tenderness. He leaned forward in his pew seat, his elbows on his knees, his eyes so dark in his face.

"That is not the violin I gave you."

I withered at the unexpected ice in his voice. "No."

"Where is it?"

"Under my bed," I said, and it was not a lie, for it *was* under the bed—my old bed, at the boardinghouse. He began to reply but my pulse jumped with sudden anger, rising to match his own.

"You stole that violin," I said, though I had no idea if this was true. Had he robbed the signore's grave like a resurrectionist straight out of an old penny dreadful? Or had he simply refashioned a similar violin to merely *look* like the signore's, initials and all? "You stole it from Domenico Picataggi, my mentor and friend."

"Little bird," the Master said, a note of warning in his tone that I did not heed.

"I don't understand how or why, but—but—the thing you gave me, it's unnatural. I played it once and it gave Emilia a nightmare, a dream in which—in which she *died*. It should have woken everyone in that boardinghouse but it didn't, it only—"

"*Colombina*," said the Master, sounding so very much like Mistress when she was cross that I spluttered to a stop. "I did not steal the violin. The signore gave it up for you."

"What?" My heart collapsed in on itself. My fury too. "Why? I don't understand, I don't—"

"Shh, let me explain," said the Master, gently enough that I could not consider it a rebuke. I folded my hands in my lap, nodding for him to continue. "Sometimes souls bring certain things with them from the mortal realm; things they had such a tight hold of in life that they simply could not let them go and still keep their soul intact and whole."

I inhaled, short and sharp, thinking of Mamma, the tube of lipstick I'd curled in her cold hand. Had she taken it with her, a tiny token of my love for her?

"But for your friend, his violin was even more than that." The Master caught my gaze and held it. "He kept his death in it, little bird. Some artists do."

I smiled a little at that. "He always said his violin was an extension of him, as integral to his system as his heart or his lungs." I paused, took a tremulous breath. "But why has he given it to me? He loved it so much—it doesn't make sense."

"It is a powerful object. Full of life, death—*magic*." The Master reached as if to touch my cheek but dropped his hand at the very last moment. "I asked if he would be willing to part with it for you. Someday you may have need of it, and so I must ask that you always keep it close. Will you promise me this?"

I could only manage a small nod, knowing that the violin was not in my room in his house, but halfway across Chicago. *I do, I promise.* With this the Master sighed, a long and steady exhale, and then he hung his head. I feared he had rooted out my duplicity, seen it written plainly across my face, but when he looked up again his eyes were not so dark, his mouth not so taut as before. When he tipped his face to mine I did not pull away. He kissed me—a real kiss this time and not simply the dream of one—and it was like falling or flying, I couldn't tell which. Up was down and down was up, and oh—how did being this close to death make me feel so alive? I heard music, though there was none. I tasted sweetness, though I was not sure there was any of that here either. I smelled the roses on him; I breathed it in and in and in.

We parted before dawn, and the air between us was warm.

"Will you marry me?" the Master asked, and I no longer flinched at the question, but still I looked away. From the moment I had first set foot in the land of the dead, I had been dazzled by the magic of Noctem—enchanted by the lost souls that came at the call of my dancing, the roses scented with stories, the deaths like delicate jewels buried in the heart or in the throat or in the head, in tears or in the fingertips, wherever one kept their sorrow, their joy and their fear and their love. But now I thought of Sig. Picataggi's violin, quite literally risen from the dead, and how the music had spilled like blood from between the bow and strings, how it had seeped into Emilia's dreams. *It is full of life, death—magic.* Yes, I had seen magic, and even wielded it myself; but we can't know the sharpness of a knife by simply looking at it, or even through the lightest touch. To understand it fully requires a serious cut.

Was this magic—the endless depths of it, the crests of it, the beauty and terror of it—enough for me to give up my beating heart?

"No," I said so quietly I barely heard the word leave my lips. "No, I won't marry you."

The Master only nodded and left me. I knew I was forgiven for my transgression that night, but still I did not bring my old violin to Noctem again.

MRS. O'DONNELL ANSWERED the boardinghouse door in a floral housedress that hung like a hospital gown over her thin frame, her yellow-gray hair in wisps around her face. She smelled of burnt coffee, and the familiarity of it nearly made me weep.

"Ah, my favorite boarder is back," she said in her faded Irish accent. "Come in, come—would you fancy some coffee? I've just put a pot on."

"Maybe another time," I said politely as I stepped into the cool foyer. Mrs. O'Donnell tried to take my hat and coat, but I gently refused her hospitable advances, smiling as she chattered on about the weather (cold, snowy, unchanging, even as we were days away from April) and the conflicts escalating overseas (Germany had recently invaded Czecho-slovakia, and Spain persisted in its civil war). I had hurried out of re-hearsal early—I'd had no excuse but hadn't needed one; when I said I needed to leave early, Mistress had waved her hand, dismissing me with-out protest—and now had only ten minutes or so before Mr. Russo came to take me home. Mrs. O'Donnell stepped back and took a long look at me once I'd entered the dim circle of light.

"Oh, my—you're nothing but skin and bones! How about a nice bite to eat, hmm? I've made peanut butter and pickle sandwiches for dinner tonight," she said. "Shall I bring one out?"

Somewhere out of sight a group of company apprentices were talking and laughing, and I felt instantly like a trespasser, that deepening certainty that I did not belong.

"Actually," I said, and swallowed against the dryness of my throat, "I've remembered that I left something behind under my old bed. Do you mind if I go and fetch it?"

"'Course not. Not a soul's occupied that room since you left it." Mrs. O'Donnell reached out then, and patted my cheek. Her skin felt like damp cloth. As kind as she'd been, I could not remember a time when she'd touched me before. "There's been little whisperings about you, my dear."

The laughter from the parlor reached a peak and died abruptly; a girl only vaguely familiar to me poked her head around the corner. She had no visible reaction when our eyes met except to quietly withdraw. From the kitchen, a smell of brewing coffee about to burn.

I watched Mrs. O'Donnell's hand fall back to her side; the fingers flex and clench.

"I won't be long," I said, and left her there.

In the stairwell, my footfalls echoed like a flock of dark birds taking flight all at once; the hallway on the third floor was silent and empty. Wallpaper and old curtains, a creak in the floorboards. Had I really once called this placed my home?

There was a smell in my room that I didn't remember, like wet leaves in a gutter, like pavement and ash. Like the city, I supposed, but quieter. I knelt beside the bed, and with hands that shook only slightly I reached underneath.

The violin was still there in the long brown box, wrapped with thick paper, polished to a dark and tremulous shine. I ran my fingertips over the wood and flipped it over, just to make sure. The initials were still there, but they appeared slightly altered to me now, the leg of the *P* shortened so that it looked less like a *P* and more like a *D. GD—Grace Dragotta*. I stood with the box in my arms like it contained a dead thing, a *memento mori*, some meat and old bones. Rotten, but precious. Fulfilling my promise.

Whispers followed me through the boardinghouse and out the front door. There were faces in the windows, a blur of parted lips and widening eyes, and I wondered what I looked like to them, if I would soon become a myth like the girl who had died in Emilia's old room. Just another girl taken by Death.

Dusk like a spreading maw, broken jaw of the moon. Mrs. O'Donnell watched me from the stoop, saying nothing. Or maybe she did say something, a few words of farewell, but I didn't hear them and I didn't reply. She waved, and I knew, somehow, that I would never see her again. Not in this world, at least.

"What do you have there?" Mr. Russo asked, as I stood once again on the curb outside the studio, shivering with the box in my arms. He opened the car door for me and I slid inside, enveloped by warmth that seemed to hover but never quite touched me.

"Something I forgot to bring with me last time," I said and closed my eyes before Mr. Russo had even begun to hum. I didn't want to talk to him or anyone, and when we arrived at the Master's house I ran straight up to my room with the box. I slotted it under my bed and breathed a sigh of relief—my promise to the Master was complete.

Then I collapsed onto the rug in front of the fireplace, rubbing my hands to get warm. Suddenly I thought of my bedroom window, and an ache so old I had nearly forgotten it gripped my throat to the point of burning. *Out the window, down the alley, through the park.* How many hours had I spent cleaning it? How many dreams had passed like light through the glass; how many breaths had stuck there like a painting that could not last?

And I had not even thought to look through my little window one last time.

"WHAT LIES BEYOND those hills?"

In the temple beside the Master, I stood with my back to the shining city and stared out at the darkness that began just past the reach of my fingertips and stretched on into infinity. That shadowy place from which the lost souls emerged, where the stars in the sky were far apart and cold before they disappeared altogether, swallowed whole.

"What lies behind your eyes when you close them at night?" the Master said, and I looked up at him, wondering if this was a trick question.

"Darkness," I said, and he smiled a little, flash of the sun.

"And what lives inside your darkness?"

Memories, dreams, bits of old, decaying meat. Strange creatures moving in the depths of me, and their names are Hunger, Yearning, Need.

"Come, little bird," the Master said, pulling me from the view of the hillside. "It is time to dance."

I WAS SO tired that even when I woke in the mornings I sometimes thought I was still sleeping, walking through the world with my eyes half closed. In rehearsal with Mistress I danced possessed, seized by the ache of the afterworld that I carried with me in my heart throughout the day, a shimmer that pulsed in my chest. I had to remind myself, repeatedly, that in the studio I was still among the living.

"Why must I dance at Near North Ballet? Why can't I dance only here, with you and the souls in the temple?" I asked the Master one evening, and his eyes were as steady on me as the wind. I never felt tired at night; the moon touched me and I was alive.

"You *can* stay here," said the Master, and left the rest unsaid: *If you give me your heart.*

But what a tragedy: I was still too in love with the sound of it beating.

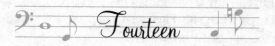# Fourteen

MISTRESS WAS WATCHING ME. I DIDN'T NOTICE, AT FIRST, BE-cause she stood in the back corner and only watched my reflection in the mirror in front of me. But when I caught her staring I smiled—wide, with teeth—and she straightened as if jolted with electricity. With a wave to Elsie she ordered the music cut, and silence settled over the studio like dirt over a grave. She walked right up to me, so close her breath puffed against my cheek.

"Are you here with us, girl?" she said, and her voice was quiet but it carried. The girls around me stiffened like corpses. "Or are you determined to make a mockery of me?"

"I don't know what you mean," I said, and I didn't; it was true. A mockery—how? I was just dancing; I was doing what she asked. Less than two weeks until *Little Bird*'s premiere.

"Don't play with me." Her words were quick and sharp. This close I noted all the fine wrinkles around her eyes, the strands of gray in her red hair, the veins bulging blue over her knuckles. "The steps, girl—my choreography. You're muddling it, making it up as you go. At first it was just here and there, small changes, and I let it slide. I thought you'd get yourself back on track. But today the whole last sequence was different, remade according to your whims. A tour jeté in place of a saut de chat, a pirouette in arabesque instead of an attitude turn. You may have the benefactor now, and he may keep you like a queen, but you are still *mine*, Miss Dragotta, and you will stick to the steps I gave you."

Her face was flushed by the time she was done. I looked down at her, into the face of the woman who had *sold* me—like fabric, like flour, a commodity desperately needed but not so very rare. All in exchange for enough money to keep her company afloat. Was her success really worth the price of my freedom? I was glad I had denied her a kiss all those weeks ago when she'd first sent me away. I would deny her the breath from her lungs if I could.

"Who are you to talk to me this way?" I said, my body burning as if with a fever. What a mistake Mistress had made, to consider me still a child. To reprimand me as if I were still hers, still clinging to what meager scraps of affection I could find. "You are not my mother."

Mistress slapped me.

The sound didn't echo so much as radiate; it had heat. Someone gasped, and I was only sure that it wasn't me. I cradled my cheek. It didn't hurt too much, not right away, but it was very red—I could see that in the mirror even between my cupped fingers. More than anything it was surprising, though perhaps it shouldn't have been. I watched our reflections, frozen like a painting, like an abandoned work of art.

A tear leaked from my eye over my slapped cheek, but not from pain. My heart was steady and sure as I looked at the faces of the girls I had grown up with—some of them horrified and others pitying. And as if something had been knocked loose in me at Mistress's violence I saw all of their deaths, a glimmer beneath the surface, a spark. There, in Anna's belly, and there, behind Miriam's eyes. There, in the palm of Isabelle's hand, and there, square in the center of Beatrice's chest. And Mistress's, the brightest of them all.

"Oh, Mistress," I said, and leaned closer to her, until there was barely any space between us. But I spoke loudly and clearly so that everyone would hear. "Your death is in your throat."

She never took her gaze from mine, but her hand went to her neck. A fingertip, pressed to the dip between her collarbones, that thin and vulnerable place. There was a pale shimmer beneath the skin to match the bright one in my heart.

"Yes, I see it, coiled there. Soft at the center but armored in harsh words and hard laughter. And that smile of yours, kind and cruel at once. Your lips, like the wilted petals of a rose that never truly bloomed. How could it, when you've planted it in such barren soil?"

"Get out of my studio," she said quite calmly, and I am still proud of myself that I was not the one to take the first step away. She backed up until her spine was nearly pressed against the glass. "And don't come back until you're ready to apologize for your behavior today."

"Mine is the face you shall see when you die," I said, and then I left them all behind.

THE NEXT MORNING I waited on the sidewalk in front of the studio for Mr. Russo to disappear around the corner, and then I ran to the bus stop at the end of the street. I took the bus southwest to Pilsen, and rang the bell of 1121 West 19th Street, where Emilia said she was staying with her cousin until the wedding. Three times I tried the bell, and I even knocked, three times more, but no one answered.

Later, in the car, when Mr. Russo asked how rehearsal had gone, I looked him in the eye and said, "Just fine."

I was grateful then to escape into sleep when he hummed me his lullaby.

IT WAS MY fifteenth night in a row in the temple, I think, or else the sixteenth. Time meant little to me then. I was distracted, restless; I could not put Mistress out of my mind. Her death in her throat, weak as it was, glistening like a sick thing, like a poison waiting to strike. I stumbled as I danced in the temple that night, and I was worried the Master would berate me as Mistress had. But he only watched, his lips parted and soft, and I knew that if I ran to him he would open his arms and let me in.

I could fall against him and the world would disappear—this one and the last one and the next one and the next. The temple was our shield and our sanctuary, a vast castle for a queen and her king with not a single beating heart between them. Luminous beings, souls dancing together forever after. All I had to do was go to him; all I had to do was say yes.

But before I had the chance, the soul of a black-haired woman stepped from the trees. It happened so suddenly that my eyes went wide as I nearly folded to my knees.

I had wondered, I had—but no, it was so long ago, surely she would have traveled on to Noctem by now, where she was dressed in silk and pearls and sat in the front row at the ballet every evening, watching the dancers floating an inch above the stage and smiling to know that some-day I would sit there beside her. And Lorenzo would sit on her other side, no longer a boy, the age he would be if he were still alive, silver in his black beard and laugh lines around his eyes. A bouquet of blood-colored carnations blooming from the hole in his chest where once a bullet had pierced him clean through the heart. Holding hands as the ballet carried on so that they wouldn't lose each other in the dark. I had imagined this so fiercely that the presence of her here, alone, her soul's light flickering like a candle touched by a sigh, shook me so violently that the Master lunged forward to catch me before I fell.

"*Mamma?*"

I pushed out of the Master's arms as she came toward me, a look of confusion on her ghostly face.

"Grazia," she said, and her voice was hoarse and low, unused. Or else used only for weeping. "You—is it you?"

I closed the short distance between us and hugged her, unsettled to find that I was several inches taller than she. The last time we were to-gether I had been a child, growing but not grown. Had she always been so small? She *felt* small in my arms, and only as solid as ice right before a thaw, like she might change, wither, or disappear at any second. I had not touched any of the souls before but the little girl's hand, I realized, tightening my hold on her.

"Ah, *bedda,*" she said, her head on my shoulder, her curls grazing my cheek. She was warm but smelled like a winter wind, clean and sharp. "I have been waiting for you. But I did not expect you so soon, my girl. Have you lived a lifetime already?"

"All this time, you've waited?" I shuddered at the horror of it, my mother deliberately lost, vulnerable to the beasts that would devour her without a thought. "But, Mamma, there's a whole shining city awaiting you."

She smiled—a kind smile. "Then let us go now."

"Oh, Mamma. I—"

I looked up and locked eyes with the Master. He stood off to the side, perfectly still, more shadow than man. He waited to hear what I would say. One word from me, and I would not need to deny Mamma our ever after. One word to give him my heart, and the mortality pulsing within, and I would be free to walk where the dead walk, no realm of soul forbidden to me. Only a moment ago I had considered it, and now here was my mother, eager to have me once again at her side.

So why—*why*—must I still say no?

"I can't," I said, and the Master turned away from us. The sky felt lower and closer than it ever had, the breath of the stars in my hair. "I— I'm still living my life."

Mamma's eyes glowed. "Then what are you doing here?"

Again I felt I might faint, but the Master wasn't there to catch me this time. He had folded into the darkness somehow, giving us a measure of privacy. Still, I whispered—this part was not for him.

"I'm a ballerina," I began, and Mamma smiled at that. Had she known? Was she still tethered to my life somehow, anchored by my love to the mortal world even as she wandered with and through shadows? "I was in the corps of a small company, and I was—happy. My best friend, Emilia—oh, she's beautiful, Mamma, you'd love her—she was the lead in every ballet. But then she fell in love and retired from the company to get married and start a family, and the ballet mistress promoted *me* to prima. I thought I had earned it all on my own, but after the first performance I learned that a wealthy man had made a generous donation to the company and requested that *I* play the Golden Firebird." I was talking too quickly, and I could see that I had confused her but I didn't stop to elaborate. "So I danced and I flew but always I wondered, I couldn't rest, because no one knew the identity of my patron. 'Why me?' I thought. 'Why me?' It was agony, it was—I thought he was a monster. And then he came, Master La Rosa, and I still thought he was a monster. He took me away. He brought me here. A prince—no, a *king*. A king came and took me away from the city and showed me the stars. I had never seen stars before." Together, we glanced up. It was a clear and glittering night. I licked my lips and tasted salt. Tears, spilling slowly. "The Master says they can be mine, if only . . . I'm like a girl in a story, Mamma. But I'm not so sure the story is mine."

Strange, but only then, in the silence that followed my confession, did I notice that Mamma had no breath and no pulse in her thin, wing-like hands. Of course not, she was dead—but it jarred me nonetheless. Because it didn't feel like an absence, or emptiness, a thing to mourn; rather there was the presence of something else. Something eternal that my temporal tongue could not pronounce.

Mamma kissed my cheek, heedless of my tears, and the genuine heat of her skin near mine was only an illusion plucked from a memory. But it was an illusion I believed in, and so it was real.

"You must *make* it your story," she said, pressing something small and hard into my hand as the Master appeared at my side. I hadn't heard him or seen him approach. Mamma eyed him warily. I curled my fist around her gift.

"It is time." His gaze turned sharply toward the dark path to the city. My gaze went there also, and Mamma's did too. She took a few steps, as if she couldn't resist its pull now that she had noticed it. I darted in front of her, blocking her view.

"But she can't go," I said too loudly, my voice slashing across the temple. The stars gleamed like salt in the wound of the sky. "We've only just—"

"She must. If she lingers too long here she will begin to fade back into the dark, and there will be no hope of finding her again."

"I won't leave without Grazia." Mamma put a hand on my shoulder. She spoke to the Master, lifting her chin, and I thought suddenly of that time when I caught her eating in the night, feasting without me while I watched, trembling in the shadows. How our eyes had met in the dark. "I go where she goes."

Her hand on me was heavier even than the weight of Death's.

"You left me once before," I said to her, trying so hard to keep the bitterness from seeping into it—but I didn't quite succeed. *Mamma, you're sick. Mamma, you must eat. More, more, just one more bite.* "You can do it again."

"Oh, Grazia." Mamma bowed her head. "I know you must be so angry with me—no," she said, when I began to protest. "Oh, *carissima*—it is all right. But please believe me when I say that I didn't want to die; I sought only an end to the pain."

I nodded but looked away. I could understand that, couldn't I? An end to the pain? I had thought I could find it through dancing, and in some ways I had. When I was in motion I didn't have to think, didn't have to feel anything but my muscles expanding and contracting, my fingers reaching, chin to the stars. Pure animal survival, no past and no future. But when I stopped, it all came back again.

I began to cry harder than ever, and I wasn't sure there would be an end to this new grief. "Mamma, Lorenzo is waiting for you. And Nanna and Nunnu. Wouldn't you like to see them again?" I exhaled, somewhere between a shudder and a sigh. "I'll be there soon, I promise."

We embraced once more, and she kissed both my cheeks, and all too soon she went fearlessly up the path to Noctem with the Master right behind. He looked back, once, lingering: *Are you coming?* I shook my head, wrapping my arms around my waist: *I can't.* He nodded, and then vanished into the darkness after my mother.

The silence was inside me, flowing like blood. The hunger of a wolf in winter, the thirst of a rose before a storm. Alone, I uncurled my fist. In my palm, my mother's gift.

A tube of lipstick: *Ancient Brick.*

SOMEWHERE BOTH UNFATHOMABLY far and very, very near, it was almost morning.

Somewhere there was a warm bed waiting for me, and too-hot tea, and snow sticking to the window glass. Somewhere there was fog, and steel, and distant traffic. Somewhere there were thick walls and locked doors keeping me out, keeping me in.

But not here.

A hazy kind of calm enveloped me. With steady hands I uncapped Mamma's tube of lipstick and brought it to my mouth, carefully tracing the lines of my lips with it; no way to tell how well it looked without a mirror. But precision here didn't mean much, only the act of the application. When it was done I retightened the cap and slipped the tube into the top of my leotard, snug against my chest.

"Take me where I want to go," I said.

The wind led me: It tugged at my hair and wrapped around my knees, surging toward the gap between two dark columns, just wide enough for me to slip through sideways. A cry rose in my throat, a throbbing knot of fear, but in the next moment I had swallowed it down, as easily, as greedily as the darkness then swallowed me. *See?* The darkness seemed almost to speak—in my ear, in my head between a dream and a nightmare, in the echoing, hollow spaces in my heart. *No need to shout or to weep, little bird, not here where the air is warm and sticky and the trees curve around you like ribs, like bones to keep you safe. Perhaps there are monsters, child, oh yes, and perhaps they are empty in the belly and slyer than you. What of it? If you cannot see them, then how can they see* you?

It wasn't a smooth path, nor was it a straight one, the soles of my slippers wearing quickly away. Not at all like the worn path over the hill to the city or the trail to the garden inside the stone church, flattened by countless wanderers. The leaves of the thin trees looked like hands against the sky, wide and reaching—until the trees thickened and I could no longer see the sky at all. The air was warmer here than it was in the temple, and humid too, and soon I began to sweat. The knot holding my skirt in place unraveled and the chiffon fell from my hips, but I did not stop to snatch it up. The darkness whispered to me in the soothing voice one uses to lie sweetly to a child, telling me there was nothing to fear, not here, even as I heard footsteps, perhaps more than one set, distant and coming nearer. I went as fast as I could, pushing aside branches with my hands, scratches on my arms and legs and cheeks, some deep; relying on my sharpened senses to detect the placement of the trees. Not quite running, but hurrying.

Hurrying.

Gradually my eyes adjusted, and I could see a little, though not much: the eyes of an owl, a thick patch of moss. The footsteps in pursuit faded for a time and then came roaring back, louder, closer, and soon were gone again. I pressed my lips together, believing in the deep magic written across my red mouth. A white rabbit hopped across my path.

I didn't stop—not once did I stop. But the darkness and the trees and the retreating and returning of the footsteps became relentlessly monotonous, and I forgot urgency. I forgot fear too. I slowed—lungs burning, lips dry, feet and calves and sides aching—and I reached out to touch the nearest tree's trunk, but my fingers met stone instead.

Rough and cold, I trailed my fingertips along it, for four steps, five steps, ten, twenty. I looked up—no branches, no leaves. Only walls, as wide as my arms could stretch, too high to see over or climb.

I had entered a labyrinth, and I was trapped.

I sunk to my knees; I did not stop. I crawled through the mud, clawing the ground with my nails, tears and sweat mixing and dripping down my face, my neck. The walls became narrower and narrower, and the breath in my throat narrowed too. Something slithered through the mud behind me, hissed.

Take me where I want to go!

Back. I wanted to go back. Not to the temple, not to the Master's house, not even to Near North Ballet. Not to my childhood, and violin lessons with Sig. Picataggi, and those spectacular nights when Lorenzo would dance with me to whatever tune crackled over the radio, spinning me round and round the living room while Mamma watched us, laughing, in the doorway, before shaking out her hair and joining in. All of that was done. Back farther than that, but in a different direction. God, how can I explain? Down on my hands and my knees in the dirt, I longed for a time that never was but could have been. A dream, I mean, a stuck place, a wish I had once buried so deeply in the hush of night that I couldn't find it again. Sometimes in sleep I would close my fist around it, up to my elbows in stars, only to wake with a gasp, empty-handed.

Out the window, down the alley, through the park.

This can't be all there is.

A thin, wet tongue licked my ankle. I whimpered but kept crawling. I did not stop. A labyrinth is not a labyrinth if there is no way out.

It began to rain, softly at first, but soon it burgeoned into a storm like the one that had meant the Master's brother was near and desperate to break into the city of Noctem to take back his lost love. Was he there now, trying uselessly yet again? As the rain soaked into my skin and hair and ruined leotard, I came to a fork in the path, the walls of stone branching in three directions. There were doors set in the stone at intervals, old wooden ones grown over with vines, but when I tried to open them I found them locked and unyielding despite the rot. Where did they lead? Where would they take me if only I could open them? *Take me back*, I thought fiercely as I rounded the corner to the right, pushing myself to a run. Another fork, another right. Another. *Take me there now.*

I saw them out of the corner of my eye, crouched in the dark along the paths I did not take: beasts of the afterlife, the lost and lonely souls, little more than moving shadows. A glimpse of hoofed feet, curled claws, a tower of antlers tangled with vines and dying roses—I dared not look at them directly. If I did, surely they would pounce and eat me, digest me until I too was part of the dark. I kept my gaze straight ahead.

I heard them, though. Shifting and scratching. And their voices were one voice, the voice of the greater darkness that had welcomed me and assured me that there was no reason to be afraid. Speaking in a language that was once a human language, stripped bare, like exposed bone; a language of pain, of tripping and falling. Of crawling on your knees through the mud, of looking up and seeing—nothing. And it was so full, the emptiness. It had no end.

So they spoke, their many voices twisted into a single voice, and I—I listened. I trembled, but I listened. I trembled, but I understood.

Lie down and let the darkness heal your wounds, mend your bones, and drain the blood from your heart. You will not need a heart here. It will only confuse you with love and fear and dreams; it will only slow you down. Think how fast you would run without it, little bird, think how far and high you could fly!

The rain turned to snow. Light and languid, it melted quickly on my feverish skin. *Take me away, somewhere safe!* With this plea, I felt immediately as if I had been turned upside down and all the blood was rushing straight to my head. Was this magic, my wish being granted? I turned another corner, and there—a light up ahead.

Noctem, I thought in both terror and triumph, and in a last burst of energy I sprinted toward it, the beast-whispers growing louder, harsher, a rising hysteria (theirs or my own?). *I will escape; I will carve out my mortality for an hour or two and slip into the safety of the city of the dead.*

But it was not the city. I was still in the labyrinth, walls on either side, and there didn't seem to be an end to them. Still, there was that light up ahead, and soon I was close enough to see that it was a streetlamp, the shape of it somehow familiar. And at the end of the path, a door. It was familiar too.

I threw my entire weight against it, the voice of the darkness behind me reaching an unholy shriek. The wide, arched door gave easily; I stumbled through and shut it with a firm shove. For a moment I leaned against it and closed my eyes, breathing hard. There was a splinter in my left palm and one in my thumb. Both stung, throbbing as quickly as my pulse. Only after my heart had quieted to a murmur did I open them and behold my sanctuary.

I was inside the church of St. Francis of Assisi.

Incense and white candlewax, a susurrus of polite conversation. The sun flared brightly through the stained glass, casting colored shadows onto the pews, the gold accents of the altar gleaming like treasure. I stumbled forward, sliding into a seat at the back, dazed as I looked around, as I felt the hard wood of the bench beneath me, solid and sure. The church was full; a few heads turned my way as I sat, and I looked down at myself in a panic, knowing I was in no way dressed appropriately for church. But I needn't have worried; my sopping, mud-stained clothes were gone. In their place, a midnight blue Sunday dress, an old favorite of mine, with ruffles at the sleeves and a widely flared skirt. On my feet, clean black flats, and my curls were clean and dry, a ribbon tied like a band around my head and knotted at the nape of my neck. My fingertips, when I brought them to my lips and pressed, came away clean.

Around me the chatter died down, and I looked up from my unstained fingertips. Into the quiet the organist began to play, tentative at first, as if feeding each note carefully into the mouth of a waiting animal. Then, stronger, more sure, a joyous tune—a wedding march. With the other congregants, I rose and turned to the back of the church.

Emilia was there, in a long white satin dress and a veil threaded with pearls, her dark hair rolled back off her face. She had one hand hooked around her father's arm, and in the other she held a bouquet of fresh pink flowers. Her eyes were on the altar, where Adrián stood in a black suit, gazing back at her. Both were smiling, so wide.

I exhaled, somewhere between a sigh and a sob.

Emilia and her father began to walk down the aisle, and as they passed my pew her gaze cut to me. She paused, her smile slipping as she opened her mouth in an expression of bewilderment, in glee and worry and wonder and confusion all at once. I knew, because I felt it too.

I'm here. I smiled, my first true smile in such a long time, wishing I could speak the words but knowing from her answering smile that she knew already what I was trying to convey. *I found my way back to you.*

The rites, the prayers, the vows, the Eucharist—it was all like a dream, but I knew it was real because I had never once been aware of my heart beating in a dream, and so steadily. Throughout the ceremony, Emilia snuck glances at me, as if checking that I had not vanished while she presented an offering to the Virgin Mary, or while Adrián slid a ring onto her finger. Each time she did I smiled, wider and wider. I felt so light, like the girl I should have been, like a girl called colombina, endeared for her strength in soaring rather than her weakness in crashing through a window. For the haunted beauty of her depths and not the trembling at the surface. Was it nearly two months since I had first departed the boardinghouse at Mistress's command, trading my calm nights for a house full of mirrors and a feast after the sun had set? And was it only hours ago that I had embraced Mamma's ghost at midnight in the ruins of a temple lost to time? I tried not to think of the Master returning from Noctem to find me gone. Would he come after me?

Well, let him try—I was beyond reach.

Happy tears and laughter were muffled by the organ's recessional song as the bride and her groom started up the aisle toward the back of the church. Again Emilia looked in my direction as she passed by, an anxious glance even as her smile stayed in place. *You won't disappear, will you?*

I nodded, reassuring. *I am right behind you.*

Once they had gone out the door, bright sunlight obscuring the city beyond, I rose with the other guests and made my way with the merry crowd toward the exit. The warm sun touched my face at the threshold, and for a moment I was blinded. Then I crossed over, and the sun blacked out. I was alone, once more, in the dark.

I tried to step backward into the church, but my spine hit smooth, solid stone. The lamp was gone, and the snow was too. A cool wind blew; my wet clothes—leotard, tights, ruined ballet slippers—clung to my skin, and I longed to rip them off, to offer my skin to the night. Was this how the Master had traveled to and from the theater for *The Firebird,* how he had appeared so mysteriously right before each performance and disappeared immediately after? Through an enchanted labyrinth with doors instead of dead ends—doors that would take you wherever you wished but only for a time, only until you passed back through the door and into the labyrinth once again? I stumbled, enveloped by a smell of old earth, of graves overturned, of screams pushed far, far down into the dirt.

An ache in my chest, salt in my throat. I wiped my mouth with the back of my hand, and it was not lipstick smeared across my knuckles, but blood.

Magic was not solid, like stone. I could not hold it in my hands. It was warm, and wet; it flowed and dripped. I could hold it only in my heart, in the dark, where I could not see. In my heart, in the dark, where the beasts roamed free.

I heard a rustling, followed by a long, low growl. A pounce, a moan, and the sound of ripping, of teeth. A meal, a feast. That smell, dry and piercing. It was the smell of hunger, and of death—they were the same. How had I not noticed until now?

A labyrinth is not a labyrinth if there is no way out.

I didn't run. I crept silently. The beasts were fearless and I was not, but I could pretend and it was almost the same.

Mired again in the murmuring dark, it took only a moment for my senses to sharpen. There were still walls around me, high and thick, but the stone was crumbling, and sickly trees and brush grew through the cracks. Spiders splayed their webs across long cuts in the stone and between round columns placed in a row. Some of the columns were obliterated down to the base.

No longer was I in a labyrinth. These were ruins—like the temple, but not quite. What was this place?

Well, whispered the voice of the beasts in answer, *doesn't every king need a castle?*

I came to an atrium of sorts, or what might once have been a great hall, a long open space. At first I thought it was empty and that I was alone, so I stopped to catch my breath. I could see the moon. Full and round, but it was split down the middle, a dark crack, so perhaps it wasn't the moon at all. Old-moon, prophet-moon. Its light did not reach me.

In the far corner, something moved. A shadow, darker than the dark, rose from a crouch, rose to twice my height. It was human in shape but elongated, thin bones bent in multiple places—three elbows and two knees. Its exposed rib cage gleamed white, even in the dim. And a heart, visible behind the sternum, absolutely still. A dead thing, wasted. It took one step toward me, and another.

I looked into its face.

It had a face like sorrow. A too-wide mouth and eyes that seethed with the dying light of falling stars. Its spindly hands opened and closed, opened and closed, as if it were trying to grasp something long gone, long forgotten. I looked at it and it looked at me and I felt pity—sorrow and pity together. It choked me. Even as the beast groaned low and began to skitter across the ruined great hall, faster than should have been possible with all its odd joints, I felt sorry for it, and sorry that I had seen its private hell and there was nothing I could do to save it. Or myself.

I only remembered to be frightened when it was too late.

I dodged to the side, but still the beast slammed into me, knocking me to the ground. My hip connected with the stones below and a jolt of pain flashed down my leg. Scrapes on my shoulder, loose rocks. The beast loomed over me, and I wanted to scream but my throat had closed and would not let it out. Claws raked the side of my neck, and warm blood spilled down. Perhaps the beast would carve the scream right out of me.

But the beast went still as a merciless roar echoed through the open hall. I twisted my head toward the cry and fresh pain shot through my neck. But still I had to see; I had to know. A shadow ran on all fours toward us, footsteps thundering. And this time I was afraid, just when I needed to be. I flattened myself against the stone, and in a blink the shadow leaped and crashed into the beast. They rolled together, away from me, a tangle of limbs and slashing claws and teeth.

It was over in only a moment—the long-boned beast gave a gasp, its head snapping up toward the sky, as if searching for one last glimpse of a constellation that was not there, before it quivered and collapsed.

And I saw, as its head fell back, that it was not a beast at all but a man—or the *idea* of a man, a man who had forgotten his true shape over time. The man's jaw was square, his hair thick and dark, and his eyes—oh, God, his eyes were brown and wide, and when they sought mine before closing forever I could have sworn I knew those eyes, that those eyes knew *me*. The voice of God, a gun going off.

Lorenzo, I whispered, or tried to whisper, but the name stuck on my lips. His face turned away from me as he shuddered his last, and he was a beast again. A curled-up, pathetic thing, and it was all too easy to convince myself I had only imagined it, the likeness in that fearsome visage. No—my brother was safe in the city of Noctem, beneath a sky of waltzing stars, where Mamma would join him soon, with a kiss and a hug that lasted a century. Where I might join them someday too.

The shadow hovering over the fallen beast stood slowly, and I saw that the shadow was the Master and that he was very angry.

He stumbled, coming toward me, and I shrank back, one hand pressed to the cuts on my neck. They were shallow but hadn't clotted yet—there was blood under my fingernails.

"No," I said, or tried to say, but still he came and knelt before me. And with his face so close I saw that he was not angry—he was afraid.

"Little b . . . Grace—" His voice cracked. He reached for me and again I recoiled, thinking of claws, but his hands were perfectly ordinary, only very large. I exhaled, released a single sob, and the Master gathered me in his arms, his warmth closing around me. He held me, not as a little bird, delicate and battered about by the wind, but as someone solid and sure who also had comfort to give, protection to give, love and warmth and strength to give too. I wanted to stay right there forever, or at least until the night had ended, with him cradling me so that my head fit perfectly in the curve of his shoulder. My eyes began to close and he said my name again, and I realized I had not heard him say it before this moment. *Grace*, just Grace. It felt like a prophecy, and a promise.

The Master held me, took my face in his hands. There was blood on his cheeks, and I could not tell if it was mine, or his, or the slain beast's. He kissed me, and I kept my eyes open. There was no ice left in my chest. He kissed me, and I burned.

Sometime later he assisted me back to the temple, holding my arm as I stumbled over the underbrush. (I would not let him carry me, though he asked more than once.) We stood, facing each other under the moon, and as he was about to say goodbye, to send me back alone, I held up my hand and said simply, "No."

He frowned, puzzled, and I took a step closer, crossing the small distance between us. I wrapped my arms around him, a strong and steady embrace.

"Come with me," I said into his chest. "Don't leave me, please. Just this once."

He sighed into my hair, and I closed my eyes, unwilling to let go. When I opened them again we were in the mirrored room, both of us reflected in the glass.

"Lead the way," he said, and holding my breath I released him from my grasp and took his hand instead, never looking back as I pulled him through to the dining room and the house beyond, up the stairs creaking beneath our weight. In the mirrors on the walls I saw him, and only him, his reflection soft, almost grainy, in the candlelight. Mirrors to reflect the dead, to reflect *Death*, and I wondered if he too feared that he wasn't entirely real if he couldn't see himself, couldn't track his movements the way I'd followed mine in the studio. Only once we had reached my bedroom, with the shadows in the corners as sharp as knives, did I turn and look at him again not quite believing that he was still there with me until he reached out his hand and touched me, his warm palm pressed to my cheek.

"I am here," he whispered, as if he knew what I was thinking. "I am here with you."

It was a kind of dance we did there in the dark, all skin and sweat and limbs. I wanted it more surely than I had wanted anything in a very long time; I chose it, and chose him, and in the choosing he was mine and I was his. I felt claws on my back, scratching so tenderly that they did not cut me open; I felt teeth at my throat, biting so delicately that they did not saw through sinew. Afterward, more tired than I had ever been, I lay my head on his chest and heard no heart beneath his ribs. I knew that mine was beating for the both of us, keeping me alive and keeping him near. I fell asleep with it in my ears like an unquiet lullaby.

Just before dawn, before he would disappear again, he asked me his question. Always, the same question. It was a rasp, a whisper in a sore throat: *"Grace, will you marry me?"*

If this were a dream, I would say yes. If this were a dream, I would watch while he ate my heart. I would bury my bones next to his and together we would run into the dark.

And if this were a dream I would wake up and carry the feel of it around with me like a strange ache, like a catch in my breath, like a dark blue bruise, touching it again and again until it faded and the exquisite hurt faded too.

But this was not a dream. Somehow, it was not. Here, the things I said and did would have consequences. I no longer cared about any of them—except Emilia.

I am right behind you.

How could I say yes without seeing her one last time?

I curled into the Master, with a deep and terrible sigh.

"Not yet," I said, as he stroked my hair, a gesture nearly too tender to endure. "Not yet."

Fifteen

I SAT IN FRONT OF THE FIRE, BUT I COULD NOT GET WARM. My memories of the night before blazed far hotter than the flames: dancing, Mamma, the lipstick, the labyrinth. The church, the ruins, claws at my throat. The beast, the battle, its last breath spent seeking stars. The beast that wore a face like my brother's. The Master holding me. The Master's hands, awakening my pulse in places I hadn't known it could beat. The Master's touch, and the Master's kiss.

I brought my fingertips to my lips. They were dry and cold.

The window was closed, frost pressed like a face against the glass. I drank one cup of tea, and then another and another. Steam, curling like a hand I could not hold. A blanket was wrapped around my shoulders, but it was as thin as a gloaming shadow. Eventually, my lips went numb.

I heard voices. At first I thought I was delirious, imagining, but no— the voices were deep and loud, and coming from somewhere inside the house. I stood, letting the blanket on my shoulders fall in a heap, and I went in search of them.

Maybe it wasn't the best idea. What if it was burglars? What if they were dangerous? But I had almost been torn open by the claws of a lost beast in the labyrinth of the dead, and mere mortal intruders didn't frighten me now. I followed the voices to the second floor and traced them behind a door, the brass knob knotted with cobwebs, a slit of dull light on the floor. Closer the voices were familiar to me, though clashing like dark and daybreak.

"She has said no to you countless times." It was Mr. Russo, fury heat-ing his voice, feeding it like logs to a fire so that it almost crackled, deep and strange. I tiptoed up to the door, pressed my ear gently to the wood. "It's past time to concede, *Master*. You've had more than enough chances."

"I do not concede," said the Master, his tone measured compared to Mr. Russo's, though I knew him well enough by now to detect the froth of anger below the calm surface. "It is not over. Despite her refusals, there is still hope. I see it in her eyes. Why else would she keep coming with me to Noctem night after night?"

"You are *deluded*. You think you can—"

"Besides," the Master cut in, "you have broken the rules of our agreement, more than once. Meddling, walking through her—"

"And what proof do you have of that, hmm? Wherever I walk, I leave little trace." A sharp breath, and then, much softer, almost conciliatory, "Just give Catherine to me now and I'll call this whole thing off. No need for you to torment the poor girl any longer, to beg for her heart."

There was a pause, pulled taut.

"Or do you enjoy it? Seeing her afraid?"

The slam of furniture, a chair knocking to the floor. I jumped and held my breath. I crossed my hands over my pounding heart, scared to stay but unwilling to go.

"That's *enough*," said the Master, and it was almost a roar. Like a beast, oh God—just like a beast. "Catherine is dead and Death does not yield. Not even for *you*."

"You knew I loved her and you took her anyway!"

I released my breath, head spinning. Catherine—*Catherine*—a name I hadn't heard before and never really wanted to hear again for the terrible way he said it, for the grief in it and the pain. Mr. Russo had loved her, this Catherine, and now she was dead and the Master would not give her back. Just like Sleep in the story of *Little Bird*, just like the Master's brother trying to break into Noctem where he did not belong. *I have been called far worse than cruel, and cursed with many a dying breath,* the Master had told me once, and here was proof of such castigations before my eyes. No wonder he kept no servants but this one, or he'd have a house full of mortals all begging for their lost loved ones. Why did Mr. Russo think it worthwhile to demand such a thing of Death, who only takes and gives nothing back? Even I had not asked for the return to life of my mother, for the signore or my brother. I would not even think of it.

"Stop this! She was already ill when you met her. She was always meant for me." The Master's voice broke, a high crack. "All mortals are."

Mr. Russo laughed, low and mocking. "Except one? Our trembling little bird—have you finally found someone you are willing to save? Or are you only in this to save yourself?"

There was a scuffle, a cry, and a grunt of pain. With some desperation—whether for the Master, Mr. Russo, or myself, I didn't know—I tried the doorknob and found it unlocked. I pushed through, with no real thought of what I would do once I was inside.

It was worse than I had imagined: fresh claw marks on the walls; plaster dust floating in the air. A chair overturned, and a sofa too, glass on the floor. Mr. Russo's nose and mouth were bloody, and blood bright between his teeth; the Master's hair was mussed but otherwise he appeared unhurt, his bloodied fists curled and ready again to strike. But when I came into the room they both stopped dead, and stared at me almost as if they didn't know me.

A silence like the sky—unknowable and endless. We were all three of us breathing hard, but I did not know who was more shocked: me at their violence, or them at my sudden and unbidden appearance. The Master was the first to speak.

"Grace," he said, and uncurled his hands. He began to say more but was interrupted by Mr. Russo, who had started to sing.

To sing? Yes, and what an odd thing to do just then, but it was a melody I recognized, the one Mr. Russo had hummed in the car. And it reminded me of the girl from my long-ago dream, the girl with a voice so powerful she could put others to sleep.

It was all too much—Mamma and Emilia and sleeping the night in the Master's arms; Mistress's ballet of brothers at odds over life and death, and me, caught in between; Mr. Russo's bloodied lips and the room all in ruins. Their voices, the Master's gloveless hands, the claws I saw there before I blinked and they were gone. Beasts, magic, lost in a labyrinth—exhaustion greater than any I had ever known seized me, and slowly, I slumped to the floor.

"Give me one more night," the Master said, looking at Mr. Russo. "One more proposal, and if she refuses again, I will concede. I swear it."

Mr. Russo nodded once, sharply, in agreement, but did not stop humming. The song wrapped around me like silk, like a blanket, and I struggled against it. I reached for the Master at the same time he reached for me, kneeling so I could lean against him as I fought to keep my eyes open. But I couldn't, I was losing; I was so, so tired.

"*Who is Catherine?*" I whispered, and it was the last thing I knew before I fell hard into sleep.

I WOKE IN my bed to a knock at the door. Too distant to be my bedroom door, but close enough that I could feel the tremor through the walls and the floor. I rolled over, a painful throb behind my eyes. I remembered a lullaby, something about a girl and a beast. It filled my head and my heart; I hummed it under my breath.

The knock came again, louder. A movement at the window caught my eye and I turned toward it absently. A flutter of white against a gray sky: the tilt of a head and the tremor of wings. A bird, a little one. It stared at me through the glass.

I know this sounds absurd, but it's God's honest truth. A dove led me here . . .

A knock. Not a knock on the door I stood beside, all quiet now on the other side, but on the front door, two stories below. I pushed away thoughts of the Master and his antagonist for now and ran.

The house was like a corpse decaying around me: sagging, squeaking floors, shards of broken glass swept into the corners, dust and wallpaper paste. Another knock came, tentative this time, quiet with a waning hope. I tripped on the stairs and gripped the banister for support, the wood swaying precariously at my touch. There was a faint smell of rot and corruption, and I tried to breathe only through my mouth. The knocking had stopped, and my heart with it. Was I too late? I reached the front door at last and yanked it open.

I was greeted by a gust of icy wind, and Emilia, with her back to me, already stepping off the porch. At the unlatching of the door she turned with a little "Oh!" of surprise. We both reached for each other at the same time.

"Em!" I cried into her shoulder as she said, "Grace!" There on the threshold we hugged each other tight. The air was bitter and biting and I pulled her inside, using both hands and a great deal of muscle to shut the door. She shook the snow out of her hair and peeled off her wet gloves, a puddle forming on the floor under her boots. Right away I led her up to my room, where we sat facing each other in front of the fire. She said nothing about the derelict state of the house outside my bedroom—either she was too polite to comment or she truly didn't notice. My focus was firmly fastened on her face, as was hers on mine. Until her eyes flicked toward the window at my back, and I twisted around to see that the dove was still on the sill, looking in. The shadow it cast was long.

"The bird," Emilia said with wonder, and perhaps a hint of fear. "It led me here, I swear it."

"I believe you," I said, turning away from the window. I didn't fully understand yet, but I knew it was true. "I'm so happy to see you."

"And I you." She took my hands and squeezed. "I was so worried about you, Grace. Last night, when you vanished. What happened?"

I stilled. "Last night?"

"At the church," she said, and I looked down at the gold band on her finger. "I almost couldn't believe it—I didn't think you would come. I haven't seen or heard from you since the night of the gala and I feared you might be . . . In all that time, I didn't know what to do, or what to think. But then you were there, at the wedding, and it was like—like a miracle. Grace, I missed you so much." One of her cheeks was flushed from the fire, the other one pale. Still I was not warm. "I think I was more emotional about seeing you than I was about the ceremony. I waited for you at the reception but you never came."

In the early morning hours, after I had returned to the house through the mirrored room, I felt that I could no longer be certain that St. Francis of Assisi wasn't only an illusion. It had been so brief, so *bright*, the sunlight slanting across the altar just so, the gold in the icons ablaze as

Emilia and Adrián made their vows. A rasp of prayers, and the music plucking at my bones. But no, this confirmed it—I had been there, truly. Same as the Master, weeks ago, slipping in and out of the theater without being seen.

"Emilia," I said, an ache in my throat. "I have a very strange tale to tell you."

I told her of a king that ruled over a city that lay between two shadows, and of a girl who danced for him and his courtiers like the petal of a rose floating on the surface of a stream. I told her of a soaring castle with spires of twisted glass, and a mirrored room at its center that showed her not her own reflection but the reflections of those she loved and longed for. I told her how the girl had discovered that the mirror could transport her to the hour and destination of her heart's own choosing, but only for a very little while, a potent but imperfect magic. I told her that the girl could not stay in the castle in the city past the dawn unless she agreed to become queen of that place, to bind herself there with her blood.

It was a fantastical story, yes—but it wasn't a lie. I didn't want her to worry, so I'd made the tale of the Master and me more of a romance and less of a haunting.

She looked at me for a long time when I had finished my tale. "Does he make you happy?"

My throat was so sore; it was a wonder I could speak.

"Not happy," I said, and she frowned. "He makes me feel as if I have no end."

It was all I could offer her. I think she understood.

We stayed like that for an hour, for two, our hands entwined and the fire burning and the sun flaring bright before it slowly let go and faded from the sky. We stayed like that until the white bird tapped on the window glass with its beak and we knew it was time for her to go. I told her about Mistress and the ballet, how I hadn't been to rehearsal in days. Then we talked about her wedding, her hopes for the future, her desire for a family. I said very little, but I don't think she minded. I was happy just to listen, and to lock away this moment even as it slipped from my grasp.

"I'm sorry I didn't play my violin for you," I said as we stood, when it was almost time for her to go. I had forgotten, until now, about her request and my broken promise. "I'm sorry I didn't play as you walked down the aisle."

She smiled and touched my hand. I knew that I was forgiven.

"Will you still see *Little Bird*?" I asked, both out of curiosity and to keep her there a moment longer.

"No, I don't think so." Emilia sighed. "Not if Mistress dismissed you. It wouldn't be the same without you on the stage."

The bird was waiting for her on the porch. There in the doorway to the Master's house Emilia said what I thought might be the last thing she'd ever say to me.

"You mustn't be afraid to say yes to the Master, Grace. You mustn't be afraid if that is what your heart wants."

I was afraid, and I told her so. But when had fear ever stopped me from doing what I must do? I was afraid when Mamma died and left me alone; I was afraid to play my violin for an audience of strangers. I was afraid when Mistress took me in, and I was afraid to perform for the Master. I was afraid of coming here, and afraid of the Master, and afraid of the dark and of the beasts and of the labyrinth. I was afraid to say goodbye to my best friend, my sister.

But all these things I was afraid to do—I did them anyway.

For a long time after she'd gone I leaned with my back to the door, wondering if the bird would return—hoping it would while at the same time wishing fiercely it would not. Contradictions, always, every beat of my heart in opposition with the thoughts in my head. I hadn't only said farewell to Emilia. I had said farewell to my life.

My life as it was, and as it once could have been.

Will you marry me?

There was nothing, anymore, to keep me from saying yes.

# Sixteen

I HAD SEEN VERY LITTLE OF MR. RUSSO SINCE FOLLOWING the Master into the land of phantoms. He no longer drove me to rehearsal—he knew, somehow, that I had been expelled. I was worried he'd tell the Master, but *Our secret,* he'd said, and that was that. Since then he'd been there at the door to my bedroom every evening to take me to dinner and that was all. I didn't mind his absence much; I barely noticed. Nothing on this side of the mirrored room felt real to me anymore. Nothing but Emilia—and now she too was gone, like someone I'd dreamed of long ago.

And so it jarred me to see him, waiting for me, sitting at the top of the stairs. His face was clear of blood but not of bruises; his jaw and cheek a livid blue. And it all came back to me clearly, the fight between him and the Master. The song he had used—like magic—to put me to sleep and wipe it from my memory. I stopped at the bottom with my hand on the banister, looking up.

"So you've decided," he said without moving. The light fell from the long window behind him, his face shaded and gray. "You will give your heart to the Master."

Pulse in my throat. "How could you know that?"

"It's not so very hard to guess." He stood and came down the stairs halfway, loping, taking his time. "You have a look about you, as if you have emerged from a battle that you have lost and are about to plunge headfirst into another."

I watched him. There were so many shadows between us. I had not noticed before his leonine grace, and I began to wonder who he was, really—merely the Master's associate, or something else? There was a similarity in the roundness of the eyes, in the long line of the jaw, in the curl of the fists. *My brother.* Mr. Russo crouched on the step, his elbows on his bent knees, so that we were eye to eye.

"He probably told you it wouldn't hurt. That it would take only a moment to crush you to death between his hands, a moment shorter than a breath."

"He is not going to *crush* my death," I said, burning with indignation. "He'll take my heart, and . . . *gently* . . ." I shook my head, because I had never really thought about the mechanics of it. I hadn't wanted to. But I was not about to let Mr. Russo know that. "I won't feel a thing."

"And you believed him, when he told you this?" Mr. Russo said, in a voice like a fresh pink scar. My palm was slick but I did not let go of the banister, I did not let go of the only thing holding me up. "Oh, little dove, how *well* he chose. A girl born in the thick of a plague, a girl who grew like a weed in the garden of death, stubbornly clinging to the soil in the midst of so much tragedy. The Mafia and the murders, the depression and the hunger. He is all you've ever known, and you've grown so tired of running, haven't you? Why not turn and trip into his arms instead? Why not eat his sumptuous lies to fill the hollow places that have sat empty for so long inside you?"

"*Stop it.*" Gooseflesh had risen on my skin. "Stop saying these things." But he did not stop.

"Once you looked for him in every face that you passed, and you were right to do so. He hides in them, and in you. In your belly, between meals, and in your heartbeat, slowly winding down. Every pulse is one you can never get back; every breath tires your lungs, just a little, just enough. Every day, you become a little less. Your eyes, straining. Your spine, hunching. He is Death, a demon, a beast that crawled out of the darkest depths of the woods. You cannot escape him. No mortal could."

The sun had moved, almost imperceptibly. But the shadows were different now, more complete.

"I don't believe you," I said, but my voice was thin and tremulous. "I will marry the Master, and I *will* live forever."

He rose and held out a hand to me. I looked up at him.

"Come," he said. "Earlier you asked after Catherine. I will show you what has become of her."

Catherine. The name pounded in my ears, tore at my chest like ragged fingernails. It was, perhaps, the only thing he could have said to make me come with him. *Catherine.* I had to see; I had to know.

"You loved her?" I said, and his entire body went rigid, his eyes dark and hard.

"Yes, and Death took her from me." He relaxed, but only a little. He stretched his arm as far as it would go, imploring. "*You* have a choice. Catherine did not. *Come.*"

I did not take his hand. But I followed him. Through the house to the shrouded dining room, through the double doors to the mirrored room, quiet and cool. My heartbeat clotted thickly in my ears.

A girl appeared in the mirror, in the distance, walking through an infinite silver world. In a gossamer gown the color of the moon on a cold night, pale lips and light steps, her red hair loose and hanging to her waist. Her feet were bare, raw with scabs, and there was dirt on her hands, on her cheeks, on her knees. She walked toward me, relentlessly, and stopped just on the other side of the mirror, as close as my reflection would be. Or perhaps she *was* my reflection, another version of me; older and with lines around her eyes, sorrow carved deep. This girl, this ghost—she didn't speak.

She danced.

And I saw the columns of the temple behind her, thick mud on the soles of her feet. A glimmer of stars, trapped there in the endless dark. The girl's face, utterly blank, sores in the corners of her mouth. And beyond her, at the temple's edge, stood the Master, his eyes like an animal's, slick and bright. I watched him watching her, and my heart was colder than it had ever been, frozen in ice so that I couldn't be sure it was beating anymore at all.

"Give your heart to him," Mr. Russo said softly, over my shoulder, "and he will take away your hunger; he will take away your yearning and your pain. You will have no need of breath or heartbeats, and your bones will remain strong, unbreakable. You will dance, and the souls hanging tight to their husks will be compelled to seek you out, seek you here, so that he may more easily lead them away to that cold, glittering place where souls go when they no longer have a body to keep them warm."

Another girl in my place. Or was I now in hers? Her red hair sticking to the sweat on her neck. Blood oozing from the sores on her lips. The souls, indistinguishable from one another, shimmers of silvery light creeping from the folds of the darkness to see her dance, drawn to her mortality even as it waned like the moon. I watched as she spun one last time before she slowly, slowly collapsed. That was more mesmerizing than anything, the fall, the way she spiraled to her knees and then onto her side, her head pillowed on her outstretched arm.

And she stayed there on the uneven earth, the Master looking on, making no move to help her to her feet. Her eyes were open, staring away from the Master and away from me, staring at something I couldn't see. She smiled—it was small, barely there—and then her face went slack and her limbs sagged against the dirty stones.

"You will dance, and dance forever—or until you can't anymore," Mr. Russo murmured, gently tugging a lock of my hair, his voice so close to my ear. "Your feet will blacken and curl, your spine will hunch, and your veins will go dry. And when at last you collapse, only a shell, with your voice peeled from your throat, then you will die, and he will bury you. And he will find some other maiden, fresh as a rose, as a spring sky, and he will bring her here and she will dance on your grave. You will feel every one of her steps down to the core of your soul and it will hurt worse than any agony you have already endured. And when she is worn through he will bury her on top of you, followed by the next maiden, and the next. On and on until the end of time." He paused, and then, "You will become just another girl in a row of perfect girls. Another face, another body in a line of similar faces and bodies, and soon you will only be remembered as *The Girl*. The girl that was loved, once. The girl that died too soon."

I made a sound deep in my throat, a cry with no more breath behind it than a sigh, my chest too tight, my heart shrunken, misshapen, a hard and painful knot. I had worked so very hard to escape the corps of Near North Ballet, and yet, here I was faced with another: a corps de corpses, of chicanery and rot. Dancing for the Master, for the souls of Noctem, I had begun to believe I was exceptional; but if what Mr. Russo said was true, I'd never been anything other than ordinary, expendable, utterly replaceable.

Can this really be all there is?

The scene before me faded, replaced a moment later by another, by a silhouetted figure kneeling over a fresh grave on the hillside, head bowed and weeping. Then this too was gone, and I was left blinking at myself in the mirror, my true reflection revealed to me at last: tangled black hair, a sore just forming in the corner of my mouth, red like disgust, and my spine curving under the exhaustion of dancing every midnight, of dancing under a moon and stars whose names I could not even guess at. There was a bruise like a petal on my cheek, and I could not even remember how it had gotten there. Mr. Russo stood a little behind me, in my shadow, his whole body tensed as if his skin might split at any second and his bones fall to the floor if he did not hold himself together by sheer force of will. But when our gazes connected he relaxed, his fists unclenching and his lips parting softly. He leaned in close to me.

"There is a way to stop all this." His voice bit at my flesh. It scraped, peeled back my skin. "To break the curse."

I turned and looked at him. Not his reflection—him.

"How?" I said.

"When he asks you for your heart, don't say no." He pressed something long and cold into my hand, something sharp. I took it, curled my fingers around it. His voice was too close, trapped with me beneath the ice. "Say never."

Seventeen

I WORE THE WEDDING DRESS MAMMA HAD BEEN SEWING WHEN she died, the bloodstain over the heart now a rusted brown. Though it was not entirely finished, and though it didn't fit me quite right, still loose in the hips and the chest, it felt right to wear it. White is for weddings, after all. I went to the window and looked at the snow and pressed my lips to the glass. A red print, the color of ancient brick.

Mr. Russo didn't come to escort me to the dining room that evening. Finally, I knew the way. It was a prickle in my fingertips, growing more painful as I approached, dulling if I took a wrong turn. I sat at the head of the table, my usual place, and I used the dagger Mr. Russo had given me to cut slices of roast beef, to peel the rinds of the grapefruit. I swallowed the wine fast; still it burned my throat, but I didn't mind; I laughed. I was alone, laughing, the juice from a thick cut of steak smeared across my cheeks and chin, and I thought of Mamma in the moonlight, Mamma eating meat. How I had watched her, my belly so empty it was full of fire, feeding on flame and ash. How I had watched her, and never said a word. Because I knew, even if I had, she wouldn't have shared, not even a morsel.

I would have done the same.

The doors to the mirrored room opened at midnight, and beyond them the Master waited. His hood was pushed back and his mouth was soft as he looked at me and I at him. As I crossed the dining room it was as though I watched the scene from over my own shoulder, trailing myself like a ghost: the dark eyes, the locked jaw, the knife behind the back.

"Dance with me," I said, but I heard the words as if someone else were speaking them. With the dagger still in my right hand, I picked up my skirt so that the fabric concealed it, and the other I placed on his shoulder.

We took our first step; the music began, and right away I realized the music was mine. I would know it anywhere, like seeing my reflection or my shadow. A violin played in the rain, played by a child's hands, shaky at first but growing slowly more sure and more strong. A simple song, one I had made up as I went along, like a story on the tip of my tongue. Now as the Master guided me in a waltz and the mirrors rose to reveal the temple with the dead gathering all around, I listened and remembered a misty morning long ago, when I stood on the sidewalk in the shadow of a cloud and kept my eyes down as I dragged the bow across the strings and forgot that I was anywhere other than right where I wanted to be. The rattle of the El over my head; fumes from exhaust pipes, footsteps and whispers and empty stares. And I had glanced up, just briefly, to see a figure with his hood pulled low against the falling rain. It had chilled me, his body angled in my direction, but I had not known why, and I did not look his way again.

Now, of course, I knew: He was Death, ever present, ever at my side, listening not to my music but to my heart. Bringing me closer to him with each and every radiant beat.

He *was* a beast.

I had not *really* forgotten, or believed otherwise, even with his claws sheathed, even with his teeth shining only dully in the light. I had not forgotten, no—if nothing else, the scars on my arm were a stark reminder. And had he not saved me from—murdered for me—that lost, haunted soul I'd encountered in the labyrinth? But the mere fact alone of claws and teeth do not make a beast, and his kindness, in time, had burned away my fear like mist in the morning sun; with my eyes fixed on his face, his smile, I'd no longer noticed the lengthening of his shadow. He had promised me deathlessness in exchange for my beating heart—and now that I had seen the truth of what Catherine had become because of him, it stunned me that I had believed him. When had Death ever given me anything? All he had ever done was take and take and take.

The song ended and the dance did too; the Master stepped back and bowed, but I didn't move. He sank to one knee, looking up at me. And I looked down, from somewhere high above both of us, inside and outside of myself at once. I clutched the dagger with fingers that were mine and not mine, that belonged to me and to Catherine, and the countless others that had come before her—before us—back and back until the beginning of time.

I raised the dagger with a steady grip, and the Master did not even look at it, did not take his eyes from my face. For a moment the glow of the moon glinted silver on the blade, piercing me with its light, and as I blinked against the brilliance the passion of the past left me in a rush like a breath. I reached for the ghosts, the used and the betrayed—but they were gone. I no longer felt them inside me. My hands were mine again.

My heart was my own again too.

"Grace," said the Master, and his voice was like snow. It settled in all of my wounds. "Will you—"

"No. *Never.*" I released my hold on the dagger; let it fall to the floor. Its clatter drew the Master's gaze but only for a moment. His mouth tightened but he said nothing. I dropped to my knees in front of him, bowing my head and clasping my hands as if in prayer. "I won't, I won't. Please, just let me—I don't want you to bury me like the others."

"The others?" he said, but his voice was choked, strained. When I looked up, he was clutching his throat.

"Master—" I watched as he tumbled from his knees to his side. His crown tipped and landed on the stone floor; his cloak was twisted beneath him. The dagger lay inches away, harmless and dull. I hadn't— I didn't—

But he was dying; I could see that. Gasping, groaning, it went on and on. Uselessly my hands hovered over him as the whites of his eyes glowed a relentless and devastating red. Not like blood—like the sky, torn apart by a storm, and like fire, the sting of smoke and flame. I covered my mouth; I began to cry. How had I thought I could kill him? To plunge the blade into the flesh and the muscle, tearing through softness and living tissue? And yet, somehow, somehow—

It was over in a minute, an hour, a century and then some: The Master went still, his body long and limp on the damp stone floor, and when

I looked around the temple the souls were gone. I was alone, and the dark was like a shriek muffled by a strong hand over a mouth. My tears fell onto the Master's cheek.

In that moment I didn't know if the tears were for him, or for me.

"You should have said yes to him." I turned at the voice and flinched as Mr. Russo stepped into view. How strange and gutting and—and wrong to see him there. This place, this temple—it was the Master's, and it was mine. I stayed utterly still as Mr. Russo walked carefully around the body and crouched down on the side opposite me, his head tilted to the right as he surveyed the Master. "He was the gentle one."

"You told me to murder him." It was as much an accusation as a question.

Mr. Russo smiled, and it was not kind. Oh, God, how had I not seen? "And so you have."

I wrapped my hands in the Master's cloak, for comfort or anchor or armor or—I didn't know what. "I don't understand—"

"It was your rejection. Part of a bargain made twenty long years ago, and damn me for not setting stricter parameters, for letting him take his time in searching for just the right lost little girl to pull into his world of darkness and rot. As you see, we agreed that if he could not fall in love with a mortal and earn the affections of his beloved in return, then he would forfeit his mortal human form, and the lost souls wandering the hills around Noctem would stay lost. Forever." Smoothly he stood and kicked the dagger across the temple. "The dagger was mostly for show."

The full horror of it set upon me like an animal crouched to spring. "Why would he agree to so high a price?" I cried. "All those souls . . ."

"It was worth it to him for what he stood to win: Another realm. Sleep." His unkind smile turned into a scowl, his tone stiff with bitterness. "No longer a king, but an emperor. Keeper of souls, and keeper of dreams."

None of this made sense. "And *you* could give that to him?" I asked.

He laughed, but it was without humor, dry and withering. "Let's just say that Sleep is a friend of mine."

I shook my head, feeling as though I might be sick. As if I might start retching and never cease. "But why would the Master—"

"Why *wouldn't* he?" Mr. Russo's tone hadn't changed, but still I flinched as if he'd almost struck me. He ran his hands through his hair and his fingers shook. "Who doesn't want to evade Death? Who doesn't cry out to curse him? Who doesn't do anything they can to keep him off a little longer, and a little longer still? *Death* doesn't even like Death! He's a terrible beast and he knows it. If he had a means to escape—to experience sleeping and dreaming for the very first time—why wouldn't he take it?"

Death is all I see when I look at a mortal, when I walk through the world, the Master had said, his loneliness and longing bleeding through the words. But was it enough to push him to agree to such terms, to place a bet knowing that all he had and more might be lost? *Death is all I know.*

In my head I believed it. But my heart refused. "No, the Master wouldn't," I said. "Look what it cost."

"The stakes had to be high, or else it was not much of a bargain." Mr. Russo shrugged. He *shrugged*, curse him, as if those souls didn't matter, as if none of this mattered. "The Master has never understood the fears and desires of mortals. The things they dream of, the urges that drive their actions, their wants and their needs. He has never understood *love*, and how complicated it can be. He believed he could merely throw some pretty flowers at you, take a few turns with you around the ballroom, and it would be enough to sway your heart in his favor. Failure never occurred to him."

"But—but that's not *fair*." I wanted to stand but my knees trembled so badly I would only collapse. "It was my right to say no. Why then should so many have to suffer for my refusal?"

Mr. Russo inclined his head in acquiescence. His dark hair was silver in the moonlight. Those eyes . . .

"You must not blame yourself. None of this is your fault. The bargain and its terms had nothing to do with you."

"Why would *you* agree to something so terrible?" Each word he said picked me apart, like a hawk prizing open its prey. Soon there would be nothing left of me but the lies I had been fed. "What was in it for you?"

"The one I love returned to me at last." He laughed, pure triumph. He took my face in his hands the way I'd taken his in mine on the stairs so many weeks ago, and said softly, almost tenderly, "Returned to me from the city of the dead."

"Catherine?" I whispered, his hands hot on my cheeks.

"Yes. My sweet Cathy, who Death took from the earth too soon, even when I begged—I *begged*—him on my knees to spare her."

"You tricked me." I remembered what the Master had said during their fight, that Mr. Russo's beloved was marked for death long before he'd met her, that she had been sick and without a cure. How had he known exactly what to do and what to say to conjure enough fear, enough fury in me to turn me against the Master? He'd convinced me I was disposable. "You and her both. Catherine never danced for the Master. You only wanted me to think so, so that I would not marry him."

"Yes, you are right." Mr. Russo released me and took the Master's crown from the ground where it had fallen. But he did not place it upon his own head. "The Master has never loved anyone."

"He loved *me*," I said, and it sounded pale even to my own ears. I remembered asking Mr. Russo what he thought the Master might dream about—*I am certain his dreams are of you.* But the Master didn't dream at all. He couldn't.

Mr. Russo only frowned, pitying.

"Come." He stood and held out a hand, the crown clutched in the other.

I was so tired then, so tired I couldn't stand, or didn't want to. My heartbeat was a blur in my chest, slow and heavy and indistinct, and my mind spinning as if I were still in a dance. It was a struggle even to raise my chin.

"Give me the Master's crown," I said. I didn't like the way he held it in his hand, as if it belonged to him, as if it had *always* belonged to him. "It is the least you could do."

"I think not. The Master never told you where he kept his death, did he?"

"He doesn't have one," I said, even with his body splayed before me. But that had only been a shell, hadn't it? Surely the Master wasn't truly gone?

"Ah, and what is death, Miss Dragotta, but eternal life?" Mr. Russo's fingers tightened around the crown, and so tightened around my heart. "His death belongs to me now. You will never have it."

My head was so very heavy.

"You were kind once." I sagged against the Master, his body still warm. "I saw it. Your smile—"

"Lips lie." He looked suddenly to the side, but when I followed his gaze I saw nothing, heard nothing. "If you want the truth, you must look at the eyes."

Again his focus snapped to the darkness beyond the temple, and I realized: He was afraid. Of the beasts in the labyrinth, of the souls whose hunger had contorted their bones and turned them inside out. Of the sticking places where the light doesn't reach. And I smiled, because he was afraid—and because I was not.

"I'll stop you too." I could not bring myself to say *kill*. So I thought it instead: *I'll kill you too, John Russo. I will.*

"Is that so?" he said, with a laugh like scraping. Around us the shine of the stars, the shiver of the leaves on the vines, the wind like a lullaby of old. The golden crown gleaming mockingly. It was a fight just to keep the gray from creeping in at the edges of my vision.

"I know you are tired, little girl," said Mr. Russo, and something struggled to come together in my mind, the very last piece: I saw myself again standing on the hill over Noctem with the Master by my side, a storm breaking the sky. It had been his brother who had lost the one he loved, trying to get into the city to save her. And if the Master was Death, then his brother was—

"*Sleep.*"

We said it at the same time, but mine was a revelation and his a command.

I obeyed.

Part Three

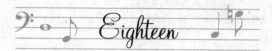

Eighteen

I THINK I WOULD HAVE STAYED THAT WAY FOREVER—ASLEEP— if it weren't for the hands on my shoulder, shaking me. Slowly at first, and then with more force. My eyes were closed and I wanted them to stay that way, at least for one moment more. I had been dreaming, dreaming of . . . something. A girl dancing on bloodied feet and a cold voice whispering lies. A dance and a plea . . . *Marry me . . . Be mine . . .*

No. Never.

"Grace, come on." The shaking turned to shoving. "Wake up now. It's not professional to sleep on the job."

I knew where I was even before I opened my eyes. It was the smell, I think: musty, an old building, dust clinging to the folds of the long velvet curtains. Worn seat cushions and electric lights and a faded mural on the ceiling, a bland depiction of angels hovering on wings that seemed far too minuscule to carry them all the way to Heaven. It's easier, after all, to fall than to fly. I would know better than anyone.

In the private box along the left wall that I had entered only once before, I sat in a chair with one of the last people I'd expected to see hovering over me: Beatrice, with her blond hair pulled tightly into a bun and her thin mouth in a frown. When she saw I was alert she clicked her tongue in annoyance.

"Anna wants to kill you, by the way," she said, sounding almost bored. She wore a gray tutu with a long Romantic skirt, her pointe shoes tacked at the ankle with pink thread. "I just thought I'd warn you."

"What?" I struggled to sit up straight, a twinge of pain seizing the back of my neck. I'd been splayed in the chair almost on my side, knees bent, with one arm tucked under me and my cheek resting against the back of the chair. When I looked down, I was still wearing the white dress, my mother's blood stained over the heart.

What had happened? There had been a dagger in my hand, and then—and then—

"As your understudy she was fully prepared to dance your part tonight, but now here you are and it's back to the corps with her." Abruptly Beatrice stood, and I tipped my head to look at her. "Mistress sent me to fetch you. You really should be in costume by now. It's only thirty minutes to curtain."

I felt as if there were gauze in my head and in my mouth and in my throat. Wounds everywhere, and gauze to stanch the blood.

"But—Mistress ordered me away," I said, and my voice was somehow steady. "How . . . ?"

"You really don't know?" A spark, and a smile on Beatrice's red painted lips. "Your patron came in about twenty minutes ago and talked to her. We listened at the door to her dressing room but we couldn't hear what they were saying. Whatever it was—well, she rushed from the room in tears. But they seemed like joyful tears, not sad ones. Anyway, you're back in her good graces, thanks to him." She perched again on the edge of the chair next to mine and leaned toward me eagerly. "Oh, Grace, he's *so* very handsome. Are you sure he's not a prince?"

I shook my head. "A king," I whispered, and the hope in my heart was nearly too much to bear—like vines, it choked me. Blooming wild, blooming fast. Perhaps those last moments in the temple were an illusion, a nightmare, only as real as a breath dissipating into the open air. *Please*. I pressed both hands to my heart. I felt it beating there, a beastly little thing. Maybe it deserved to be devoured. Even now I don't know if I wished the Master were alive again for his sake, or for mine.

"My patron," I said to Beatrice, and there must have been something in my face, my eyes, my tone, that made her go still. "He's here?"

"Of course."

"Where?"

"I'm not sure. He said he told you to wait here while he spoke with Mistress, and when they were done they sent me to come get you." She smoothed the voluminous tulle of her skirt over her knees. Her hands were so thin—it was like none of us would ever have enough to eat. "But I'm sure he's still in the theater, somewhere. He's not about to miss your first performance as the little bird in *Little Bird*."

I rose, and Beatrice did too. My heart was getting away from me, running, and I wanted to follow it. But I stayed where I was, sensing that Beatrice had more to say.

"I envy you, Grace. And not because of a prince." She looked up at the angels on the ceiling as she spoke. "I'll be here dancing until my body breaks down, until I can't dance anymore. And what then? I'm not that special, really. I see all these girls in the corps who are younger than me. Still learning, but God—they're so hungry. When I'm done they'll replace me, and I'll be forgotten. And eventually someone will replace *them*, and on and on until—who knows? Forever, I suppose."

It was a story she was telling me—the same story I was told by a man I should not have trusted—and yes, there was some truth to it.

"I think that's just life," I said, and still she looked up. "But that doesn't mean you're not special while you're here. While you dance."

She rose on her pointes—I'm not sure she even knew she was doing it. Closing the distance between her and the angels, just a little bit. "At least you have an escape."

"No," I said, and parted the curtain of the private box. "That's the great secret. There is no escape."

I COULD SAY something here about hope. About how having it is glorious but losing it is gutting. How it's a bit like wine—too little and you won't feel anything, too much and it will make you sick. I could say that all hope has edges, sharp ones, and even the shallowest of cuts will sting.

But if you are human, or if you were once, long ago—I think you already know.

It was not the Master waiting for me backstage. It was Mr. Russo.

Did he see me? I don't know. There were so many people around him. Praising him, thanking him for all he had done as a patron of the company. Of course, they'd never seen the Master, and so it didn't make any difference to them that this man and Master La Rosa were not the same. Mistress was among the preening crowd, but as soon as she saw me in the hallway she pulled me into the dressing room. It happened so fast—a kiss on the cheek, a tight embrace, a whispered, *Ah, colombina*—and then there were a dozen girls around me as well, whirling and fussing, helping with my makeup and my tutu and the pointe shoes I had left with my things at the studio the last time I had been there, when I'd walked out into the cold with nothing, with not even the intention to return.

My face was pale in the mirror as Beatrice rubbed rouge on my cheeks and threaded a needle with which to tack the ribbons at my ankles. Even Anna hovered nearby with my headpiece, an arrangement of white flowers with a clip to attach it to the side of my bun. I murmured a thank-you to each of them in turn. When I was ready—hair up, costume on, shoes tied—I went back to the hallway outside the dressing room, but my new patron was gone.

I thought about leaving. I thought about running away. *Out the window, down the alley, through the park.* Perhaps Emilia could have helped me, even given me a position in her family's bakery. I could start fresh. I'd done it once before, when I'd come to Near North Ballet—why couldn't I do it again?

But I knew running wasn't an option, not really. I wouldn't only be leaving the ballet behind, I'd be abandoning Noctem too. Who would look after the souls, if not me? Who would dance in the temple and lead them safely from the snapping jaws of the beasts to the sanctuary that sparkled like a second chance in the moonlight? It wasn't noble, this desire to return—it was utterly selfish. My heart was dark and overgrown with trees; so many nights there had made a forest of me.

I would have gone there at once, if only I knew the way. But I had never seen the path to the house in Hyde Park, and I suspected I would need a certain driver—or a mysterious white dove—to find it. Magic, once stumbled upon, isn't so easily caught unawares a second time. Maybe if I pleased Mr. Russo tonight, he would take me back. After that I could figure out a way to stop him.

The only way forward now was to dance.

ACT ONE OF *Little Bird*.

It used to be that when I was in the theater, nothing existed outside of it. Not the city and its lights, not tomorrow or yesterday, not winter and ice, not hunger and heat. There was only this, the fantasy—the music and the steps and the story.

But that was before I had danced beneath an open sky.

I sat on a bench in the center of the stage, alone. Behind me a glittering backdrop of the city, buildings lit against the starless darkness that seized the sky just before dawn. The first notes of the music swelled like a cloud with rain as the curtains parted, and a spotlight fell over me like the conical glow of a streetlamp. There was a book in my hands, a prop with empty pages. I was supposed to be reading, but instead I looked up.

Mr. Russo smiled when our eyes met.

I'll kill you too.

My partner, Will, walked onto the stage from the wings, idly strolling toward the bench where I sat. Once he was Ivan and I was the Firebird, and here we were again, destined (or doomed?) to repeat ourselves, wandering forever from fairy tale to fairy tale. He nearly walked right past me, but then the girl with her head bent over a book caught his eye. And so Sleep, an immortal being, falls in love with a mortal girl who is already marked for Death.

Nothing frightens La Rosa. Though, if he were wise, there is one thing that should.

And what is that?

Sleep.

Sleep, brother to Death, whose dominion was dreams. *Sleep comes to mortals every night of their lives, while death only comes but once*, the Master had said, and I began to see it, there upon that stage: Death takes, but Sleep *invades*.

I felt like a bird flying into the wind as I danced, soaring too high to breathe. Stretching and jumping and bending and turning; and all the while my gaze kept straying to Mr. Russo in the Master's box, in the Master's seat, smiling wide as he watched me—the inimitable smile of someone who has won.

Part of a bargain made twenty long years ago.

There was a girl beside him. I caught only snatches of her between steps, glancing up and to the left every chance I could get. She wore white, a gown not at all dissimilar to the one I had been wearing up until only half an hour ago. Straight spine, shoulders back, the regal delicacy that came with training for years and years in ballet. With learning the language of magic, of the cracks in the face of the world where fantasy lived and breathed, of monsters and the maidens who loved them, often in secret. A small mouth and red hair, quick eyes that seemed to find Mr. Russo's as often as mine.

And on her head the Master's crown.

She was familiar to me, and not only because she was Catherine, the girl I had seen in the mirror. Gone were the sores, gone was the blood, and the dirt too had been washed away. Or perhaps it had never been there to begin with.

Lips lie. If you want the truth, you must look at the eyes.

My pas de deux with Will ended, and I exited the stage. Mistress was in the wings, hugging herself as she smiled and watched, but she wasn't watching the dancers—no, her eyes were up, toward the Master's private box. A tear rolled slowly down her cheek. I had never seen Mistress cry.

"He loves her for her dreams," she whispered, and I moved closer to hear her better. She never once tore her gaze from Mr. Russo and the girl in splendor beside him. "They're so bright, he said, more intricate and more *real* than any he had ever encountered before. He would live with her there, if he could. In her dreams where everything her dear heart wants is hers. But always she wakes up. He can only have her here, where Death touched her and took her away."

At that moment, Catherine leaned over and kissed Mr. Russo's cheek. He took her hand and brought it to his lips. Pressed his smile to her knuckles. Not kind, not cruel. Only triumphant.

"Grace."

I jumped at my name. Mistress was a step closer than she had been before. She reached for my hands but I hid them behind my back.

"Yes?" I said, in as detached a manner as I could manage. I gazed down at her and felt like an angel, a seraph of the highest order—that is to say, without mercy. How could she bear to look at me without burning?

"Grace," she repeated, and sighed. Twice now she'd said my name, and it rattled me more than it should have. I couldn't remember ever hearing it from her before. Always I was her little bird, colombina, or Miss Dragotta—but never simply Grace.

I wanted to tear my name from her mouth, and from her memory.

"You've done so well," she said, and behind my back my hands were trembling. How long had I waited to hear this? "Whatever happens now, just know that I am proud."

There were so many things I could have said to her then: *I thought you loved me. I am nobody's bird. Why me, why me, why me?* But the words jammed in my throat, and all I could do was stand frozen while I watched over her shoulder as Sleep begged for his beloved's life. Death was implacable, dismissive, his steps tight and controlled: *She is mine now. Find another to love.*

What do you know of love? Sleep swept across the stage, low and lithe. *You who are as cold as a stone under snow? You who takes and takes and takes?*

Death was unmoved and unmoving. *I know enough.*

At this, Sleep only smiled. *If you know so much, then I propose a deal: Fall in love with a mortal and earn her love in return. If you do, I will give up my realm to you. But if you don't you must forfeit your mortal human form, and all the lost souls of Noctem will remain forever lost.*

The bargain had never been part of the plot of our ballet, but I saw it now, saw how Mistress had choreographed it in anyway, even if she and I, the Master and Mr. Russo, were the only ones who would understand. And because none of us had known how the bargain would end, the second act was about the girl who died—Catherine—wandering the underworld while Sleep pined for her and cursed his brother. Had the Master known that Mistress would tell this part of the story? Maybe. Maybe he had even counted on it.

All along this ballet had been meant as a message to me, a way of revealing the terms of the bargain without telling it directly. Why else commission such a spectacle, one so specific to the very story playing out around me? But only now that it was too late to change anything did I see what had been right there in front of me.

"I was elated when Death chose you, of all my girls," Mistress whispered, and when I turned to her it was like the world was showing its true face again, pits for eyes and mold on bone. She placed her hands on my cheeks and tipped her forehead to mine so that her dark eyes filled my entire vision, blocking the stage and everything beyond it. "Little bird, I knew you would *fight.*"

It was all I could do to breathe in, to breathe out. To not use my air to scream. "What are you saying?"

"You brought my Catherine back."

It fell over me in a rush: rumors of Mistress's daughter, a girl no one in recent memory had ever seen; Emilia telling me of a girl who had died in her room at the boardinghouse, but before it was a boardinghouse at all, when it was still Mistress's house; a sickness that stole her slowly until all at once she was gone. Mr. Russo and the Master, fighting over a lost love. Over *Catherine.*

Mistress's daughter.

I grabbed her wrists and ripped her hands from my face.

"You knew." My God, my heart was beating so fast, and I was so dizzy it was a miracle I could still stand. For so long I had wondered if she thought of me as a daughter, as someone she could love unconditionally. Now I knew: I was her bird, but she did not love me. How could she? A dove is not a swan, even if they have feathers of the same color. "You knew who and what the Master was, and yet you gave me to him willingly. A sacrifice."

Carefully, Mistress wiped her wet cheeks with her sleeve. She said nothing, and I still do not know if her silence was an admission of guilt, or guiltlessness. No denial—she had done it. But was she sorry? Even a little? Onstage the music was quieting—it was nearly my cue. The girl had to die now, to lie in Sleep's arms and take her last breath.

I waited for that old protective shell of ice to freeze around my heart, but it didn't—it couldn't. Ice cannot form near a fire.

"What if I had said yes to the Master? What then?"

Mistress's gaze went again to her daughter, and to Mr. Russo sitting beside her, watching this ballet based on their story. All this time I had pitied the withering girl caught between two godlike brothers, and I had even felt rage on her behalf; anger for the girl who had not been given a name in the context of this ballet.

But I realized now that the only nameless girl was me.

"It doesn't matter," said Mistress, and a smile I knew well stretched her thin and pallid lips. All this time she had worn kindness only as a mask for cruelty. She turned away from me. "You didn't."

I DIDN'T LOOK up at the private box again. For the rest of the act, I bled my soul upon that stage, a spill of gore and guts, a deluge of everything I had been holding on to these last months. I let the fire of my rage melt the ice of my sorrow and let the water douse the fire, until I was all cool and clean inside, a benumbed state of grace. I could give no less, or else Mr. Russo might have seen it, written there plainly upon my face: I finally understood the story I was in.

I thought of the Master in the garden—all those roses, all those stories. This ballet, *Little Bird*, too was a story. A story, and a gift.

Once upon a time I had wished for a power like the one possessed by the girl from my dream: a voice so beguiling it could put my enemies to sleep. A power Mr. Russo himself had wielded against me so many times—in the car on the way home from rehearsals, and in the house after I'd found him fighting with the Master—and always so I would not ask questions. I did not have a voice like that, and surely I never would.

But there was one more gift the Master had given me, one Mr. Russo had delivered to me, but he must have not thought much of it or else he would never have sung me that song, effectively revealing the way to use the Master's gift against him. The one I'd played only once, and that had given Emilia a bad dream. The dark wood, the taut silver strings, wrapped in paper as thick as skin: devastating, dazzling, Sig. Picataggi's resurrected violin.

The curtains had barely even closed on Act One before I opened my eyes. I sat up quickly, still half-cradled in Will's arms, and raised my gaze in the direction of the private box as if I could see it clear through the curtains.

I had killed Death. Now, I would sing Sleep to sleep.

Nineteen

RUNNING WAS FAR TOO SUSPICIOUS; I FORCED MYSELF TO walk. Through the wings, down the hallway, to the backstage door. Intermission was twenty minutes, plus the thirty minutes of Act Two before I was set to appear. In my long white tutu, in my flowered headpiece, in my scuffed pink pointe shoes, I went as calmly as I could to the backstage door. But as I approached, already reaching for the handle, I heard someone behind me calling my name—Beatrice? Mistress?—and so I crossed the last few steps in a lunge, yanking it open and throwing myself through.

But when I looked up, my heart in my throat and in my fingertips and in my ears, it wasn't the alley outside that I saw. No—it was stone and vines and leaves. Walls, narrow but crumbling. And darkness, devouring. The click and slither of unseen beasts.

I turned but the door behind me was already sealed and gone—only a smooth stone wall, only a glaring dead end. I pressed my palms against it, pushing uselessly, closing my throat against a scream, a cry that would wake the birds, that would call the wind, that would pull a cloud over the moon like a heavy curtain. There was no going back—only through.

A labyrinth is not a labyrinth if there is no way out.

I did not have time to feel sorry for myself, or even to curse Mr. Russo's name for neglecting to drive me through the city as a mortal would; for dragging me through the labyrinth of beasts so that as soon as I left I would end up here, back at the beginning. What had he sacrificed of himself to make the journey? What had he offered to the teeth of the wind and the sky?

He must have carried me, and I shuddered to think of it: Like a bride in his arms he had carried me across the hillside and through the labyrinth, time twisting strangely around us, warped so that a week became an hour, a minute only a moment, and with my head hanging heavy as the hot breath of the hidden beasts stirred my hair and let him know they were close. Avoiding their feral stares he carried me through the immovable stone door that the Master had once used to enter the theater all those times before just as the show had begun, entering and exiting without being seen. I don't think we were seen either. He set me in a chair and left me there for Beatrice to find.

Rage opened like a wound within me, deep in my tissue where there were already so many scars. Fear cauterized it quickly—not forever, only for now—as I bowed my head, listening. The beasts were coming. Clawing and hissing, too many teeth. Souls corrupted, open mouths like open graves, no longer in possession of a voice with which to speak their names. If I looked at them, I was lost. Eaten, gone, forgotten. Hunger, incarnate. Hunger, without end. The beasts were coming for me.

So I would not look at them. I closed my eyes and cupped my hands, right palm under my left, and soon I felt a weight there, warm and wet and beating. Strong and lighter than I would have expected, with waves of blood dripping between my fingers and falling to the stone beneath my feet.

Let me pass. I took one step, and another. I held my hands out high in front of me. *I bare my heart to you.*

I veered left when it slowed, and right when it raced, and straight when it beat loud and steady. This was my death, and it was mine to hold and wield as I pleased, like a weapon or an offering. Beneath my feet the stone soon turned to dirt and then to mud, a smell of rain just past and soon to come again. Around me the beasts clicked their teeth and clamped their jaws and scratched at the walls; a warning breath wafted on my neck. Smacking lips, flapping wings, a hum of distant thunder. The heat from their bodies, the light from their scars—they were close in front of me and behind. If I stopped, I was lost.

So I did not stop. It was only an illusion to believe that they could hurt me.

The beasts began to weep, an all too human sound. Fingertips brushed my shoulder, and those felt human too, save for the burning on my skin their touch left behind. I wondered what I looked like to them, what I smelled and sounded like. A miracle—or merely a meal? I tripped on a root or a twig, I didn't know what, and though I stumbled I didn't fall. My heart grew slick and heavy in my hands, so heavy that my arms trembled under the weight. But I held them high, and my head high too. The beasts walked beside me now as if I were leading them, or they were leading me, and I could feel their shadows on me as surely as the moonlight, scraping me to the bone. The darkness was pressed like a hand to my eyes, a slight and subtle pressure. *Don't look, don't look.* I didn't.

The rest passed like a dream. I *knew* I would make it through, and I think that's the only reason I did. In my mind, I was already in the mirrored room. Alone, no beasts. They fell away one by one—I was aware of their absence as if a scab had been peeled away, revealing the shiny new skin where once there was a wound.

How long did I walk? Until the end of time. I stopped only when my heart stopped, an abrupt and muscled beat. Then silence. I opened my eyes and was met by my own pale face, reflected a dozen times. My hands were empty but bloody, my heart once again beating in my chest, sore and hollowed out, and at my feet was the Master's body, perfectly preserved.

"Shh," I said, as if he were only sleeping. I stepped over him, past him, beyond. "I'll return soon. I promise."

THERE WAS NOTHING left of the feast but bones, tiny ones, and wine stains on the once white tablecloth, a shriveled apple core. Somehow, though, the room smelled sweet, like flowers flourishing in rot. It was dark—the candles had burned to nothing, useless clumps of wick and wax—but it didn't matter. My eyes adjusted and I could see as well as any animal. I left the dining hall, and now I didn't need my heart to guide me. It was silent anyway.

I saw myself in every mirror I passed. The dark hair, the torn tutu, the hands dipped in blood. I paused only once, to tear the ruined, dirty shoes from my feet, blisters on my bare toes, and felt at once the strength that comes from touching holy ground. How much time had passed since I left the theater? How much time did I have left? The house was a tomb sealing slowly around me.

My room was just as I had left it: the bed made, the window open, a cup of tea on the nightstand. The fire, though, had died in the grate, and the wind had blown the ash across the floor in streaks. I dropped to my knees and reached beneath the bed to where I had stowed Sig. Picataggi's violin in its box, beside my old violin in its case. I pulled out the box with trembling hands and lifted the lid.

If I look, I am lost. If I stop, I am lost.

Tears fell on the violin. Were they mine? I touched my cheek, and yes, they were mine. I raised my cold eyes to the window—a dove was perched on the sill. The slanted light from the setting sun cast a long, dark shadow into the room. The bird reminded me of the hunger once in my belly, of tales from before the beginning of time.

"Hello?" A familiar voice called out behind me, close and getting closer. The dove tilted its head. "Grace . . . are you here?"

I turned to see Emilia step into the doorway, raising a hand to shield her eyes against the angled, dying light. "Grace?"

I rose, and she gasped at the sight of me. It was right that she should gasp and cover her mouth in horror, because transformation is always alarming, and I was only halfway there: outside a mortal, inside undying, a beast with the face of a girl once known and beloved. My heart was still beating, but under a different sky. Even standing there in the Master's house I could feel the terrible thrill of my blood soaking into the soil, no different from the rain, christened in lightning and a dark chant of thunder. Someday I would give my bones as well.

And so I rose before Emilia, and flinched at her gasp even though I could not blame her and never would. My soul was my own but it was in pieces.

Oh, but—she didn't gasp in fear of me, only fear *for* me, as was made plain a moment later when she dropped her hands and rushed to me, when she swept me into her arms. At her touch I knew that my tears were mine without checking. She recalled all the human parts of me, and kept them firmly at the surface where she could see.

"I thought I might never see you again," she said, and I trembled all over—from joy, relief, sorrow, grief. At my back, the dove in the window spread its wings, and I watched with my head on Emilia's shoulder as its shadow elongated on the wall in front of me. "Oh, Grace," she said, with a deep and shuddering sigh. "What happened to your king and his kingdom?"

THE DOVE ON the windowsill flew into the room and landed on the bedpost, its black eyes unblinking.

Hurry, hurry.

Emilia searched the wardrobe for a suitable pair of shoes while I washed my hands in an old pitcher of water left by the bed. My mouth was dry; my jaw ached. I was covered all over in scrapes and bruises, in smears of mud like little shadows, but still I was not tired, not even a little. Would I ever sleep again, dream again?

"Our little friend kept flying past my window, trying to get my attention, and I thought you might be in trouble." Emilia, having found a pair of boots, came to stand next to me, watching the water in the pitcher turn brown. "Clearly, I was right."

The house let me go without a fight. Perhaps it knew that it didn't need to keep me there by force any longer, that eventually I would return on my own, bound to it with my blood. Adrián waited for us in his borrowed car by the curb, the engine idling.

"River North Theater," Emilia said after we'd slid together into the backseat and he asked, with some bemusement, where we were going. But he pulled onto the empty street without further questions, and I sighed with the violin in its box on my lap, shivering.

"Are you cold?" Emilia held my hands in hers as I took a deep breath to begin my story anew. How had it been only a day since I'd seen her last? "Your hands are like ice."

No, they were not like ice, but I didn't say so; they were like death, nearly a corpse's hands, not cold but absent warmth. Had they always been so? Was this the last illusion, the self-deception that I had somehow stumbled into a destiny never meant for me? But no—destiny is not destiny if it is not yours from the start, and so maybe I was always a little burning beast in my heart.

Time passed oddly in the labyrinth, so that a week had gone by while Mr. Russo had carried me through to the theater, and only a blink of an eye had passed while I fought my way back. And so, for me, it felt like only yesterday that Emilia and I had sat before the fire in my room in the Master's house, where I had told her of a king from a land farther than the closest star and a girl who danced in the hold of his shadow from dusk until dawn. It was a fairy tale, through and through, a shining bone with bits of gristle—a gift. I had only been trying to make things seem lovelier than they were, and though there was truth in it, that truth had been knotted with lies. I unraveled them all for her now, sparing nothing, not even the blood on my hands; I did not try to shade the darkness with light. She listened, with a silence like a deep cut clotting, and Adrián listened too, though I do not know if he believed me. I didn't need him to—only to drive, as fast as he could, before the second act of *Little Bird* began and Mr. Russo realized I was missing.

When I think now of that ride—which was both too long and much too quick—I remember church bells ringing all across the city. Big ones and small, crying out as if in surrender to an advancing enemy, and that enemy must have been me. Well, maybe enemy is too strong a word— more like skin expelling a splinter of wood. Is there a word for that? I did not belong there. Maybe I never had.

It wasn't that I was stuck between this city made of brick and steel and another made of stone. It wasn't that my hands weren't cold, only not-warm, and it wasn't that I had to remind myself now to breathe and to blink. It was that, as we approached the Loop and the tall, rigid buildings rising into the sky, I looked out the window at the people on the sidewalk, faces blanched in the streetlamp light, and I could see right through their flesh to their deaths, as I had that day in the studio when Mistress had slapped me. Pale and glowing, beating like a pulse; in the chest, the knees, the back of the skull. Everywhere death, and what a terrible and secret knowledge to possess. I trembled under the weight of it. It was difficult even to look directly at Emilia as I spoke, for fear of seeing it there, her death. Clean and glinting, mockingly bright.

But I could not avoid her eye forever, and when I finally acquiesced at the end of my story, breathless, I looked and there it was—Emilia's death in the tears on her cheeks, luminous and clear. I could have reached out and wiped them all away if I'd wanted.

"It is a fairy tale, after all," she said, with a squeeze of my hands like she would never let go, not this time. How could she bear to still touch me after what I had just divulged? I tried to take my hands from hers but she would not release me. "It merely isn't finished yet."

Twenty

ACT TWO WAS WELL UNDER WAY.

They'd looked for me everywhere, scoured the entire theater during intermission, the dancers and the stagehands and even some members of the orchestra, but when I couldn't be found Mistress had swiftly plucked Anna from the corps—again—and put her in my second-act tutu—a gray skirt with black lace on the bodice and a single white lily in her hair. As she was my understudy, it was only right. I would do no more dancing that night.

When I walked through the backstage door and through the hushed and narrow halls to the wings they did not even see me. I was more of a ghost then than I had ever been before or would ever be again. A gift, I think, from the violin, the box held tight to my chest. An enchantment that kept their eyes and minds averted from me, like the beasts of the labyrinth macabre—if I did not look at them, they would not bare their teeth to me. I let myself smile, feeling deliriously nocturnal, an animal in the dark. It was a last moment of peace before the breaking.

The lights were so bright on the stage. God, how could they dance with all that light shining over everything, their skin and their hands and their faces? Harsh, and grating, and inelegant. No wonder the stars are so far, admired best at a distance, made soft by the surrounding darkness. The music was like a kiss on the side of the neck, gentle but chilling, or like a fog descending, obscuring the path forward and back. Mistress stood in the wings, watching the shades of the underworld bourreé in a circle with their wrists crossed over their chests. Anna too, waiting for her cue. I knelt in the corner, as far from the stage as possible in that tight space. As soon as my box touched the ground, the spell it had cast over me was broken.

Mistress turned, and I felt the moment her gaze locked on to me, like a jaw biting down. I shivered. Not a cold kind of shiver—I was sweating as if with a fever—but a shudder of loss and its plaintive echoes. I was not her bird, and never had been. *Stars burn—and burn out*, she had told me once, as both warning and comfort, and it was true. I *had* burned, and burned to ashes, but now I would rise from the ruins of myself, and this time my flames would sustain me rather than consume. A dove is a beautiful bird, but a phoenix—a *firebird*—cannot be caged.

"Miss Dragotta," Mistress hissed, standing over me, *"where have you been?"*

When I looked up, I saw Mistress's death gleaming like a jewel at her throat, brighter than any death I had yet seen, as if it were full to bursting, about to crack open and flood her soul with its ghostly light. I smiled at her, kind and cruel at once.

"Somewhere you will soon follow." A whisper only, but it reached her—she straightened as if slapped. I didn't wait for her response, returning to my task. I raised the lid of the box and peeled back the paper. At long last I grasped the violin, lifting it like an infant, like something with muscle and a beating heart.

With a calm like night, I rose to my feet. Mistress reached for my arm, but I looked at her sharply, and when our eyes met she paused, her hand hovering in the air.

"If you touch me," I said, "you will burn."

After a moment, Mistress lowered her hand. Anna stood behind her, gazing at me as if she'd never seen me before and did not know me. I still wore my dirty white tutu, the boots Emilia had found for me in the closet, and withered flowers in my hair, which had fallen out of its bun and puffed around my shoulders in ragged spirals. Surely, I could not go onstage like this. But it didn't matter now. Beatrice finished her solo as the Queen of the Shades, and I wondered if this role too was meant as a message to me from the Master, a reminder that someone must always be there to summon the lost souls of Noctem. But how? How to carry on with the Master gone? As the enthusiastic applause for Beatrice died down, she noticed me in the wings and nodded, summoning me from the shadows. With my chin raised, I stepped onstage.

A few of the girls gasped at the sight of me, and stumbled off their pointes. I walked past them, looking directly at the pale faces in private box number one. And before anyone could say or do anything to stop me, I raised the violin and began to play.

I had meant to start softly, a true and haunting lullaby. A gentle humming tune, leading them lightly into dreams. But there was so little mercy left in me; I could not unclench my teeth. All those eyes, widening. All those mouths, inhaling. All those lights, excruciating. And so my song began like grinding bones, high and sharp, a note to rouse the dead and send them walking the earth again. A pause, and every person in that theater stopped breathing to listen.

It was memory, and dream, and weeping; it was winter, and summer, and a moon like melting ice. It was worship, and prayer, and the terror of eternity. Ritual and blood and saints lying still in the snow. It was clasped hands and horrors unspoken, breaking glass and a tap on the window at your back. Let it out; let it in. I played with abandon, and I did not stop.

Not once did I stop.

The dancers onstage fell asleep first. Already fatigued, they required little coaxing. It didn't happen all at once—they sank slowly to their knees, tulle skirts piled around them, and then they collapsed, spilling sideways onto their shoulders, cheeks to the floor. Graceful as always, even in this. Pointed toes and soft fingertips.

The orchestra soon followed—they set down their instruments, mesmerized, and slumped forward in their chairs as a few people in the audience rose from their seats, uncertain. Some even made it to the aisles before they succumbed to the somnolent pull of the violin, fainting on the worn carpet, limbs limp and eyes closed.

But—what of Mr. Russo? All this in the theater I was aware of, but I wasn't watching them. My eyes, as ever, were up.

It was like he was drunk. He stood at once and stumbled, catching himself with a hand on the back of his chair. He closed his eyes, swaying there, and when he opened them all I could see were the whites, expanding like a luminous void. A shudder went through him and he bowed his head, clutching the chair so hard his knuckles were bent and pale. And I thought it was over, I thought he would fall, but after a moment he raised his head and his eyes were dark again, dark but clear.

Oh, how he smiled then, crust of the moon, and like a man intoxicated he stumbled from the box, pushing the curtain aside to let him through. He was gone from sight, but I knew, I knew: He was coming for me. Sometimes sleep comes quietly, and other times violently, gradually or all at once, but always it comes and always it claims you, holds you fast until morning, holds you close.

This time, though, he would not let me go, he would keep his arms tightly around me until I choked.

I kept playing, faster and faster.

Catherine took no notice of him or of his absence, only sat with her small hands in her lap, her head tilted slightly to the side as she listened, the crown secure on her head. She showed no signs of sleep—but none of vigor either. And I was sorry for her that her second life was about to end so abruptly. I was sorry she'd had a second life at all.

Behind her, a familiar figure crept closer—Emilia with her ears stuffed, a clean wad of the lamb's wool we used to wrap our toes inside our shoes. I held my breath as she reached a small and trembling hand toward the crown.

I had wanted Emilia to go home, to forget all this and be safe, but when we finally reached the theater I realized that I couldn't do this alone. While Adrián had gone to park the car, I stood with her on the sidewalk under the theater's marquee, the pop and flash of a hundred tiny lights, and I sighed long and heavily into the night.

"I hate to ask this of you," I'd said, but Emilia had shaken her head.

"You can ask me anything."

"I need you to be my hands." She had nodded as I'd told her my plan, such as it was.

Now, I will sing Sleep to sleep.

It would all be for nothing if we didn't claim the Master's crown. We were close now. So close.

A hand darted out and grabbed Emilia by the throat.

Mr. Russo had lunged back into the box, and now he swung her around, away from the red-haired girl, who continued to sit peacefully, insensible of her surroundings. He held Emilia over the ledge of the balcony, the backs of her knees pressed against the railing. His face was flushed, covered in sweat, blue veins stark under the skin that looked almost like marble in the dim. Hard, unyielding. Emilia clawed at his hand, to no effect, and he pushed her still farther, holding her there, his intentions clear. If he let go, she would fall.

If he let go, she would fall and fall and fall.

I slowed my song, a lullaby at last. The melody the same as the one Mr. Russo hummed to me. Imperfect, but then, it is hard to make a clean cut, a straight line, a parallel edge. It was daybreak, and birdsong, and little bells chiming; it was countless small hurts, compiling. A splinter, a bruise, a break. It was wings, opening wide.

It was a plea and a promise both: *I will stop you. I will kill you.*

Ah. Still no mercy in me.

There was none in him either. I could see it, *feel* it, even from so far away, his yearning to throw her over the balcony and be done with it. It was in the quiver of his lower lip, the muscles straining in his arms, the feral shine of his eyes. He was a beast, after all, and isn't that what beasts do? Rend and gnaw and take care to step only in shadows? The fault was mine for ever putting Emilia in his path, like sending a rabbit to parade before a den of starving foxes. My fault, for not looking past the glare of his smile to the sharpness of his teeth.

My fault, for fearing Death instead of Sleep.

All this time, Mr. Russo knew me in a way no one else ever could, no one else ever *should;* he had walked through my dreams and used them against me. My dreams like a hand curled around a candle to protect the flame, desires burning in the lush darkness of my soul. My longing for greatness, for magic, for more than the world had to offer. *Out the window, down the alley, through the park.* My dreams like a breath desperate to blow the fire out, my fears growing in the far shadows until the heat of them was all I could feel: fear of dying, fear of a life half-lived, fear of fading away, unloved and utterly forgotten. *Just another girl in a row of perfect girls.* Dreams, true dreams, both frightening and divine, that were just too big, too messy, too precious, to be hidden inside an egg inside a casket.

What is there to fear from sleep? I'd wondered once, but now I understood: Death was in my heart, but Sleep was in my head—and had been all along.

From my dreams, did he know how much Emilia meant to me? Did he know that hurting her would destroy me? But Emilia would not die today, no—her death was not in her throat. It was in her tears, and there were none of those now. My song was darkness, and it is a lie to think darkness is cruel and nothing else. Like all things—even light—the dark has many faces, many voices, and some of them are kind.

Mr. Russo's fingers loosened. Slowly, but they loosened. The dark in me called to the dark in him. It roiled there, beneath sinew and skin. *Step back. Step back, and let go.* A command, and one he obeyed. He stepped back from the ledge, and as he did his hand fell away and Emilia stumbled forward, choking for air. Choking, but she was free. Mr. Russo gazed at me—not once had he looked at Emilia, even with his hand on her—and bit his lip so hard a drop of blood welled and dripped down his chin. Fighting me, but he would not win. He tilted on his feet, and just before he fell in a heap his eyes turned up to the angels. There was a flash of something—pity, or rage, or regret, or all three. This war between us wasn't over forever—but it was over for now, and that was all I could ask. He folded to his knees, and then out of sight behind the solid railing of the balcony.

Asleep.

Asleep and wading through dreams of his own, leaving the dreams of others well alone. I imagined Sleep's sleep as a long and difficult labyrinth, a beast lurking in every shadow, a pale sun cloaked in mist that never rose, never set, only hung like a painting on a wall so that he could not tell east from west. Maybe someday he'd escape. But not for a very, very long time.

Emilia put a fist to her heaving chest, as if she could soothe her racing heart with a touch. In front of her, Catherine had not moved. My music held her in thrall, but I couldn't play much longer; it was like speaking with a sore throat. The violin was hot, almost burning, in my hands. Emilia had only to reach out and take the crown from the enchanted girl's head.

From so far away and with the music like the wind in my ears, it was impossible that I should hear the boneless thud of the girl crumpling to the ground when Emilia lifted the crown. But I *felt* it—in my bones and in my chest and in my teeth. Like being shaken roughly from a dream. Emilia stood tall with the crown in her hand, breathing hard.

Someone screamed.

I didn't realize it was a scream, not at first. It was a sound like rain falling from a dark cloud, filling every dip and crack and crevice, relentless. It was pain and anger and hope swiftly crushed. It was a human sound, natural yet unnerving, and I finally lowered my violin, turning toward the source of it.

Mistress.

The woman was on her knees, with fresh scratches down her cheeks as if she had tried to tear off her own skin. She held her arms straight out in front of her, locked at the elbows. Wrists up, palms up, pleading with some unseen entity for clemency. Death was there in that room and I think she knew; it glowed white-hot in the back of her throat as her scream went on and on.

I thought they would wake up—the whole theater, everyone. But not a single eyelid twitched. Not a single body stirred. Mistress soon ran out of breath, and the silence that followed was worse than the scream, louder somehow and more disconcerting. But still no one woke. No one made a sound. My spell was cast, and it would hold until I was long gone and far away.

"I am sorry, whatever you think." Even now I am not entirely sure if I said this aloud, or only thought it in my head. The silence swallowed everything, even the sounds inside of me. "But *you fed me to the beasts.* What did you suppose would happen?"

Mistress's eyes swiveled like mad, rolling balls, bloodshot and bulging. She tried to speak—or perhaps she merely gasped for air. Finding none, she too fell to the ground in the same manner as her daughter: heavy and unceremonious, a body stripped of its soul. Her eyes were open and staring.

The quiet then was like the quiet in church—grave and reverent—and I wondered if this was also the sound at the beginning of the world and the one that would be there at the end. It was comforting, in its way. Like walking the edge between ecstasy and oblivion.

For a long moment I stood there onstage in the glare of the lights, swaying, clutching the neck of the violin in one hand and the bow in the other. Tired? No, I would never be tired again. Death was dead and Sleep was asleep, both their mortal shells felled by my hand, yet I was still here, still whole, and my heart beat as loudly as a scream within me. Dropping the bow, I placed a hand over my heart and curtsied to an audience of none, sinking all the way to one knee. A final reverence, the performance complete.

Twenty-One

I DON'T REMEMBER LEAVING THE THEATER. ONLY THAT I DID, and that somewhere along the way the violin and bow had crumbled into red dust that stained my palms like dried blood. I hoped that it was not entirely gone, that the soul of the instrument had returned to Sig. Picataggi in Noctem. And then I was outside, under the marquee lights, and Emilia's arms were around me. That she should comfort me was absurd—she was the one with a band of red ringing her throat—but she stroked my hair and said sweet words and I let her, I let her hold me and soothe me like I was a child again, more for her sake than for mine. I watched our shadows swaying as one on the sidewalk.

The crown, when she gave it to me, was heavy. Heavy and cold.

In a pile of tulle, I rested the crown in my lap as I sat in the back of Adrián's car. No one spoke all that drive back across the city, and it felt much longer than it had earlier. Adrián's hands were tight on the steering wheel, and he kept darting glances at Emilia beside him, at the mark stretching crudely across her throat. He had only entered the theater at the end of our great spectacle, and Emilia had hurried him out before he could take true stock of the carnage, of the sleeping bodies—and of the two dead. And so he was angry, almost shaking with it, but he didn't know whom to be angry with, and I knew Emilia would never tell. She hummed a pensive lullaby under her breath, and it took me a long while to recognize the song as my own. It chilled me to hear it on her soft lips. When Adrián's eyes met mine in the rearview mirror, pleading and forlorn, I sighed and looked away.

The dove did not appear, but we didn't need it now; the way to the house in Hyde Park was fixed like the brightest of stars in our minds—though I suspected that it would soon fade. Magic is tricky like that—it is thick like blood, a life-giving ichor, but you cannot hold it in your hands. And blood, once spilled, is gone forever, a memory like any other. Through the window, I watched the city slip by.

The house was a shadow unmoving, its windows shuttered and lonely. There was a flutter inside me at the sight of it, something dark coming alive. Was it my heart, or something more vital? Adrián pulled the car to the curb and left the engine running. Curling his hands tighter over the steering wheel, he didn't intend to stay long. Nevertheless Emilia climbed out of the car with me, and then we stood on the sidewalk, facing each other. I held the crown with both hands.

"Grace, I am so sorry." Emilia looked at me, so open and earnest, like a girl at the beginning of her story, and I saw in her what I could have been if the Master had never come for me. But that story was not meant for me, and I felt no remorse for a life I'd never live. "I didn't understand. I didn't want to. All this time it was easier for me to believe you were on some wonderful adventure with a handsome prince in a house of gold. I didn't want to think of you suffering. I didn't want to think of you getting hurt."

If my heart had still been my own it would have fallen and kept falling. This was an apology I could neither accept nor deny. If I accepted, she would think she had done wrong by me when she had not, and if I denied it, she would feel the need to offer penance again and again, even after I had gone.

"Emilia, my love," I said as the clouds above us thickened and the wind blew like a sweet breath. "You and I are the same—we romanticize our pain, even at the price of our own destruction. We'd rather live with magic and a hole in our hearts than with a whole heart and no magic to be found anywhere in this world."

She shook her head, her mouth set in a stubborn frown. Her hair was wild, matted on one side and a black puff on the other. "No. Magic isn't supposed to be like this. Magic is—is—is finding an old love letter pressed between the pages of a used book. Or the sun warming your skin on a harsh winter day. It's the way Adrián makes me feel." She exhaled, long and low through her teeth. "It's not death and sleep and violins and—and beasts. It's not hearts exchanged for passage through a dark wood. It's not spells cast with a scream."

I smiled at her sadly, because I knew—and I think she did too—that magic was all of those things and more.

"Stay here." Though her shoulders slumped with exhaustion, her eyes were bright and her voice was too. She stole a glance at the house, shifting her feet. "Stay here with me. You can live with Adrián and me until we find you a place. You can dance and—and be *free*. Stay, Grace. Please?"

"Oh, Em." The crown was so heavy; my arms were beginning to ache. "I think you know as well as I do that once you find fairyland you can think of nothing but going back. That's where I belong, and always have, even before I knew it was there."

"Then I'll go with you," she said at once, and I laughed—not out of scorn, or spite, or incredulity. I laughed because I loved her so much, because the warmth of it couldn't be released any other way. With the crown between us, I leaned forward and I kissed her cheek and hoped that that one press of cold lips against warm skin said all the things that could be understood without words: *Thank you for being my hands in the theater. Thank you for being my heart long before that.*

"Near North Ballet needs a new mistress," I said quietly, and Emilia breathed in sharply. She had thought of this too. I kissed her cheek a final time and whispered, "Keep the Master's box open for me."

Emilia didn't cry, and neither did I. Adrián climbed out of the car and came to put his arm around her, hugging her close. I smiled at her as I turned away.

It was no more than thirty steps to the house. And yet, didn't it take an hour to traverse, a whole night and a day? Didn't it pass like a sunset, like a scab formed, like ice when it melts—slowly? Was Emilia still there behind me as I walked through the doorway, away from the world that was normal and familiar to me? Were the lights of the city still lit, were there cars on the street and people to drive them? Was there love, and was there life? I didn't know. I never looked back.

The crown seemed to lighten the closer I came to the house. Now it was as weightless as a feather—a strong breeze could blow it away. But, if I gripped it too tightly, it would disintegrate into ash in my hands. And so I balanced it carefully on my palms and I walked, alone, into the dark.

THE MASTER WAS right where I had left him. The curled hands, the dark hair, the cloak fallen over him like a blanket. But of course he was—I had killed him. With a word, I had done it. In the dim of the mirrored room I could almost trick myself into seeing the rise and fall of his chest. Fantasy only. I knelt beside him with the crown in my lap and touched his forehead with the back of my hand, caressing. His skin had gone cold.

Around us, the mirrors glowed like ice in the moonlight. I could see the temple in them. Birds winging through the darkness, leaves fluttering in the wind, constellations like the notes of a song. My tears fell onto the Master's cheek, running down toward his chin as if they were his own.

"I said no to you so many times," I said in a voice like coming up for air. "Why was the first not enough to fell you?"

My fingers trembled as I traced them down the line of his face, his jaw. Lingering, for just a moment more.

Then I lifted the crown and placed it upon my head.

An awakening within me, every nerve in my body touched by fire, by light. My death had cracked open; it flowed through my veins alongside my life, dancing together like partners in a waltz. My heart stopped, but only for a moment; with a breath, my heart began to beat again, slow and strong, and I laughed through my tears to hear it. It was the sound of heavy rain, and running footsteps, and magic. I felt it pounding in my chest and in my fingertips and in my throat. A shiver ran through me, and when I looked down my tutu was clean and ivory again, pale pink slippers on my feet. I stood, with one hand on the Master's shoulder, and as I rose the glass of the mirrors melted into a clear stream of water that ran over the stones beneath my feet, nothing now between me and the temple and the souls still lost there. It was dark, a dark devoted to me utterly, and I knew it was a living thing, that we shared one heart between us. *Worry not*, I thought. *I will keep it safe.*

I turned at the sound of someone approaching through the underbrush, snapping twigs and the rustle of leaves, but there was only a bright white bird on a low slab of eroded stone, staring at me with black and shining eyes. I smiled and went toward it, stepping carefully around the Master's mortal body. The bird didn't startle as I neared, and it didn't fly away. I came very close before I stopped and gave a small curtsy.

"Good evening, colombino," I said. "I was hoping to see you here. Shall we?"

The dove inclined his head.

I walked through the hills with my eyes to the sky and the dove soaring close above, though he was not always a dove; sometimes he was a shadow, and sometimes, even, a man. Sometimes I felt it: the brush of the back of his hand. He was all of these at once, a many-faced god, a beast walking beside me. You cannot kill Death, not truly, and I would see Sleep again when I closed my eyes at first light. But it was I who wore the crown, and it would not be easily taken from me. It was I who would dance until the end of my days, coaxing souls from the shade and into the city of Noctem to face whatever came next. It was I, a frightened girl no longer afraid.

It was I, Eternal Life.

I heard the beasts before I saw them, just before I reached the stone church and the garden within. But they didn't groan, or even hiss—no, they *hummed*, a deeply enchanted lullaby, familiar to me now. It filled me up and fed me, sweeping away my hunger—not a song to fall asleep to, but one to wake me up. They crawled from their hiding places tentatively, and I saw that they were not really beasts at all but souls, souls that were bruised and battered and flickering with a long-lost light. I looked for Mistress among them but I believe she is still out there, hiding from me until she's ready. Singing softly all the way, they followed me to Noctem.

And there in the temple of an ever-present god I danced, and I am dancing still. Sometimes a dove perches on the cult statue or the broken stones, watching silently, and other times there is a shadow spinning me round and round, warm to the touch. And for every soul that comes to find me, a fresh flower blooms full in the darkness in the church the Master once showed me. Roses upon roses, and I will tend them until the end of this long night.

I held my breath the first time I walked through the gates of Noctem, unsure what I would find. But the dove flew above me and I was not afraid; a light as bright as the sun cut into my eyes as I passed through the wall and in the brilliance I heard music, a special song. I squinted as the light began to dim, and just saw the edge of a lipstick smile the color of ancient brick before being pulled into a tight and unwavering hug. And a hand on my shoulder, accompanied by a voice: "Hey there, Gracie girl. It's been too long."

I am not without nightmares. If I close my eyes even for a moment I am haunted by dreams of a smile like a sudden, frozen gust of wind. Catherine is still waiting for him—I'd seen her once, wandering through the crowds of Noctem, alone—and someday Sleep may find a way to return in a different form. But for now Noctem will not grant him passage; the gates remain closed to him.

Not like me. The hills, the labyrinth, the city of the living, and the city of the dead; the darkness beyond it all. I can run anywhere I please.

Acknowledgments

Grazie mille to the following people:

My agent, Penelope Burns. Your enthusiasm is truly what keeps me going, and there is no one I would rather have in my corner. If I had the Master's golden crown, I would give it to you.

My editor, Anne Groell, for taking the scattered stars of my vision for this book and these characters and arranging them into a constellation. Thank you for helping me push this story to places I never dreamed it could go, and making it better than I ever hoped it could be.

The truly wonderful team at Del Rey that makes dreams come true: Bree Gary, David Moench, Jordan Pace, Adaobi Maduko, Ashleigh Heaton, Sabrina Shen, Tori Henson, Maya Fenton, Scott Shannon, Keith Clayton, Tricia Narwani, and Alex Larned. Cassie Gonzales and Regina Flath for the beautiful cover design. And Jana Heidersdorf for capturing the soul of the book in the cover illustration.

My friends at BAL and CLPL. Library people are the best people!

All my talented and supportive writer friends, especially Kelly Jensen for the writing dates (until Covid derailed us). I worked on this book while sipping coffee with you and I'm so grateful for your encouragement.

Judith Svalander and all my instructors throughout the years for teaching me how to dance. My dancing days have informed my writing in so many ways. My sense of rhythm and poetry on the page is a direct result of the grace and finesse of motion you taught me to harness in the studio and pour onto the stage.

Vanessa, my sister by covenant if not by blood, for dancing and choreographing and laughing and crying with me (sometimes all at once).

Connie and Jerry Wees, for all your love and support.

Gram, who lived in Little Sicily as a child and whose mother was a seamstress, just like Grace. Who lived a good, long life and had a huge, loving family. We miss you every day.

Dad, for driving me seven hours to an audition and then seven hours back immediately after. You're the best dad a girl could ask for.

Mama, for coming to every performance, for being backstage and in the audience. For seeing *The Nutcracker* so many times you could pretty much dance it yourself.

Kara, for getting me like no one else does. I promise someday I'll write a story with centaurs in it.

J.D., fellow library guy and my favorite little brother.

Fightmaster and Lady Slippers, for the snuggles and keyboard smashes made with your tiny, perfect paws.

And Frank. There would be no book without you. Thank you for always believing in me, and for gently reminding me that utter despair is just a natural part of my writing process. *Vivi con me per sempre!*

If you loved *Nocturne,* be sure not to miss

WE SHALL BE MONSTERS

the next enchanting novel from

Alyssa Wees

Here is a special preview.

*M*AMA BRUSHED MY HAIR AS I SAT ON A WOODEN STOOL IN front of the mirror, my little television on mute in the corner, flickers of color and light. The hairbrush was old—a century old at least—and one of her most prized antiques: sterling silver, with thick yellow bristles like discolored teeth. I knew from experience that the handle was always icy cold, like it had just been plucked up from the snow, but Mama wielded it as if it didn't bother her at all. It was the only item she ever refused to sell, even though she kept it in the display case at the back of the shop when she wasn't using it on me. Like a secret, except it wasn't a very good one. It was dull in the light, even after a polish.

Outside the clouds gathered like blackbirds on a branch, peeking through the window. Staying very still, I told Mama about the boy I'd seen at the edge of the woods. But she said never mind, it was only a shadow. And I said no, too pale to be a shadow, and she said well, a rabbit then. Bigger than a rabbit I said, and she said hush. She always said that. *Hush.* So all I was left with was the sound of my pulse in my ears and the bristles of the brush scraping my scalp and my big eyes blinking back at me. I sat very straight and pressed my knees together, waiting for it to be over.

Hush.

I was not allowed to go into the woods because of the monsters there. I did not know what a monster was, only that it would eat you. I did not want to be eaten, but I did so long to see a monster. Mama would not describe them to me. *Nightmares,* she said. *You will have nightmares if I tell you. You will never sleep soundly again.*

I tried to tell her that I had nightmares anyway—sometimes before I went to sleep—even though I had never encountered a monster. I would be lying there in the dark and all of a sudden my heart would begin to beat very fast, like a fox's in an open field. I would sweat a little and my breath would come in gasps. And I was so afraid, only I didn't know what I was afraid of. And that fear was worse than the fear of any monster, because I could see nothing, hear nothing, feel nothing there to frighten me. At least, if I saw a monster, I would have a reason to be afraid.

Hush.

I did see a boy in the woods, though. He was a fairy prince.

I knew he was a fairy because his voice was like the leaves curling in autumn, and I knew he was a prince because of the crown he wore in his thick brown hair, laurel and berries as red as fresh blood. Also, he told me so.

He told me lots of things.

Like how to tell a poisoned apple from a sweet one, and how to call the sun to come out after the rain. How to listen to the trees when they are telling you that an enemy is approaching, and how to waltz in the high fairy fashion: swept up on the wind, gliding a foot or more above the earth. He taught me the proper way to curtsy before his mothers— the queen and queen consort of the fairies—for when he brought me before them one day, after he had vanquished the dreadful Hunting Beast who was known for snatching fairies from their beds and eating them up. With his silver sword and scabbard, with his shield blessed by the Great Ensorceller of the Hidden Moon, he would slay the monster that came hunting every few years and free his people from its chilling shadow. And once he had completed this most noble quest—*One cannot become a hero without a quest,* he told me—there would be a feast that lasted days and weeks held in his honor, and there would be song and dance and revelry that would light up the night sky as if it were noon.

He told me I was invited.

But—he was still very young, and still in training, hardly older or stronger than me, a girl of only twelve. And a half.

"We must be patient," said the fairy prince to me, "because I will have one chance to kill the Hunting Beast, and only a fairy full grown can do it."

Only a man and not a boy, even if he was a prince.

"And why must *you* be the one to slay the creature?" I asked, my heart tangling with fear for him. "Why can't the queen do it, or the queen consort? Or some other soldier so you don't have to be in such danger?"

The fairy prince smiled in that way that made me blush down to the bones in my cheeks, and he leaned very close. "Because it was foretold, my Gemma Belle, that the very bravest of knights would vanquish the Beast once and for all, and the stars are never wrong."

(He called me that, his Gemma Belle, and it was like a song.)

I didn't tell Mama any of what he told me, because I wanted these things for only the two of us to share, the fairy prince and me. But I didn't like keeping secrets from her. It made my throat feel raw. So that night while she brushed my hair, I told her just a little: just about the fairy feast we'd have after he slayed the Hunting Beast, about the music and the dancing. I longed to show her how I would curtsy before the queen and her wife but she would not stop brushing my hair.

"And why must the prince murder this Hunting Beast?" she said when I was done, in a tone like anger but under glass, and I didn't like that, that one word she'd said: *murder*. The fairy prince never said murder, only slay or kill or defeat—a noble act, heroic. Murder, though; it made me shiver and made my heart spin, dizzy.

"It is for glory," I said, and that was a word I liked: *glory*. Glorious. It had a melody. I let myself get wrapped up in the fantasy—fairy lights and vining waltz, the prince's hands in mine. Mama watched me in the mirror, watched me with her wide, dark eyes that could see things about me that even I didn't know.

"Maybe," I began, but my voice was too loud and I lowered it. Quiet, like sleep. "Maybe, at the end of the night, he will even give me a . . ."

"Kiss?" Mama finished for me, just as the brushing was done. One hundred slow strokes, no more and no less. My scalp tingled where the bristles had been, almost painful. Mama looked at me in the mirror, unsmiling, tilting her head so that a lock of dark hair fell across her neck like a wound.

"Go to bed now," she said. "Sleep well."

Strange, but when she said these words I was still sitting on the stool, and the next moment I was tucked up in bed. I didn't remember the walk up the stairs or changing into my nightgown, or even laying my head upon the pillow. I had been telling her something while she brushed my hair—but what?

That night I dreamed of berries, crushed underfoot.

IN THE MORNING, a Saturday, I wanted to play outside but Mama said no, she needed help in the shop. I asked if I could go out after and she said all right in a voice like melted ice. Dusting, it was always dusting she wanted me to do, and there was always so much of it. In school, while I sketched a boy wearing a crown of leaves in the margins of my Lisa Frank notebook, we learned that dust was just bits of shed skin. Dead skin, skin that flaked and fell off and settled on every surface because it had to go *somewhere*. I only wished it could float on the air and stick to the ceiling instead, and we could all just politely agree to look anywhere but up.

Mama sat in her office with the door open, going over accounts. It seemed like she was always going over accounts, or else talking on the telephone in a tone too whispery for me to understand. I grabbed the duster off the hook in the closet and then I started in the back of the store and worked my way forward. The space was so crowded it was easy to miss things, and I carried around a small stool to stand on when items were piled too high, stacks on stacks in narrow rows. There was little logic in the way the shop was arranged: tea sets next to crumbling texts next to bookshelves next to an armoire. A hand-cranked Singer sewing machine, a chess table, even an ax, slightly rusted around the edges. There were hats with feathers around the brim and ribbons to tie it under the chin, and a line of dress forms wearing lacy, yellowed wedding gowns. I noticed patterns in the dust, thicker in some spots than in others, the places I had missed the week before. Sunlight came through the windows, but it was the kind of sun you only see and don't really feel on your skin, an empty glimmering. I moved through the shadows, shivering.

I saved my favorite room for last. The Glass Room, I called it, because there was nothing else in it but mirrors and chandeliers. Blackout curtains were closed tightly over the windows so that the chandeliers could shine. And the many mirrors of all shapes and sizes reflected the glow, intensifying it: like standing close to the stars, or inside a kaleidoscope. I used to think it was a portal to some strange and radiant world.

Lots to dust in the Glass Room—each arm of the chandeliers, plus the frames of every mirror. There was a smell of lavender about the room, dying petals, delicate rot. My arms were aching by the time I was done, and I wished—I *wished!*—that I had a little brother or sister to help me with the cleaning. Or to do *all* the cleaning, since I would be the elder and could boss them around. I would make them do the dusting while I went to play in the woods in secret.

I was not allowed to go into the woods because of the monsters there. I didn't know what a monster was; only that it would speak in a voice like deep water, and when it called to you it was impossible to resist. Always in shadow, one step ahead, so that you were achingly curious to draw closer, to see what couldn't be seen. With its voice of black and blue, the monster would lead you into the dark and into the trees, a long and winding way, far from home and far from the path. And those who wandered never came back.

Fearsome, Mama said, meat of nightmares, ax on bone. But, oh—how I longed to go and see it for myself! To know just what it was that separated a fairy tale from every other kind of story we tell. I begged her to show me but she wouldn't—or couldn't—and sometimes, in my most secret heart, I suspected that this was because she was making it all up. Like how pirates bury their heaps of jewels and coins on a faraway island and then draw dragons on the maps between here and there so that others would be too scared to sail through those waters and steal their hidden treasure.

What was Mama hiding in the woods?

An hour passed, maybe two, before every mirror and chandelier was crystal clean, spilling diamonds of light on the dark wood floor. A treasure room, with my face reflected all around and everywhere. I smiled at myself, a many-headed creature, and gave a little bow. *Ta-da! The End.*

I heard something then. A voice, Mama's, and at first I thought she was singing to herself . . . but no. There was another voice, one I didn't recognize right away. Soft, but echoing.

"Virginia, I may have a lead."

The shuffle of papers, a chair scraping against the floor. A little cough, a clearing of the throat. Mama took her time to reply, but when she did her voice was steady. "You're sure?"

"Yes. I should know in a week."

"My God," Mama murmured, and I tiptoed out of the Glass Room, edged around an armoire, and crouched behind a bookshelf filled with tomes so old that they didn't even have titles on the spines. In my hands I clutched the duster like a magic wand; my fingertips felt numb. I had thought there was someone in the office with her, but it was just the telephone on speaker.

"My God," Mama said again. "This could all be over in a week?"

I peeked around the bookshelf and saw that she had her hands over her face, bony fingers splayed wide, but then she peeked through her fingers and saw me. She clicked a button to take the phone off speaker and I shrank back behind the bookshelf, feeling like a naughty sneak.

"Thank you, Clarice," she said formally, and the name sent an ache through my heart. She was talking to my grandmother, who I hadn't seen in a while because she was "away." Almost a year, actually. When I asked Mama where she was and when she was coming back, all she said was *hush*.

Already my grandmother's face had started to fade from memory, but I still remembered that she wore dark pink lipstick and that her smiles were like shooting stars: rare and hard to find but dazzling if you were lucky enough to catch one. She was always touching the top of my head, pressing her cold palm to my crown and asking wouldn't I like to cut my hair so short I would never need to brush it? Easier to take care of it that way, she said, but I didn't want to look like a boy and also what would I do with all my scrunchies if I couldn't wear a ponytail? I told her this and she nodded like she understood. *All right*. But later she'd ask again.

With my head bowed, I slunk back to the Glass Room.

Mama found me there. I pretended to dust a gilt-framed mirror I'd already dusted, acting like I'd been there the whole time and not spying on her phone calls. I prepared to be reprimanded and sent to my room.

"Not finished yet?" she said behind me, and when I turned at the lightness of her tone I saw a laugh in her eyes that didn't quite make it out of her mouth—but still, it was there, shocking me into silence. "Go ahead, Gem. Go outside and play."

I SAT ON the little stool in front of the mirror, but my legs felt wobbly—even while sitting—and I couldn't stay still, knees bouncing and fingers twitching. Mama saw and paused with the bristles of the brush still buried in my hair, my scalp tingling where it touched. I had lost track of the number of strokes.

"Gemma, is something wrong?" said Mama, and I couldn't tell her about this afternoon—it was too frightening to recall!—but I *had* to, didn't I? It made me so itchy to keep secrets.

"Well," I said, trying so hard to hold it in. But it was like trying not to throw up when you had a bellyache. The story came pouring out, burning my throat and my mouth. *"Well."*

Earlier, after I had dusted the Glass Room and Mama let me play, it had started to rain. Just a drizzle, but I didn't like to be wet and I didn't want to go back inside where there was little to do and the air was so stuffy and smelled like all the old objects filling it from floor to ceiling. A curious thing, though: It was raining in the backyard, but it wasn't raining in the woods. There was sunlight slanting between the branches, and as I crept closer to the trees, I could even feel its warmth. Would it be so terrible, really, to seek shelter under the leaves, just for a moment? *No,* I decided as I inched beneath the nearest tree, careful to keep an eye on the house behind me. *It's only for a moment.*

But I was in the shade, and it was a little cool there. Only a few feet into the woods there was an unfiltered patch of sunlight—close enough to where I stood that I would still be able to see the house, so what was the harm in venturing just a little farther inside? I stepped over a fallen log and went to stand in the sun, the light like a warm hand on my forehead, comforting and bright. The rain continued to fall beyond the edge of the woods, coming down harder now. I backed up a few more steps, just to be entirely clear of it. Then I heard a sound behind me—a snif-fling, snuffling sort of crying—and I thought I'd better follow it to make sure whoever was making it was okay. That was permissible, wasn't it? Noble, even? To want to help someone who might be in distress? It was a quest, and quests were always noble. (Someone told me that once, but I couldn't think who.) I left my patch of sunlight, my heart thumping like a rabbit on the run, and walked swiftly toward the sound.

It had not seemed far away from where I had been, but I walked for a very long time, the sniffling growing louder but its source still out of sight. Finally I came to a clearing, where a very thin woman knelt with her head bowed among some of the strangest things I had ever seen growing in a twisted kind of garden. Short plants with leaves that looked very much like skin; a bone-white tree bearing brown fruit that twitched as if from muscle cramps. Mushrooms oozing something sticky and rust-colored from their caps; flowers whose petals opened and closed as if with a breath. When I peered closer, I saw that there was a tiny pair of brown lungs attached to each stem, filling and deflating and filling again. Trying to ignore what looked very much like dirty human fingers pro-truding from the dirt not three feet away—roots, they were only roots, I told myself—I called to the woman, whose face was obscured by a thick curtain of long white hair glowing almost blue in the light.

"Hello, are you all right?" I had not thought to be afraid, despite the strangeness of the scene, but then my whole body went cold and clammy and I realized that maybe I had made a mistake. I stayed to the side of the clearing, not daring to enter it, and I was glad I didn't when the woman looked up, her hair falling away and over her shoulders. She was beautiful, but in the way a poisonous flower is beautiful, or a brightly colored venomous snake—beauty to tempt and reel you in be-fore it strikes. I had the peculiar sense that she wasn't young even though her skin was smooth and unlined. Her eyes were silvery-blue, her lips red and curved into a smile like a cut.

"Oh, what a pretty little thing you are," she said, her voice as high and clear as a songbird's trill. "How old are you, my sweet?"

"Twelve," I said, mesmerized. I had the uncanny feeling that I was talking to a phantom, something dead that had come back to life. "And a half."

"A wonderful age, your magic just about to bloom." She closed her eyes and sniffed the air. "Yes, yes—I can smell it on you."

"I don't have magic," I said, taking a step away.

"Not yet, but it will come. The Touch is like that; it develops in ado-lescence." The woman's eyes flashed gold and red before settling back into silvery-blue. "You're a bit skinny for my tastes, but I like the bones best anyway. Ah, how fortunate for you that I already ate."

A whistle came from somewhere beyond the clearing and I jumped. I was already stepping backward, readying to run as far and as fast as I possibly could. The woman stood, unfolding, and she was taller than any woman I had ever seen—a giantess looming over me even though she was still halfway across the wide clearing.

"My handler's coming. Don't tell her you saw me." And with that, she sped off on her very long legs into the shadows of the trees. I wasted no time in leaving that strange place behind, sprinting back the way I'd come, and I did not stop even as the rain hit my face and soaked me to the bone.

Now, in the mirror in my room above the stool, Mama's face had gone pale as I told my tale. She started brushing again, faster, my head pulling back as the bristles caught on the tangles and knots. My brain went cloudy, sort of numb, and in another moment I couldn't remem-ber what story I'd been telling, or if I'd been saying anything at all.

"You are not to go in the woods, Gemma," Mama said, and she sounded very far away even though she was only right behind me. In the mirror, I watched her touch a spot on her chest, pressing a fist to it like it hurt. "How many times must I tell you that?"

"What?" I said, confused, because I had never been to the woods. I had never seen a monster there, though I so desperately wished to meet one. How would I know what makes a hero if I'd never encountered a hero's equal and opposite?

"*Hush*. Go to bed now," Mama said in a much gentler voice. And I was so tired suddenly, so tired I almost didn't make it to bed before I fell asleep. Before that one word echoed across my dreams.

Hush.

IT WAS THE most unpleasant part of my day, brushing my daughter's hair. It shined in my hands; it gleamed. Surely, if this were a fairy tale, a rich king would fall in love with such hair and never look her in the eye all her life; all he would see is the dark of it, the fantasy. One hundred perfect strokes, and I could think of nothing but one hundred ways she could lose her heart. And with every stroke my chest burned, the magic extracting a bit of my vitality in exchange for the memories I stole. It was unpleasant, yes, but I had to do it. It was best to forget the woods and everything in it; best to shove the monsters back into the shadows where they belonged. Best that she never think about monsters at all. Some memories were too frightening to keep, and so I unburdened her of them, one brush stroke at a time. One hundred strokes to complete the spell, and a fog came over her eyes, creating gaps in her mind that she would fill in time with pleasanter things: open skies and summer nights, future hopes and dreams. No fear, and no nightmares either. The spell wouldn't last forever—like all things, even magic decays—but it was enough for now.

Then I put her to sleep.

These evening hours were mine, the only time that no one expected anything of me. I put the hairbrush away under the glass in the counter at the back of the shop, where everyone could see it but no one could buy it. A private little joke, it was my way of taunting the one I had stolen it from. I weaved between the tight aisles of antiques, some of them scuffed and some pristine: end tables and china cabinets and Tiffany lamps, carved music boxes and Madame Alexander dolls with bright painted cheeks. A jewelry box, a grandfather clock, and everywhere dust and creaking.

Precious, pretty things. All of it useless to me.

I stepped out onto the porch and closed the door behind me with a faint ring of the bell. The air was cool and damp, and when I passed from the wooden stairs to the grass a shiver went through me. The road beyond was silent; it was the one good thing about living at the end of a dead end. The only ones who used this road were the ones that came to my shop. A lonely life, but I preferred it. And I wasn't alone, not really. There was my daughter, and the wind, and the birds.

And the woods.

It was dark as I walked around the side of the house. Cold, pale stars. Fading moon. And all around me trees, quiet and still.

On the east side of the house I stopped and looked up to Gem's bedroom. I made sure that there was no light behind her curtain, that she was asleep and not simply staying up past her bedtime to read. She did that sometimes—flashlight under a blanket, an old copy of *The Perilous Gard,* dog-eared and beloved—and she thought I didn't know. I didn't mind it really, as long as she was not by the window.

But the room was dark and I exhaled, goose bumps rising along my spine. I faced the woods and waited.

There was movement at the edge of the trees, but it was too far away to see clearly. I stood still and didn't take my eyes from the spot.

I was lost in these woods once, years ago. There was this game I used to play with myself after my mother forbade me from entering the woods but before I believed that monsters were real. (Before she *made* me believe.) How far was I willing to go to defy her? How far into the trees and the shadows between? I would step backward into the brush, feeling behind me with my feet and my hands, careful not to stumble on a fallen branch or boulder. Eyes fixed ahead (behind?), locked on the clean light at the edge of the woods from which I had come and to which I would return, always in sight even as I ventured farther.

When I could no longer see the light I would pause a moment, listening to the scurry of small creatures, the whisper of leaves, the reverent song of the birds. I imagined a monster creeping closer behind me, dark eyes glowing hot in its head, knees bent backward, and pale skin draped like curtains over the ribs. The Hunting Beast as I pictured him to be, a creature straight from a nightmare. And when the thrill of it—the terror—became too much, I released my breath and ran fast along the path I had made, bursting back into the bright. I would laugh, high and shaky, triumphant over the "monster" I had thwarted, unable to follow me and capture me there in the daylight.

A game of imagination, it was always the same. Until the time I took one step too many and felt a cold hand wrap around my wrist.

Now, standing beside the white brick Victorian where I had lived all my life, I watched through the dark as a figure stepped from the trees. Too tall to be a man, too thin to be anything else. Gnarled hair, twisted antlers like a deer's, a slow and scraping gait. Precisely the monster I had envisioned, once upon a time, now here in the flesh. Not the Hunting Beast—I'd never actually encountered *him,* only his victims—but a monster all my own. He crossed the distance between us, but before he was even five feet past the trees, I was walking—then running—toward him to meet him halfway. Just like the night before, and the night before that, stopping just short of running into his arms the way I would have done if he had not forbidden it. The last time I'd tried—years ago now—my cheek had been pierced by the thorns that jutted from his shoulders like those on a rosebush, and the skin of my arms had been scraped from moving against the roughness of his own, coarse and furrowed like bark. So we didn't embrace, but still I reached for his hands and he reached back, the heat of him flowing into my palms, close to burning. His long fingers curled gently around mine before squeezing once and letting go and my heart fell. Too brief a touch. It wasn't enough—it would never be enough—and I didn't care if it hurt me. I just wanted to be near him.

As if sensing my longing for more, he took a step back, cloaked all in shadow except for the eyes that glowed, and waited for me to say that I had found the thing that would save him. *A mirror to show one's true reflection.* We had two and a half years left, but the days were slipping away so fast. So little time before he became a monster in full, in his *soul.* So little time until he would hunt me down and eat my heart, whether he wanted to or not.

"Not yet," I whispered, and he bowed his head. I wanted to keep from crying, so I made my voice hard instead. *"Not yet."*

ALYSSA WEES grew up writing stories starring her Beanie Babies, in between training in ballet and watching lots of Disney movies. She earned a BA in English from Creighton University and an MFA in fiction writing from Columbia College Chicago. Currently she works as an assistant librarian in youth services at an awesome public library. She lives in the Chicagoland area with her husband and their two cats.

alyssawees.com
Twitter: @AlyssaWees
Instagram: @alyssa_wees